DAMBALLA

AIRSHIP 27 PRODUCTIONS

Damballa
© 2011 Charles R. Saunders

An Airship 27 Production
www.airship27.com www.airship27hangar.com

Interior llustrations © 2011 Clayton Hinkle
Cover illustration © 2011 Charles Fetherolf

Editor: Ron Fortier
Associate Editor: Ray Riethmeier
Production and design: Rob Davis.

ISBN-13: 978-0692460900 (Airship 27)
ISBN-10: 069246090X

third edition

Printed in the United States of America

10 9 8 7 6 5 4 3 2 1

DAMBALLA

by Charles R. Saunders

Dedicated to the Three Amigos
Mike Ambrose – Larry Dickison – Al Manachino

CHAPTER ONE

A POMP PARTY

Music stirred the sultry night air of Sugar Row. The syncopated sounds of smooth jazz wove magic in the June heat and brought quick smiles to the lips of the men and women of all shades of darkness who walked past the mansion from which the music emanated. But none of the pedestrians climbed the flight of stone steps that led to a brass-bound door that looked like the entrance to a castle.

Or, in the minds of some, a fortress.

For nobody entered the palatial abode of Madame Delia Pomphrey without an invitation engraved in social-class standing, which was worth more than gold. And Madame Pomp, as she was called out of earshot, had already issued all the invites she'd intended for this night. Those who had not received RSVPs were far from surprised, as Delia's snobbery was acute even by the standards of the Row.

Ordinarily, some of the faces that glanced at the imposing door would have sneered at the pretensions of the doyenne of Sugar Row, regardless of the sublime music that caressed their ears. This was not an ordinary night, though. And these were not ordinary times – not by a longshot.

Madame Pomp's was not the only name whispered on the lips of residents of other fine houses on Sugar Row, as well as employees who hid their envy and resentment behind carefully cultivated masks of indifference. Any job was a good job these days, even a job working for people who looked down on their own color for no reason that made any sense at all.

The other name on the minds of everyone on the Row, as well as the rest

1

of Harlem and the whole wide world beyond belonged to a man who was not even in attendance at Madame Delia Pomphrey's function, though she did not feel slighted by his absence. It was a name that had first captured, and now commanded, attention for the past three years: the name of the heavyweight boxing champion of the world: Junius "Jackhammer" Jackson.

In little more than a week, the Jackhammer would be defending his crown against the formidable challenge of Wolfgang Krieger, the "Aryan Adonis" of Germany, in the most compelling prizefight since black champion Jack Johnson defeated "White Hope" Jim Jeffries back in 1910. Now, twenty-eight years later, the Jackson-Krieger bout promised to be even more controversial, with war clouds looming over Europe and economic unrest simmering in America.

Such was the occasion for Madame Pomp's pre-fight party, which the society columns touted as the swankiest soiree thrown by anyone – white or colored – in the history of New York.

Even as the strollers sashayed on the sidewalks and late-model coupes glided along a thoroughfare flanked by brownstones and manses that suffered in comparison with the house known as the Pomp Palace, a voice on the street offered its own evaluation of Madame Pomp, her event, and Sugar Row in general. The voice muttered deep and guttural from the darkness inside one of many automobiles parked street-side.

"Yeah, uh huh," the man in the car snarled, his tone low as the growl of a lion. "We gon' see how high-and-mighty you is. You up now, but you comin' down soon. Real soon … "

❈ ❈ ❈

"Well, Delia, you've certainly gathered the *crème-de-la-crème* here tonight."

Delia Pomphrey looked at the man who had spoken. Before she could respond, he applied the needle.

"The dark *crème*, at least."

Uncertain laughter greeted the man's remark. The music from the Crossley gramophone quickly superseded the forced chuckles.

The small knot of guests in Delia's place of honor near the bar fell silent during the interval in which a dark-skinned waiter clad in a scarlet jacket and black pants changed the record. He picked from the top of a stack of disks bearing the names of the dukes, counts, and ladies of jazz. Then he stood like an acolyte at the side of the tall hardwood cabinet console.

Delia could have hired any of the bands who had cut the records to perform at the event, but chose not to, saying that she didn't want the ones who were not chosen to feel slighted.

On the wall above the gramophone, a portrait of Jackhammer held pride of place. It depicted the champion in his fighting stance: smooth muscles coiled beneath his coffee-colored skin, gloved fists poised to deliver lightning-quick blows, broad-featured face devoid of emotion. Delia glanced up at the portrait before she spoke to the man whose comment had caused the moment of discomfiture.

"Kurt, you are so…droll."

"Better droll than dull," came the response. "And you, my dear, have never had a dull day in your life."

Kurt van Vallen was one of a small number of whites among the select crowd at the Pomp Palace – although some of the Negroes were so light-complected that the difference was scarcely noticeable. A lean, middle-aged man of medium height with receding blond hair, Van Vallen was a writer of lurid, racially-themed novels. His latest featured a thinly disguised version of the woman who stood beside him. So far, it had outsold all the rest of his books combined, which was the main reason he had been invited to Delia's pre-fight party, and why she now purred: "You ought to know, darling."

Van Vallen smiled at Delia's display of *sang-froid* – and other attributes. So did the others who surrounded her like members of a queen's court. Although she was approaching the half-century mark, neither her fine-featured face nor her hour-glass figure betrayed the years of her age. A shimmering black evening gown molded her ample curves, and several strands of diamonds, pearls and gold hung across her deep décolletage. Her hair, pure ebony without a trace of gray, was piled like a crown atop her head.

Her skin, which was light-caramel in hue, glowed with the cosmetics that had made her fortune and paid for her mansion, jewelry and numerous other possessions. "Enlightenment" was the name of her brand, and its double-meaning escaped neither the buyers nor sellers of her products.

Delia's male companion for the evening decided that the time had come for him to rescue the conversation. His name was Lennox Levere, and among the people in the salon, his prose and poetry were better-received than Van Vallen's – not only because Levere possessed greater talent, but also Delia and her crowd preferred his work. And it was no secret that Madame Pomp was attracted to the two-decades-younger Levere in other ways as well.

"Too bad the champ couldn't be here," Levere said as smoke curled languidly from the cigarette nestled in the holder in his hand.

"He can't break training," a gruff voice commented.

"Especially this close to the fight," said another.

"Really, Lennox, you should know better," Van Vallen chided.

"Kurt, you know I'm a writer, not a fighter," Levere returned.

The two earlier speakers shared a wry glance. They were Arnie Ruland and Joby Washington, co-managers of Jackhammer Jackson. Ruland was white and Washington was black. Known far and wide as the "Salt and Pepper Twins," the pair had steered Jackhammer to the championship only four years after he made his professional debut. They were hard-faced men, veterans of an unforgiving sport. They looked uncomfortable in their tuxedos, and generally out-of-place in the Pomp Palace. Ordinarily, they would never have made it past the front door. But in the absence of the champion, their presence as his representatives was tolerated.

"He can't even break training for *me*," a pouty voice broke in.

All eyes turned to the new speaker: Lola Thorne. Lola was a singer, actress ... and fiancée of the champion. She was the only woman in the room whose presence could rival Delia's. She was two shades darker than Madame Pomp, two inches taller, two dress sizes slimmer, and too many years younger. Delia's eyes narrowed every time she looked at Lola. But the older woman knew better than to instigate a catfight on a night like this.

Still, she couldn't resist a subtly ambiguous barb.

"The man's discipline is ... admirable."

Before Lola or anyone else could continue the conversation, the gramophone's needle suddenly scratched with a banshee-like screech across the record on the turntable. And the lights in the salon blinked off, then on, in rapid succession.

CHAPTER TWO

NO BIG STEAL

The man in the car parked across the street from the mansion smiled in the darkness as he watched the flicker of the lights in the windows. It was indeed fortunate that no passers-by witnessed that baring of teeth. Some would have stopped in their tracks at the sight of it. Others would have run away. Still others might have sought to summon the police.

After the man in the car closed his mouth, his lips remained lifted in a grin no less discomfiting than his shark-like smile. He continued to stare at Madame Pomp's ostentatious dwelling. No longer did the lights flash on and off. Now the electric illumination blazed unabated.

The man in the car knew what the light revealed to those inside the house. Again, he smiled. …

❈ ❈ ❈

Before Delia and her guests could react to the flicker of the lights and the scratch of the record-player's needle, a series of new sounds claimed their attention – and added to their state of shocked confusion.

Serving-trays clattered noisily to the floor. Glasses filled with liquor shattered and sloshed. Hors d'oeuvres plopped quietly while other food items made more substantial sounds as they dropped. And a voice cut through the sudden babble of consternation as the last waiter let his tray fall.

"Keep yo' hands where we can see 'em, ladies and gen'men," the voice commanded. "Case yo' ain't figured it out yet, this heah's a stick-up!"

All eyes focused on the speaker, who was one of the waiters. The tray he'd carried moments before lay on the floor. Now his hand held a pistol – a cheap-looking weapon, but lethal enough in a room full of unarmed people.

Other waiters had also bared weapons previously concealed beneath their red jackets. Most carried guns. A few held wicked-looking knives with razor-sharp blades. Three of the nearly dozen-strong gang produced large pillowcases, the purpose of which was plain even to the most dumbfounded of Delia's guests.

The servile mien had dropped like a discarded mask from the face of the leader of the waiters-turned-bandits, and from the rest of the gang as well. There was a hard-edged darkness about them now: not only in the shade of their skin, but also the gazes that focused hungrily on the jewelry that glittered at the throats and wrists of the women, and the stickpins that secured the neckties of their escorts.

"Who put you up to this?" Madame Delia demanded, in a flat tone that was unlike any her guests had previously heard from her.

"Somebody you use to know," the gang leader replied. "No, there ain't gon' be no more talkin' heah. My ... 'associates' ... gon' be minglin' amongst you. All you got to do is drop yo' sparklers and yo' money in their bags. And don't be holdin' nothin' out on us, y'hear? And don't none of you gen'men try to play hero, or you'll end up with more holes in you than the Good Lord gave you when you was birthed."

He paused. Then a sneer of bitter contempt worked its way across his broad-featured face.

"Hope I done made myself clear," he said. "Everybody understand what I'm sayin'?"

Nods and muttered words of affirmation greeted that question. At a gesture from their leader, the bandits with the pillowcases circulated among the frightened party guests. Manicured hands reluctantly unclasped necklaces and slid off bracelets and rings. Men pulled stickpins from their ties and bills from their wallets. The loot clinked and rustled as it fed the open mouths of the pillowcases. No one said a word – not even Madame Pomp, who hesitated only a moment before adding her considerable share to the thieves' bounty.

Like others who had retained at least some presence of mind, Delia wondered why the thieves hadn't bothered to cover their faces. The implied answer to that unspoken question unnerved her. She struggled to control the tremor in her hands as the crooks gathered the last of the swag.

"Very nice," the leader said. "Very good. But you know, I got to wonder if some of y'all holdin' out."

He turned to one of his crew.

"What you think, man?" he asked.

"They could be hidin' stuff under they clothes, boss."

"Yeah," the leader said. "We need to find out."

"Sure do."

Then the lights went out.

❋ ❋ ❋

The head of the man in the car shot bolt upright as Madame Delia's windows darkened.

"Too damn soon," he growled.

The lights did not come back on. The man in the car scowled. Something had gone wrong. He had expected to see another blink of the lights – the signal that the job was over, and his gang was headed out the back entrance of the mansion, where the vehicles of the waiters were parked. The chained and weighted bodies of the real crew that was supposed to be serving that hinckty bunch of swells at Madame Pomp's were lying on the bottom of the East River. By the time they were missed, it would be too late to matter.

"Somebody fricked this thing up," the man in the car said in a near-whisper.

Starting his coupe's engine sooner than he had planned, the man pulled away from the curb. His hirelings were going to have to fend for themselves. Hell, they didn't even know who'd hired them – although their leader thought he did.

Right now, the man in the car needed to be gone from the vicinity of the Pomp Palace. And, more important, he needed to be even farther away from the people who'd hired *him*. ...

Careful not to go too fast, the man in the car drove down the length of Sugar Row. He was so intent on trying to figure out what had gone wrong that he failed to notice the car that eased out of a dark side street and began to tail him.

❋ ❋ ❋

"Who turned the goddamn lights out?" the gang leader raged above the other outcries that greeted the sudden darkness.

No one answered. The wan street-light that came through the windows was not bright enough to show anything other than a confused kaleidoscope of bodies stumbling, flailing and lurching into one another. Shouts, curses and screams punctuated the gloom as the lights stayed off.

Then another sound intruded: the pounding of a drum – a single conga, beating an insistent rhythm that was not metronomic, but variegated, like a call coming from deep in the Congo. ...

"Somebody get them lights back on!" the gang leader yelled – just before a slight, puffing sound cut off further outcries. A strangled wheeze was followed by the slump of a body to the floor.

The sequence was repeated: puff, wheeze, thud. Even as the eyes of thieves and victim alike began to adjust to the feeble illumination, their vision could not focus on the blurred black figure that glided among them like a phantom – seen, heard, but never touched.

For a few moments longer, the chaotic panic persisted. Then two gunshots exploded. With inarticulate outcries of alarm, Madame Delia and her guests dove to the floor. Some of them landed on bodies that were already prostrate. The guests didn't care that they might have fallen on top of the thieves; they just wanted to get out of the line of fire.

No more shots rang out. No more bodies fell. No more puffing sounds were heard. The only sounds in the salon were unsteady breathing and the rustle of clothing. The drumming had ended, to be replaced by a soft, hitching noise.

Slowly, cautiously, people began to move. Though they could see each other more clearly now, they did not know whether they were still in danger. Then, abruptly, the lights came back on. Adonis Levere was standing by the switch. Evidently, he knew his way around the mansion.

Gasps of shock escaped the throats of the party-goers as they stared at what the illumination revealed.

The thieves lay strewn like red-jacketed refuse across the floor. Some were prone; others face-up. Their weapons rested beside them. So did the pillowcases loaded with the loot Madame Delia's guests had reluctantly donated. But it was not the recumbent position of their erstwhile despoilers that caused the guests' eyes to widen, and their mouths to gape inadvertently. It was a grayish-black powder that claimed the guests' attention. The dust clung mask-like to the faces of the thieves.

The color of the powder caused the faces of its victims to resemble bone rather than flesh – an impression heightened by the skull-like rictus in which their teeth were bared. However, the notion that the thieves had died was quickly dispelled by one of the guests, who was a prominent physician with a large clientele on Sugar Row. After kneeling and placing his hands on the necks and wrists of the robbers, the doctor looked up at the party-goers.

"They are still alive," the physician said. "But it's as though they've been put under some sort of anesthetic."

As though the doctor's words were a signal of some sort, others began to speak almost simultaneously.

"Tie them up!"

"Break their heads!"

"Call the police!"

"Dump out those pillowcases!"

"No! They're evidence!"

"'Evidence,' my foot! I've got a five-hundred-dollar necklace in there! I want it back!"

Delia paid no attention to the storm of suggestions and imprecations as she made her way to the gramophone. A record was still spinning on the turntable, and the needle at the end of the tone arm skipped aimlessly in the blank circle beyond the disk's grooves.

Immediately, Delia saw the difference between this record and any others that were in the stack at the side of the Crossley. This one had a label as black as the disk itself. And its title, which she could not read from her present distance, was printed in crimson letters.

Replacing the tone arm in its cradle, Delia lifted the record from the spindle and brought it closer to her eyes. When she saw the name the blood-red letters spelled, she whispered it in a low, almost inaudible tone:

"Damballa ... "

She felt a presence behind her. Turning, she saw Van Vallen. For once the writer's habitual smirk was absent. He looked as though he were struggling hard to conceal his fright. Delia knew he had seen the name on the record label. She wondered how he would respond to it.

"Looks like the party's over," was all Van Vallen said.

Above them, the likeness of Jackhammer Jackson gazed impassively at the confused scene in the salon.

Had the man in the car remained in his parking spot, he might have caught a glimpse of a figure in the shadows between Madame Pomp's mansion and its left-side neighbor. Only for a moment, he might have seen the suggestion of an arm, a leg, a cloak-like garment, and a strong-featured profile half-hidden by a hood. The sight would have been so momentary that the man in the car might well have doubted the vague evidence his senses had provided.

Nor did anyone in the small crowd attracted by the previous blasts of gunshots and the current wail of approaching police cars' sirens see the partly obscured shape before it disappeared. It was as though the mysterious figure had materialized momentarily out of the darkness itself, then quickly subsumed back into the gloom from which it had emerged.

❃ ❃ ❃

Detective Errol Bynoe slowly turned the "Damballa" disk in his slim brown hands, as though the grooves on its black surface could somehow provide the facts he sought. A tall, slender, impeccably dressed man who looked younger than his 35 years, Bynoe was a native of the American Virgin Islands who had come to New York with his family when he was a child. Even then, he had aspired to become a police officer, at a time when only a few blacks wore the blue, and the notion of a Negro detective was unthinkable.

Not to be denied, Bynoe had joined the uniformed ranks. Through hard work, persistence, and imperviousness to endless insults both overt and implied, the West Indian rose to become one of the first Negro detectives in the history of the New York City Police Department.

He knew the score: the department's brass had decided to let the colored ride herd on the colored, just as the Italians rode herd on the Italians and the Irish rode herd on the Irish. That reality didn't prevent him from aspiring to be the best detective in the city, regardless of the color of his skin.

He laid the record on the table in front of him, picked up his pen and notebook, and looked at Madame Delia, who sat across from him. They were in one of several lounging-rooms in the Pomp Palace. Other police officers and detectives were still in the salon, interviewing guests and supervising the return of the abandoned pillowcases' contents to their rightful owners.

It was late, past midnight. Bynoe had interviewed already Delia along with the others. Now, he wanted to speak with her alone, without a gaggle of courtiers surrounding her.

"You've had some time now to think and remember, ma'am," Bynoe said in a tone that retained a West Indian lilt. "Is there anything at all you can remember about Damballa?"

Delia shook her head. She had donned a dark-blue caftan that covered the splendors of her gown and jewels. A scarf of the same shade as the caftan covered her hair. Under her makeup, her face looked drawn and worried. But she maintained her poise.

Her eyes narrowed for a moment. In Detective Bynoe, she recognized a fellow striver, a breaker of barriers. But Bynoe didn't have very much to show for his efforts, other than his rank in the police force. If he did, he would be living on Sugar Row, like her and most of the party guests.

"Why do you keep asking about Damballa, Detective?" Delia inquired. "You're not suggesting he could have been behind a robbery he foiled, are you?"

"He operates outside the law, and that's cause enough for concern," Bynoe returned, ignoring Madame Pomp's subtle sarcasm.

"Be that as it may, I never got a good look at him," Delia said. "I don't think anybody ever has."

The detective let that comment pass.

"We talked before about who might have hired those hoodlums to take the places of the real waiters," he said. "The owner of the service in which the real waiters were employed is in the clear. He says he knows nothing about the substitution, and I believe him. The real waiters are most likely dead."

"How awful."

Bynoe couldn't tell whether her concern was genuine. He pressed on.

"This could have been just a simple robbery, ma'am," he said. "But the way you and the others described it – what the robbers were about to force you and your guests to do before Damballa intervened – suggests that humiliation might have been a motive as well. Who might have wanted to humiliate you?"

"As you most likely know, Detective, I have two former husbands. And three estranged children. They may not like me very much, but they're not about to harm the goose that lays their golden eggs."

"How about former suitors?"

"None of them would have the nerve, Detective. Actually, none of them are even in town, as far as I know."

"Business rivals?"

Delia smiled.

"I have no 'business rivals' to speak of, Detective."

"Perhaps someone you drove out of business decided they wanted revenge."

"None of them would have had the nerve."

Pride goes before a fall, Bynoe thought. He decided to change tack.

"You haven't always lived in New York, have you, Mrs. Pomphrey?"

"It is common knowledge that I was, indeed, born and raised in New Orleans, Detective."

"Is there anyone from your past there who might have carried a serious grudge against you over the years?"

Madame Pomp's fabled composure showed a crack then. Her eyes avoided Bynoe's unblinking gaze. Her posture appeared to sag ever so slightly beneath her caftan.

"There is such a man," she whispered.

Bynoe's pen scratched rapidly across the pages of his notebook as Delia spoke on, reluctantly but informatively.

CHAPTER THREE

WORDS IN A WAREHOUSE

The man who had been in the car parked across the street from Madame Delia's mansion wasn't in his car anymore. He was tied to a chair in a room that would have been pitch-black had it not been for the bright bare light-bulb hanging directly over his head. There were three other people in the room with him. Although he could see them only as vague silhouettes, he didn't need more detail to know who they were. And that knowledge made him far more fearful than he would have been had they been strangers.

Memories strobed through his aching head. *A big car roaring behind him, passing him, cutting him off, forcing him to stop … men with guns in their hands piling out of the other car, dragging him out of his own vehicle before he could even try to get away … a hard blow to the side of his head, catapulting him into oblivion … waking up in this chair, in this room, and having no answers to the questions that he knew were coming … hoping that the moments of life that remained to him would be short rather than long …*

Two huge men flanked his chair. They stood slightly behind him. The third man sat a couple of yards in front of him, his face little more than a pale blur in the semi-darkness. No one had said anything to him since a bucket of cold water splashed into his face brought him back to consciousness. He knew the silence wasn't going to last much longer.

"You failed, Jones," the seated man finally said. "Why?"

The man's speech was tinged with a suggestion of a German accent.

13

"Ain't no 'why,'" the bound man, whose street name was "Bullets," replied. "Just a 'how.' Lights in the place went out when they wasn't supposed to. I wasn't stickin' around to find out what happened. I figured the word'd come back soon enough."

"Such a shame," the seated man said. "All your men captured ... and nothing to show for it."

"Captured?" Jones expostulated. "How did – "

At a slight nod from the seated man, one of the huskies hauled off and landed a hard blow to Jones' left shoulder-blade, almost breaking the bone. Jones cried out in agony, and if the other big man hadn't caught him, he would have toppled over, chair and all.

"Boss! Boss!" Jones pleaded. "Them lugs I hired don't know nothin' about you. The cops'll never find out – "

"Silence," the seated man said.

Jones shut up fast.

"The police do not concern me, you *verdammt Schwarzer*," the seated man said, his German inflections thickening. "My concern is someone else ... someone you did not deign to mention to me."

"Someone who?"

"Damballa."

"Bullets" Jones' eyes bulged as he went rigid in his bonds.

"D-D-Damballa?" he stammered. "What that damn hoodoo-man got to do with this?"

"He was the one who – how you say – crashed the party," the seated man said. "One man, who bested nearly a dozen foes who were armed and, at least minimally, competent. You know, at first I thought this 'Damballa' was nothing more than a product of your people's primitive imaginations. Or, perhaps, a fiction, like the ones in those silly newsstand magazines. Then I came to realize that he may not be make-believe, after all."

After a moment of silence, the seated man continued.

"How do you suppose Damballa discovered our plan, Jones?"

"All I can say, Boss, is he didn't hear nothin' from me. I ain't never seen or talked to no Damballa."

"I believe you, Jones," the seated man said. "And I also believe that the activities you instigated at Delia Pomphrey's mansion accomplished at least some of their objectives. There is still a problem, though. It is true that your men had no direct connection with me. But ... you do."

If Jones' skin could have turned pale, it would have then, because he knew what those last words portended.

"Please, Boss," he moaned.

The seated man gave another barely perceptible nod. But before anything further could occur, one of the men guarding Jones uttered a short outcry of pain, then slumped to the floor.

❖ ❖ ❖

Jones' bonds prevented him from moving as the second husky dropped with barely a sound. And he was unable to turn around to see the source of the soft, nearly inaudible noises behind him. He could only stare wide-eyed as his interrogator quickly rose and reached into a pocket in his jacket.

"*Hurensohn!*" the man swore as the grip of a gun began to emerge from the opening.

From behind, Jones heard a soft, almost inaudible sound. Then a cloud of gray powder shot like a blurred arrow toward the face of the German, who had pulled the gun nearly all the way from his pocket.

When the powder reached the German's face, it clung to his skin like a translucent film. The man's face froze in an expression of fear and rage. Slowly, he dropped backward and landed in his seat at an awkward angle. In little more than an instant, he was rendered as unconscious as his henchmen.

But not before his finger tightened reflexively on the trigger of his gun, sending a bullet through the cloth of his jacket and into the floor.

The blast reverberated like thunder in the enclosed space. Even as the echoes died away, distant shouts could suddenly be heard, as well as the faint, repetitive tap of running footsteps.

Jones heard a muffled sound that was wordless, yet still betrayed frustration. He opened his mouth to cry out, but was silenced by a hiss that he was not about to disobey. For Jones had a good idea as to who the intruder was. And with that knowledge, his fears multiplied.

Another puffing sound caught Jones' attention. He saw a small, dark object speed toward the exposed light-bulb. A moment later, the entire enclosure was plunged into utter darkness as the bulb broke. Jones was about to cry out inadvertently when a tiny pinprick against his neck sent him into unconsciousness, even as a thin blade sliced through his bonds.

And he didn't hear the commotion created by nearly a score of men blundering in the darkness.

❖ ❖ ❖

Despite the burden of Jones's limp body slung over his shoulder, Damballa moved quickly and confidently through the darkness of the warehouse. Even in the near-total absence of light, Damballa's senses – including vision – functioned far better than those of other men. Jones was bulky. But Damballa carried him easily.

Damballa was making more noise than usual. Speed was of the essence now, though, and any sounds he made would be muffled by the shouts, curses and stumbles of the Germans who were looking for a light, as well as the source of the gunshot.

That shot ...

It was the first setback Damballa had suffered since he had foiled the holdup attempt at Madame Pomp's. When he'd exited the mansion, he had spotted Jones's car as it eased away from the curb. Then he saw the other car slide out after it. Moments later, Damballa had reached his own vehicle. Driving unobtrusively, he followed the two cars. He saw the second vehicle cut off Jones' car. After Jones was accosted and abducted, Damballa continued to tail both cars – one of the abductors had taken Jones's machine.

The grim parade had continued to the warehouse district, a vast warren of low-slung buildings that loomed dark and silent in the night. A watchman had waved the two cars through the gate in front of one of those buildings, which was not very different from the others on its row. They all had German-looking names painted or embossed on their identifying signs.

The watchman never saw Damballa, for the crime-fighter had left his car some distance from the gate and had climbed – unseen and unheard – over the fence. On foot, he trailed the now slow-moving vehicles to their destination. He watched them carry Jones inside, and saw that Jones' car was being driven elsewhere. Not a good sign for Jones. ...

With the darkness helping him to avoid detection, Damballa had gained access to the warehouse. In the cloak of the shadows, he observed the interrogation of Jones. Damballa had intended to corral both Jones and his mysterious interlocutor, for he had questions of his own. The spasm of a trigger finger had put an end to that plan.

There was no time to secure both men. The questioner was too far away from Damballa for quick action. But Jones was right in front of him. After taking out the three men and breaking the light-bulb, Damballa slung Jones over his shoulder and faded deeper into the darkness.

Damballa cared nothing for Jones. Even so, he was loath to leave him in the hands of the Germans. And he was certain Jones had information of value – although less so than the facts the interrogator might have provided.

With his free hand, Damballa touched the warehouse wall. He could feel the outline of the obscure hatchway through which he had gained entry. Had he been alone, he would easily have escaped unnoticed. Burdened by the unconscious Jones, the task had become more difficult.

But not impossible.

Reaching into one of many pouches and pockets hidden inside his cloak, Damballa's hand closed on the grip of an automatic pistol. He preferred to use weapons that were quieter and more enigmatic. Sometimes, though, an obtrusive weapon was the best option.

Damballa pulled out his gun and fired several shots toward the metal ceiling of the warehouse. Ricochets spanged throughout the dark enclosure, giving the impression that more than one gunman had loosed the volley of bullets. Oaths in German and English tore from the throats of men who dove to the floor. At any moment, flashlights would be found and lit.

But the moment gained from the distraction his shots had caused was all the time Damballa needed.

He dragged Jones through the opening. Then his keen night vision scanned the area in front of the warehouse, searching for any watchmen who might have been alarmed by the gunshots. None appeared; the one who had let the two vehicles past the gate must have gone into the warehouse to investigate the tumult.

Hoisting Jones' inert bulk as though it were weightless, Damballa hurried toward the fence at a point well away from the warehouse entrance. Extracting a metal-cutter from his cloak, he slashed a large opening in the wire mesh, through which he quickly dragged Jones, making certain that the unconscious man's clothing did not become caught on the jagged edges.

Then he carried his burden to his vehicle. By the time a throng of dark-clad men poured out of the main door of the warehouse, even the sound of the motor of Damballa's car was long gone.

He slashed a large opening in the wire mesh, through which he quickly dragged Jones.

CHAPTER FOUR

THE LIBERATION OF BULLETS JONES

For the second time in a matter of hours, Bullets Jones awoke from an involuntary state of unconsciousness. This time, he felt only a mild echo of the pain that had stabbed through his skull on the earlier occasion. A bitter taste lingered in his mouth, though … a taste that reminded him of some of the hootch he had knocked back during Prohibition.

He blinked his bleary eyes. Once again, he was sitting on a chair in a cocoon of darkness, broken only by a single source of light. Instead of a bare bulb hanging from above, this time the illumination was provided by a large black candle positioned in the middle of a low table. Objects lay in patterned rows across the table: small bundles of cloth; feathers tied to the ends of sticks; small glasses filled with liquids that smoked and bubbled; skulls of tiny animals carved with arcane designs …

Only a few of those objects were familiar to Jones. And those few, he feared deeply.

No ropes tied Jones to the chair. But when he tried to get up, he found that he could not. The bonds that kept him motionless were intangible. But they were undoubtedly effective.

"Hezekiah Jones," a voice whispered. It seemed to come from the darkness beyond the candle's glow. At the sound of his first name, Jones became even more disoriented. Few people knew the name his mother had given him; fewer still had spoken it. He preferred the nickname he had given himself after he had left home.

"Do you know who I am, Hezekiah Jones?" the voice asked.

Whatever it was that held him immobile did not prevent Jones from speaking in reply.

"Damballa," the gangster choked out.

"Why did you try to loot Delia Pomphrey's party, Hezekiah Jones?"

Jones wanted to say nothing, or at least concoct some desperate lie. Instead, he found himself spilling his guts like the most abject stool pigeon. He was unable to halt the flow of words from his tongue. As he talked, the sour taste in his mouth grew stronger.

"I knew Delia back in New Orleans, during Prohibition," Bullets said. "I had me a hootch racket; she was just startin' to make them beauty chemicals. She needed a backer, and didn't care where the money come from. She come to me, and I helped her out. She paid me back right on time, without no arguments. Didn't have no trouble from her – then.

"She move on up here to New York. I stayed in New Orleans, 'cause my business was goin' good there. When Prohibition ended, I went bust, like all the other hootchy-men. After a while, I figured I'd come up here to see Delia. Woman owed me a favor. But when I find her, she don't give me the time of day. Figured she was way above 'low-lifes' like me now."

"Did you threaten her?" Damballa asked.

"Damn straight I threatened her! Her and her high-and-mighty ways! Who the hell she think she is?"

"But you could not do anything to her at that time, because you are small-time. You needed help. That is where the Germans came in."

"Yeah. They say they front me enough dough to hire some bad-boys to hit her big to-do. We would all get a good share of the swag."

"Was killing the real waiters your idea?"

"Naw. The Germans come up with that."

"Do these Germans have names?"

"They never give us no names. They act like they didn't really want nothin' to do with coloreds if they could help it. But they had to use us cause the job was in Harlem. We less conspicuous there."

"Did they give any indication that your robbery would have anything to do with the Jackhammer Jackson fight?"

"They never say nothin' about that. And I never thought nothin' about it. All I was thinkin' about was gettin' back at that Delia."

Damballa did not ask any further questions. The silence stretched uncomfortably. Finally, Jones could no longer contain his fears.

"What you gon' do with me, Mistah Damballa?" he asked, his voice little more than a thin croak.

A black form emerged from the penumbra beyond the candle's light. The shape was man-like but indistinct, as though it were part of the night. For a moment, Jones thought he could glimpse pale, linear markings, like outlines of bones.

Then Jones' throat constricted in terror as an ebony hand picked up one of the glasses of dubious liquid. Another hand wrenched Jones' head back. The glass rose to Jones' quivering lips. Then a burning fluid rushed past his teeth and down his throat. And the gangster knew no more.

❉ ❉ ❉

Delia Pomphrey woke a split-second before a hand clapped over her mouth, cutting off any outcry. Before she could sink her teeth into the palm of that hand, a voice whispered a word in her ear.

"Damballa."

Delia nodded. The hand slipped away from her mouth. Delia sat up in her spacious bed and pulled the fleecy duvet up to her shoulders, which were bare save for the straps of her thin nightgown. Instinctively, she reached out to turn on her bedside lamp.

"No lights," Damballa commanded.

As her eyes adjusted to the dim light that filtered through the curtains of her bedroom, Delia could make out a dark, man-sized shape standing at her side. But she could not discern any features.

A breeze stirred the curtains. Delia knew she had closed her window before going to bed. She suppressed a shudder. Throughout her life, she had been able to manipulate men as though they were putty. Only one had ever proven to be immune to her wiles: the one of whom she had spoken to Detective Bynoe. Now, though she had never met Damballa before, she knew she had encountered another who was impervious to her influence.

Silence stretched. Delia spoke first.

"I owe you a debt of gratitude for stopping that horrible robbery."

"No need to thank me, Mrs. Pomphrey," said Damballa. "However, I have come here to tie up a loose end."

Loose end? Delia thought. She immediately became angry at what she thought Damballa might be implying.

"Are you insinuating that I had something to do with the attempted robbery of my own party?" she asked in a steely tone.

"Not at all, Mrs. Pomphrey," came Damballa's calm reply. "I merely wanted to let you know that you have no further need to be concerned about the man who was behind that robbery."

"You mean Bullets Jones?" Delia asked, her fear returning in a rush. "I told the police about him. ..."

"The police will soon discover that Mr. Jones has ... disappeared."

"You killed him?"

"No. I ... *persuaded* him to leave town. Believe me, Madame Pomphrey, he will never come back here again."

"I believe you."

"I must take my leave now, Madame Pomphrey. Enjoy the fight."

Delia heard nothing, but a moment later, the shape at her bedside was gone. She saw a blurry silhouette at the open window, and then nothing. Whipping the tangle of covers aside, she ran to the window and stared out. No Damballa ... no ladder or rope ... no indication of how he had managed to climb up the outside wall of the Pomp Palace and make his way into her bedroom.

Delia closed the window and crawled back into bed, huddling under the covers as though they were a refuge. Morning was still hours away. But she knew she would not sleep again this night.

❀ ❀ ❀

"Wake up, boy! Last stop!"

Hezekiah "Bullets" Jones opened his eyes. Immediately, he realized he was on a passenger train. It was a Jim Crow car; all the passengers shuffling toward the exit were black. Only the red-faced, impatient-looking conductor was white. Jones' thoughts flowed like sludge as he stared up at the conductor.

"Where I'm at?" Jones mumbled.

"Atlanta, dammit! Isn't that where you wanted to go? Now, get out! Sleeping all the way down here and acting like you're sleepwalking when you're awake ... Swear to God, you've got to be the laziest nigger I ever did see!"

Still muddled, Jones rose from his seat and joined the others leaving the passenger car. *Atlanta*, he thought.

Home ... but ain't New Orleans my home?

No, said a voice that was not his, but still in his mind. *Atlanta is your home ... Atlanta. ...*

While the other passengers wrestled with their luggage, Jones wandered along the platform, heading automatically toward the doors of the train station. He knew where he was, but he didn't know why he was there. He didn't know where he had been when he got on the train. And he didn't know why or how he had been away from Atlanta in the first place.

His mouth was hot, as though he had swallowed a bottle of Tabasco sauce. A voice echoed eerily in his mind, but he could not make out any words. Words were not necessary, though. Suggestions echoed deeply within him. A name skittered ahead of his memory like a rabbit that couldn't be caught. He tried very hard to remember who he had been before he woke up on the train.

But he couldn't.

He saw a reflection of his face in a windowpane. The visage that stared back at him was not the one he only vaguely remembered. He was no longer who he had once been. More words murmured in his mind as his feet shuffled mechanically forward.

He needed a job.

He needed a place to live.

He needed a name. ...

CHAPTER FIVE

JACKHAMMER

The champion stared across the ring at his latest sparring partner. This was a new guy. Jackhammer Jackson was known to be hard on his spar-mates, and not many of them made it all the way through one of his training camps.

"If I let up in sparrin', I might let up in a real fight," Jackhammer once told a sportswriter. "Ain't no sense in that."

Jackhammer studied the man in the opposite corner. Even though the newcomer was sitting on a stool, Jackhammer guessed that he stood an inch or so taller than the champion's six feet. But at slightly more than two hundred pounds, Jackhammer was at least ten pounds heavier, maybe more. This new guy had one of those deceptively lean frames that would make him look thin under clothing. Stripped down to boxing trunks, though, his wiry muscles were clearly defined under skin as black as midnight.

The champion had caught only part of the man's name: "Kid" something-or-other. He'd never heard of him. A friend of Joby Washington, one of Jackhammer's managers, had sent him to the camp "as a favor."

Gittin' in the ring with me is a "favor?" Jackhammer thought. *Some "favor."*

"Ready, son?"

Jackhammer turned and looked at Chum Williams, who had been his trainer since the day the Salt and Pepper Twins had seen the fighter plow like a bulldozer through the field of an amateur tournament in Chicago.

Most people only looked at Chum once if they could help it. He was an ex-boxer, a veteran of the hard old days of the sport, in the years immediately following the turn of the century – and it showed. Scar-tissue had narrowed his eyes to slits, and his nose was flattened and bent. Another scar, inflicted by the blade of a knife during an altercation outside the ring, marred the right side of his ginger-colored face from lip to ear.

A majority of the people Chum Williams knew were scared to death of him. His nickname was rich in irony. But he had taken to Jackhammer right away, and had molded the wild-swinging amateur into what one sportswriter called "the deadliest predator on two feet."

"Ready," Jackhammer said.

"Joby say this guy supposed to be fast, like that Aryan," said Chum. "Show him you fast, too. Just act like you got that Aryan in front of you right now."

Jackhammer looked at the dark skin of "Kid something," and uttered a snort that might have been laughter.

"Yeah, Chum," the champion said. "I'ma do just that."

Chum stepped down from the ring. The few people the Salt and Pepper Twins had allowed to remain at the training camp this close to the fight gathered around the ring. All of them wondered how long the new guy would last. Not long, most of them decided. He didn't even have on one of the padded vests most of the other sparring partners wore to blunt the impact of Jackhammer's body shots.

"Time!" Chum shouted, in lieu of a bell.

❧ ❧ ❧

The fighters shuffled from their corners. Their oversized sparring gloves probed the air. Jackhammer peered at the parts of the new guy's face that his helmet revealed. There wasn't much to see, other than his eyes. The helmets were another safety precaution. A spar-mate could refuse the body protection, but not the helmet – not since Jackhammer sent somebody who wasn't wearing one to the hospital. Jackhammer wore a sparring helmet only to prevent inadvertent cuts that might affect his fights.

Jackhammer's face was as expressionless as its likeness on Delia Pomphrey's wall. So was the new guy's ... except for the eyes. There was something peculiar about those eyes. ...

Refusing to allow any further distractions, Jackhammer decided to introduce himself to his spar-mate. One moment he was moving toward the other man, cutting off any avenue of escape. The next, his left hand shot out three times, in rapid succession, to the head, body, and head again.

The first two blows landed. The third didn't.

You good, bub, Jackhammer thought. Not many fighters could have avoided any of the punches in that one-handed combination of jabs. And even fewer could have set themselves quickly enough to counter with a right. Jackhammer saw it coming and shifted his head aside, but the spar-mate's blow still caught the champion high on his helmet.

The blow didn't hurt. But it made Jackhammer hesitate for a fraction of a second. And in that brief interval, "Kid something" ripped two punches to Jackhammer's body, then glided away from the ropes and bounced at the center of the ring. Those shots bothered the champion a little.

Jackhammer went after him again. This time, he kept his jab high. "Kid something" tried to block and duck those jabs, but he couldn't avoid all of them. And he had to be remembering how quickly Jackhammer could shift his jab from head to body, with devastating effect.

The spar-mate continued to retreat. Jackhammer was having trouble herding him into the ropes and corners. And the new guy kept firing sneaky counterpunches that were substantial enough to disrupt the champion's rhythm, even though they didn't dent his iron jaw.

Usually, the ringside crew bantered loudly during Jackhammer's sparring sessions, with plenty of comedic commentary on the action – mainly at the spar-mate of the day's expense. Not this time, though. This session was turning out to be more competitive than some of Jackhammer's real fights.

Chum's voice rose above the muted murmur of the spectators.

"Quit playin' around, son," he said to the champion.

What in the hell makes you think I'm playin'? Jackhammer thought as yet another of "Kid something's" blows managed to find his face. The spar-mate's jab was not as strong as Jackhammer's, but it was almost as quick, darting in and out like a snake's tongue.

Even as he struggled to cope with the spar-mate's unexpected speed, Jackhammer noticed a strange habit the man had that didn't have anything to do with boxing. Every now and then, one of "Kid something's" legs would lift slightly, as though he were about to launch a kick. Then he'd put his foot back down, as though he was consciously suppressing the impulse to do something that was outlawed even under the old bare-knuckle prizefighting rules.

Jackhammer had not yet thrown a right-hand punch. His right was even more powerful than his left. But Chum had taught him to use it sparingly, so his opponents would always be wondering when he was going to unleash it. While they were wondering, Jackhammer carved them up with his left.

So far, Jackhammer had been biding his time with "Kid something," waiting for an opportunity. *Bidin's over,* the champion decided.

"Kid something's" leg lifted again. This time, Jackhammer's right hand shot out. It didn't travel more than six inches before colliding with the spar-mate's solar plexus, a vulnerable area under the ribcage. "Kid something" tried to block the blow with his elbow. But his leg-lifting motion had cost him too much time, and Jackhammer's blow struck true.

"Kid something" staggered backward a few steps. Then his legs refused to hold him up any longer, and he sat down hard, with his back resting against the bottom rope and his gloves on the canvas.

"Time!" Chum yelled.

Jackhammer walked over to the fallen spar-mate and helped him to his feet. He noticed that the man got his legs under him more quickly than most who had been struck with a similar punch.

"You had me goin' for a minute there, bub," the champion said. "You step pretty good. How come I never heard of you before?"

"You have," the other man said in a whisper-like tone. "But under a different name."

Before Jackhammer could ask "Kid something" what those cryptic words meant, Chum's voice cut him off.

"Hit the showers, son," the trainer said as he climbed into the ring. "No more sparrin' today."

Jackhammer stared quizzically at the older man. Usually, his sparring sessions lasted a lot longer than this, especially at this point before a fight. He trusted Chum implicitly, though, and he knew the old man never did anything without a good reason, even though he sometimes kept his reasons to himself. Nodding to his spar-mate, the champion slipped through the ropes and headed toward the building that contained the showers, as well as punching bags and other equipment.

Then Chum turned to "Kid something." He stared hard at the sparring partner, who returned his gaze impassively. After a few moments, Chum pulled his wallet out of the back pocket of his pants, extracted several bills, and stuffed them into one of "Kid something's" gloves.

"Get the hell out of here, whoever you is," Chum grated. "And don't ever come back. Ya hear?"

"Kid something" didn't say anything. Chum knew he wasn't going to get any answer to his question. Indeed, he was finding that this man was one of the few he wasn't able to stare down. Finally, the trainer clambered back out of the ring and made his way toward the rest of the training-camp staff. The now-former spar-mate left the ring a moment later.

CHAPTER SIX

LOCKER-ROOM TALK

Jackhammer sat on a bench in the locker room adjacent to the shower stalls. Ordinarily, this whole place, which was named Compton Lakes, was a resort in which he and most of his staff would not have been allowed to set foot, had they been ordinary Negroes. But because he was the champion, and had money to burn, Jackhammer was accorded exclusive use of the resort as a training camp to prepare for his title defenses. During those times, the very same people who would have objected vociferously to his presence found their own entrance barred.

As he pulled on his pants, and then his socks and shoes, Jackhammer didn't reflect on that irony. He liked to be alone after his workouts, so he could have time to think about how far his fists had brought him, and how much farther he intended to go, and what he needed to do to get there. This time, though, he also thought about "Kid something." It wasn't often that a sparring partner gave him so much trouble. He wondered if that meant he would have more difficulties ahead when he got into the ring against the Aryan.

Then he wondered why he suddenly had the feeling that he was no longer alone in the locker room. ...

Still bare-chested, Jackhammer looked up from his shoes. The room was only dimly lit, and the rows of lockers cast deep shadows. In one of those pools of semi-darkness, he saw a hazy shape. He knew it hadn't been there a moment ago. It was a human form, seemingly part of the darkness itself.

29

A cloak covered the body of the intruder. Its hood was drawn back. The only features clearly visible in the dark smudge of the man's face were his eyes … eyes that shone preternaturally … eyes Jackhammer had seen before, not too long ago. …

"I'll be damned," Jackhammer said softly. "You weren't lyin' when you said I know you under a different name, bub. Looks like I been in the ring with Damballa himself."

He spoke that name with as much respect as a heavyweight champion of the world could muster. For in New York City and elsewhere, it was the only name mentioned in the same breath as Jackhammer's, among colored and white alike. The difference was, Jackhammer lived under the constant glare of the spotlight, while Damballa operated in the darkness of night. Jackhammer ruled the ring. Damballa's domain was … larger.

Jackhammer knew little of Damballa, besides his reputation and description. In that lack of knowledge, the champion was far from alone. Nobody knew Damballa's true name, but his deeds were as legendary as they were amazing. He was the implacable enemy of Harlem's criminals, be they whites taking advantage of blacks or blacks dragging one another down like crabs in a barrel. But the law didn't trust him because he kept his identity hidden. And some of his methods were at odds with what the police were permitted to do.

Because the name he chose to be known by was that of a West African serpent god, many thought Damballa came from the Dark Continent, or perhaps somewhere in the West Indies. Some people thought he was a conjure-man, or maybe even a hoodoo – a spirit that had not been left behind when colored Americans' ancestors were taken from Africa.

Even before he had come to New York, Jackhammer had heard of Damballa. He just never expected to meet him … especially in a sparring session.

"And I've been in the ring with Jackhammer Jackson," Damballa said. His voice was low now, not whispery. It was reminiscent of the growl of a great cat. Nothing in his intonation suggested either the slow drawl of the South or the flashy cadences of the North. There was no trace of any accent Jackhammer could identify.

"Why you want to spar with me?" Jackhammer asked. "Couldn't've been for the thrill."

Damballa laughed quietly.

"No, Champ," he said. "Not for the thrill. If I hadn't been careful, you would have knocked my head off."

Questions crowded Jackhammer's mind. The one that came out of his mouth surprised even him.

"Who taught you how to throw hands?"

"Jack Johnson."

Jackhammer scowled and snorted.

"That ol' sumbitch?" he growled. "He ain't never had a good word to say about me since I made it to the big time."

"He's just jealous, Champ. You've stolen the man's thunder, and naturally he doesn't like it."

Jackhammer let a moment of silence pass before he spoke again.

"Let's get down to it, Mr. Damballa. Why'd you step in with me?"

"Champ, if I'm willing to take a chance in the ring with you, maybe you'll be more likely to trust me, despite what you may have heard about me."

"Trust you? From what I hear, trouble's always around you. You sayin' trouble's comin' around me, too?"

Jackhammer was on his feet now. Damballa did not move.

"Champ, you know that most of America is in your corner in this fight you've got coming up," Damballa said. "Black, white … for once, color doesn't matter. But even so, there are people who don't want you to win."

"Yeah. Like your buddy Johnson."

"No need to worry about him, Champ. He's just trying to get attention. In his mind, he thinks he should still have the crown you're wearing now."

"Tell me somethin'. Does what you getting' at have anything to do with that mess at Madame Delia's last night?"

Damballa's eyes widened in surprise.

"You are not as isolated here as it seems," the cloaked man said.

"Hmph!" Jackhammer snorted. "Them managers of mine might be able to keep my woman out of here, but they can't shut everybody's big mouth. I heard it was you that busted up the robbery. I got to thank you for that, bub. If anything'd happened to Lola …"

He frowned then – an expression even more disturbing than his usual deadpan stare.

"You think them robbers was really gon' do somethin' to Lola in order to get to me?" the champion demanded, taking a step forward.

"I don't know yet," Damballa said calmly. "It might have been just an opportunistic heist. But there's more going on than just that robbery. I am doing everything I can to find out what might be happening, and put an end to it. That is all I can tell you for now. I *will* get to the bottom of this.

And I will help you if you need it. But you've got to trust me, Champ. Do you?"

Jackhammer gave Damballa a long look, as though he were trying to read a message in the other man's eyes.

"If you crazy enough to step in the ring with me, bub, then I guess I'm crazy enough to trust you and your hoodoo," he said at last.

A smile flickered across Damballa's shadowed lips.

"So be it," he said.

"I wan' ask you one thing, though."

"Go ahead."

"When we was sparrin', you kept liftin' your leg up like you was about to take a piss. What was that all about?"

Damballa chuckled.

"I've learned many different ways of fighting, from all over the world," he replied. "Feet can be more effective than hands. You left some openings my feet could have exploited. I had to stop myself from taking advantage of them. There are fewer than half-a-dozen men who could have hit me while I was lowering my leg as quickly as you did, Champ."

"Do tell."

Suddenly, both men heard a noise at the door to the locker room. Jackhammer turned toward the door, then decided to turn back to Damballa instead. But the cloaked man was no longer there. He had vanished without a sound. There was no indication that he had been in the locker room at all.

❊ ❊ ❊

Jackhammer shook his head as he put on his shirt.

"Hoodoo," he muttered under his breath.

Rising from the bench, Jackhammer exited the locker room. As he opened the door, he saw what he expected to see: Chum, still unbending from the crouch he had assumed when he put his ear against the door. An indignant scowl stretched the scar on the trainer's face.

"I know you likes yo' privacy, son," Chum said. "But you was in there so long that if you was takin' a shower all that time, you musta damn near drowned. Then I heard some talkin'. You talkin' to yo'self now, son?"

"Well, you know that old sayin', Chum," Jackhammer replied. "When you talk to yourself, you know you ain't talkin' to no fool."

"Son, I ain't playin' with you," said Chum. "Somethin' ain't right. I was meanin' to talk to you about the way that joker almost made a fool out of you durin' your sparrin'. But somethin' else goin' on here … and I need to know what it is. Now, talk to me."

Chum fixed Jackhammer with a gimlet glare. Many people in and out of the fight game dreaded that glare, and with good reason. Years ago, Chum had spent time in prison for killing a gangster who had tried to force him to take a dive against a lesser opponent. And there were plenty of rumors floating around about things he had done that should have landed him in jail again, but didn't.

Jackhammer wasn't afraid of Chum. But he had more respect for Chum than he had for any other man in the world – including his father, who had died in a factory accident before Jackhammer had taken up boxing. Jackhammer's mother was gone, too. His brothers, sisters, aunts, uncles, and a flock of cousins from who-knows-where looked at him more as a meal ticket than a relative now that he was champion.

And Lola … Jackhammer knew damn well that if he didn't hold the title, she would never have given him the time of day. He loved her, but he didn't know whether she loved him, or his fame and money. But then, would he have loved her if she wasn't so doggone fine?

For a long time, Chum was the only person Jackhammer trusted. For all his misgivings about her, he was thinking of adding Lola to that list. Now, Damballa had asked Jackhammer to trust him. And he did. And now he needed Chum to trust the cloaked man, too. He had never kept anything from Chum, and he wasn't about to start now.

He opened the door wide and motioned his trainer to follow him into the locker room.

"We got to talk in private, Chum," Jackhammer said. "About that guy I was sparrin' with … that 'Kid something.'"

CHAPTER SEVEN

SUSPICIONS

Joby Washington was sorting through a pile of last-minute ticket requests for the Jackson-Krieger fight when his partner, Arnie Ruland, walked into the office the pair had rented to accommodate them as they did business in New York. In their home base of Chicago, an entire building served as their headquarters. Still, their New York suite suited their purposes well – and impressively – since the fight's main promoter, Jarvis Hatchford, had offered it at a cut rate. Considering the magnitude of this much-anticipated match, nothing was too good for the Salt and Pepper Twins. ...

"You hear about something queer happening at our training camp?" Ruland asked as he eased into one of the seats in front of Washington's desk.

"Naw," said Washington, looking up from the tangle of papers. "Besides, what could be queerer than that mess at Madame Pomp's?"

The two men looked at each other. They had both been in the boxing business for many years, and they'd known each other during most of that time. They hadn't always been partners, or even friends. But they were both honest – a rarity in the fight game. And when Washington discovered Jackhammer, Ruland was the one he turned to for help in navigating the shark-infested passage that led Jackhammer from obscurity to the heavyweight championship of the world in a remarkably short time.

"I heard that a ringer of some kind was sparring with Jackhammer," Ruland said. "Jackhammer decked him, but Chum cut the session short.

Only time he'd do that is when the sparring isn't doin' Jackhammer any good."

"Which sparrin' partner was it?" Washington asked.

"Fella named 'Kid Ebony.' Chum said you gave the OK."

Washington ran a hand across his close-cropped, graying hair.

"Yeah," he agreed. "My old buddy, Sam Belford, said this 'Kid Ebony' has a lot of speed, like Krieger. I can't picture Sam double-crossin' me with no ringer. Say, was Chum the one told you about this?"

"Naw. It was one of the other sparring partners. Fella named Louis."

"Louis is an OK cat, Arnie."

"Well, still … there's some funny stuff going on. I'm still trying to figure out whether the hold-up at Madame Delia's had anything to do with the fight. And who knows what those damn Germans are up to? They've got Krieger's camp sealed up tighter than Fort Knox. Maybe we ought to do the same at our camp."

"You might be right, Arnie. Tell you what … I'll call Sam right now and find out what's what. These movie stars and whatnot can wait a little bit for their tickets."

"Hold on a minute," Ruland said as Washington reached for one of the telephones on his desk. Washington pulled his hand back. A quizzical expression crossed his round, dark face. Ruland's face, which was just as round but a lot lighter in shade, revealed nothing.

"You know anything about this Damballa character, Joby?" Ruland asked abruptly.

"All I know is, he saved you, me, and a lot of other people from gettin' robbed and maybe worse."

"You haven't heard anything else?"

"You mean, from the colored grapevine? The jungle telegraph?"

Ruland shrugged, and his eyebrows rose beneath the brim of his fedora. Washington sighed.

"All I can tell you, Arnie, is that you don't ever want to get on the wrong side of Damballa, no matter what shade your skin is."

"You think we're on his right side?"

"Yeah."

"OK, Joby," Ruland said as he rose from his chair. "Talk to you again later."

Washington watched his partner's exit from the office. Then he picked up his telephone and gave the operator Sam Belford's number.

❀ ❀ ❀

Slowly, Sam Belford replaced his telephone receiver on its cradle. Belford was a small, cocoa-colored man who dressed well and ate well, despite the bad turn of economic times. At the moment, however, he didn't look as though he felt well.

Belford had just finished speaking with Joby Washington, his fellow manager of colored ringmen. Joby'd had some pointed questions for him. But Belford had all the right answers.

No, Kid Ebony wasn't a ringer. ...

Yes, Kid Ebony had some experience. He had done most of his fighting in Europe and Africa, which was why his name wasn't familiar. ...

No, Kid Ebony wasn't around anymore. Belford hadn't seen him since he'd sent him to Jackhammer's training camp. Maybe Jackhammer hit him so hard, he's laid up someplace. ...

No, Belford had never heard Kid Ebony's real name. ...

Yes, Belford would be at the big fight. Wouldn't miss it for the world. ...

Belford opened a desk drawer, pulled out a flask of whiskey, and took a long, deep swallow. He did not flinch as the liquor seared a path down his throat. However, his hand showed a tremor as he capped the flask and put it back in the drawer.

He had said to Washington exactly what Damballa had told him to say. And he hoped he had seen the last of the man in the black cloak.

❈ ❈ ❈

"The commissioner will see you now ... Detective."

Errol Bynoe directed as bland a countenance as he could toward Sergeant Hall, who sat at the reception desk that was the barrier between the office of the New York City Police Commissioner Bertram Wheelwright and the rest of the world. Bynoe could not have missed the condescending tone in which Hall had pronounced the word "Detective."

Hall was one of many police officers who resented Bynoe's rise in the ranks. But the commissioner had personally promoted Bynoe, and among the enforcers of the law, Wheelwright's word was a law unto itself.

"Thank you ... Sergeant," Bynoe said.

Hall frowned as Bynoe walked past the reception desk and tapped lightly on the commissioner's door. The detective was more than capable of inserting a subtle needle of his own.

"Come in," said a voice from the other side of the door.

Bynoe entered the office and closed the door behind him.

"Have a seat," said the commissioner.

Bynoe lowered himself into one of the plush armchairs arrayed in front of the desk. He looked at the commissioner – the man who had placed his own reputation on the line by elevating Bynoe to his current rank.

Wheelwright was a slender but broad-shouldered man in his mid-50s, with a full head of carefully combed iron-gray hair and a trim mustache of the same hue. His blue eyes gazed unblinking behind a pair of rimless spectacles. Although those eyes could cow even the most hard-boiled criminals, Bynoe could not read anything in the commissioner's current mien.

"What's the status of the Pomphrey case?" Wheelwright asked.

"Almost finished, sir," Bynoe replied.

"'Almost'?"

"The belongings of the guests at Madame Pomphrey's party are all accounted for," said Bynoe. "Only minor injuries were incurred. The suspects are all behind bars. Their leader is still at large, but thanks to information provided by Madame Pomphrey, we believe we know who he is: 'Bullets' Jones. We're looking for him. He's the only loose end."

"The only one? What about Damballa?"

For a moment, Bynoe's composure slipped. He recovered quickly, though he was certain that Wheelwright's keen eyes had detected the lapse.

"Damballa is always a loose end, sir," the detective said.

Wheelwright looked at Bynoe over the rims of his glasses.

"Do you think this robbery attempt had any direct connection to the upcoming Jackson-Krieger fight?" the commissioner asked.

"No, sir. I'm certain it was just a crime of opportunity – a temptation too great to resist. As well, information obtained from Madame Pomphrey indicates there might have been a personal element. Apparently, there is a history of bad blood between her and Jones."

The commissioner fell silent again, and steepled his fingers. Bynoe found it difficult to prevent himself from looking away from Wheelwright's gaze, or shifting nervously in his seat. He wished he knew what Wheelwright was thinking. What he did know was that speculation was useless – a realization reinforced by the commissioner's next words.

"I want you to suspend the Pomphrey case."

"Sir?" Bynoe almost choked.

"Ordinarily, I would want to see Jones brought to justice," the commissioner continued. "But with the fight coming up, we've got to devote as much manpower as possible to making certain nothing goes wrong.

"I want you to suspend the Pomphrey case."

"As you are well aware, Bynoe, this fight is going to be the most significant sporting event in history – more so even than the Olympics in Germany two years ago. Public passion is running as high as it was for the Jack Johnson-Jim Jeffries fight – although for different reasons. This time, the fight's not just a race issue. It's an international issue."

Bynoe nodded.

"We both know how important it is that nothing happens to either Jackson or Krieger before, during, or after the fight," said Wheelwright. "We are receiving assistance from both state and federal authorities in that regard. I don't have to tell you what kind of microscope that puts us under. I need your full focus to be on security for the fight."

"Understood, sir," said Bynoe. "I won't do anything else to find Jones until after that German gets on the boat that will take him and his Nazi entourage home, win or lose. And I'll keep Damballa out of my thoughts."

"Good. There's one more thing, though."

"Sir?"

"Damballa really gets under your skin, doesn't he?"

Bynoe could only nod. He didn't trust himself to speak. His opinion of Damballa was hardly a secret, anyway. Not from Wheelwright nor from anyone else in the department.

"You think he's stealing your thunder," the commissioner continued. He lifted a hand to forestall an angry protest from Bynoe.

"I know what is said about you on the street, Detective ... that Damballa is the real protector of the colored community, and you are merely a 'white man's lackey,' or an 'Uncle Tom.' Well, I don't believe that for a minute. If I thought that would be the outcome, I would never have made you a detective. Now, go do your job ... and if Damballa crosses your path, let your own judgment and discretion guide you. That will be all."

"Thank you, sir," said Bynoe.

The detective rose and departed from the commissioner's office. He did not even bother to glance at the sour-faced Sergeant Hall, much less accord the man a farewell salutation.

CHAPTER EIGHT

THE LAIR OF THE WOLF

Wolf Krieger's training camp was, like Jackhammer's, located in an out-of-the-way area, far from the teeming city. The difference was, no protesters picketed the champion's camp. At the challenger's headquarters, however, demonstrations occurred daily, with more people participating as the date of the big fight drew nearer.

On this day, a couple-hundred souls had been willing to travel along remote roads to walk back and forth in front of the high walls and barred gate that guarded the camp, which had once been a state prison called Balrogorra: abandoned, but not yet demolished. Sentries in brown, military-style uniforms manned the watchtowers. Their weapons were pointed outside, not inside, the walls.

Some of the demonstrators looked up at the cold-eyed guards, who stared back impassively. If the words on the protest sign offended the guards, no outward indication was given.

The signs bore explicit messages:
NAZIS GO HOME
TO HELL WITH HITLER
A WOLF IN WOLF'S CLOTHING
NO FASCISM ALLOWED IN AMERICA
STUFF YOUR SWASTIKAS
Other than the occasional shout, the demonstrators were quiet. They preferred to allow their presence and their placards to speak for themselves.

Nonetheless, a small cordon of police stood between the protesters and the gate, in case the undercurrent of tension suddenly escalated.

Most of the protesters were men. Many were Jewish. Only a few were black. And those few were very brave indeed, for it was far from acceptable for a Negro to express disapproval of a bout that involved their people's hero, Jackhammer Jackson. The ones who turned out for the protests did not want to see a Nazi have the opportunity to wrest a hard-earned prize from a colored man's hands.

But the vast majority of Negroes in America wanted to see Jackhammer beat the "*heil*" out of the German. So did most whites, other than a virulent faction that could not countenance the existence of a black champion, and had never gotten over their hatred of Jack Johnson.

Despite the lack of violence during the demonstrations thus far, the possibility of disruption or sabotage was a constant concern for people like Police Commissioner Wheelwright. On his orders, the police were prepared to intervene at the slightest sign of commotion.

Trouble-making was not on the mind of one of the protesters – a new one, who did not say much as he carried his sign. His gaze roved the towers and walls of the erstwhile penitentiary. He was seeking a way inside ... for another time, another day, after nightfall.

❋ ❋ ❋

Inside Balrogorra, no one gave any indication of unease over the protests on the other side of the gate. A small knot of people gathered at the side of a sparring ring set up in what had been the main yard of the prison. No reporters were present. The press had been barred since the day Krieger's crew set up camp. All information from the Germans was provided outside the facility, primarily through press briefings at various venues in the city.

"Security," Krieger's press spokesman Gunther Weiss always said when asked about the lack of access to the fighter.

Weiss, a dapper, brown-haired man of medium height and slight build, was among the ringside observers. So was Krieger's trainer, a squat ex-boxer named Franz Kohlbrecher. Krieger's manager was there as well: Hans Wimmer, a lean, saturnine-looking man whose black hair and swarthy complexion were at odds with the Aryan ideal, though his fealty to the Party was beyond question.

Two other men stood apart. One was an awe-inspiring figure indeed: a broad-shouldered, shaven-headed giant with a thick, dark mustache under a hawk-like nose and hooded blue eyes. Clad in a black uniform that was neither regular military nor SS, he was known simply as *"Der Tod,"* German for "The Death."

Neither title nor rank was necessary to enhance the fear the large man's name induced among those who'd had the misfortune of crossing his path. Yet *Der Tod* displayed a deferential attitude toward the less-physically imposing man who stood beside him.

The top of the other man's head barely reached *Der Tod's* shoulder. His own shoulders were narrow, as were his features, which were distinguished primarily by a short, square mustache mimicking that of the Führer. His thin gray hair was combed straight back from a high forehead furrowed with deep lines. A white laboratory coat swathed his body like a shroud.

This was *Herr Doktor* Claus von Dunkel, a physician and researcher second only to Josef Mengele in the Party's science establishment. No outsiders knew that Von Dunkel had accompanied Krieger from Germany to New York. His presence was the main reason for the phenomenally tight security at the training camp.

From time to time, *Der Tod* glanced down at the doctor, as though his gaze alone would attract the other man's attention. But he ignored *Der Tod*, as though signaling that the big man was not worthy of even cursory acknowledgment. After a while, *Der Tod* redirected his attention to the ring, along with the other watchers.

There, two men in boxing gear faced each other from opposite corners. The ring-men eschewed helmets. The face of Wolf Krieger, heavyweight champion of Germany and Europe and winner of the Olympic gold medal only two years before had become almost as familiar to the world as that of Jackhammer Jackson. Krieger's clean-shaven countenance, with its thin-lipped mouth, aquiline nose, deep-set blue eyes, and close-cropped blond hair, had appeared on thousands of propaganda posters extolling the Aryan ideal.

It was Krieger's physique, though, that was the reason he had been dubbed the "Aryan Adonis." At two inches over six feet in height and 220 pounds, he was not as large as *Der Tod*. But Krieger's body looked as though it had been hewn from white marble by Praxiteles or some other sculptor from ancient Greece. Krieger's muscles were smooth and well-defined, and capable of phenomenal strength and speed. Next to him, *Der Tod* looked like an oversized lump of flesh.

Krieger stared across the ring at the other boxer. The German knew this was no ordinary sparring partner. The man's face was nowhere near as well-known as those of Krieger or Jackson. In boxing circles, however, he possessed a degree of notoriety. He boxed under the name of "Cro-Magnon" Connolly. He was also known as "The Man Who Won't Be Floored."

Connolly's boxing skills were, at best, rudimentary. It was his inhuman ability to absorb punishment that had earned him his nickname, as well as a foothold in the ranks of heavyweight title contenders. The sandy-haired Cro-Magnon boasted of never having been knocked off his feet, either in regular fights or sparring sessions. Even Jackhammer had not been able to do it in a 10-rounder that was a major rung on his ladder to the championship, though he had won by a wide decision and left Connolly a battered, bleeding hulk.

Krieger's management was paying Cro-Magnon top dollar to put his reputation for durability to the test – though far from the prying eyes of the press. Neither the manager nor trainer of Connolly had been allowed into Balrogorra. The Germans had promised to take care of "everything."

"*Zeit!*" barked trainer Kohlbrecher, signalling that it was time for the action to begin.

Cro-Magnon shuffled toward Krieger. Three inches shorter than the German but approximately equal in weight, Connolly approached in a low crouch, from which he would throw swiping punches that wore down the resistance of opponents who lacked courage or stamina. He was certain Krieger possessed an abundance of both qualities. Even so, Cro-Magnon was determined to put the German to the test. Connolly was, after all, being paid just as much for this sparring session as he would have been for a regular match.

Krieger glided in classic stand-up style: left hand extended, right cocked to fire as soon as he saw an opening. He bent his knees slightly more than usual, to accommodate Cro-Magnon's crouch. With a quickness that belied his size, the German circled the Irish-American. Krieger's hands snaked out in feints he hoped would draw Connolly out of his stance.

Instead of falling for that maneuver, Connolly swung both hands toward Krieger's midsection. Krieger blocked the punches. Connolly immediately drew his arms back to protect features blunted by the many hard blows that had caressed his homely phiz over the years.

Suddenly, Krieger fired a stiff left jab. Even though Cro-Magnon was bent over and his gloves were held high, Krieger's punch caught him high on the forehead. Connolly stumbled a moment, then pressed forward again. The punch stung. But he had survived many similar shots from

Jackhammer, and he was confident that he could absorb anything the German had to offer.

Cro-Magnon abruptly rushed Krieger into the ropes, where he proceeded to maul the taller man with a volley of legal and illegal blows. Inside action like this was Cro-Magnon's bread and butter. Without a referee to break the boxers from the inevitable clinch, Krieger was going to have to fight his way off the ropes – a prospect Connolly clearly relished.

That relish turned to consternation as Krieger surged forward, fists pumping like pistons. Forced to back up, Cro-Magnon wrapped his gorilla-like arms around Krieger to buy a moment of breathing space. Connolly thought he, not Krieger, would be the one to bring the clinch to an end.

But it didn't happen that way. With a wrenching motion of his arms, Krieger broke the clinch and sent Cro-Magnon staggering halfway across the ring.

Cro-Magnon's eyes widened in shock as he fought to maintain his footing. He prided himself on being physically stronger than any opponent he had ever met, which was his answer to their generally superior skills. But the German had just manhandled him as though he were a mere schoolboy.

And now Krieger was coming toward him, eyes cold in a face devoid of emotion. Quickly, Connolly crouched and crossed his arms in front of his face, a defensive posture that could be penetrated only at great risk to his opponents' hands, for only the top of Connolly's hard head was available to hit.

But Cro-Magnon's gloves didn't fully cover his chin. With amazing agility, Krieger dipped even lower than Connolly. Then Krieger straightened his legs, while at the same time lifting a right uppercut that connected explosively on the vulnerable point of Connolly's jaw.

Connolly catapulted backward. With a resounding thud, his back hit the canvas. He lay motionless: eyes closed, mouth open, mandible askew. The rise and fall of his broad, hairy chest provided the only clear indication that Cro-Magnon Connolly was still alive.

Krieger stared impassively at his fallen spar-mate. The German had just accomplished a feat that had eluded every other fighter Connolly had ever faced – including the one Krieger would be facing at Yankee Stadium in a few days' time. Even as Kohlbrecher and the others climbed into the ring, however, Krieger's countenance remained dispassionate.

CHAPTER NINE

THE TWO FACES OF *HERR DOKTOR*

"How are you feeling, Wolf?" Von Dunkel asked.

"Super," Krieger replied.

The doctor smiled at Krieger's response.

"*Ja*, Wolf, you should indeed feel 'super,' considering that you are the super man of the ring. A true super man, not some costumed character in a silly American comic book."

Krieger grunted noncommittally at Von Dunkel's witticism. He was sitting quietly on an examining table in a room that had previously been the prison's medical dispensary. The original equipment and supplies of the facility were long-since gone. Now training-camp materials such as bandages, gauze and unguents rested on shelves that had been meticulously cleansed of the dust accumulated during Balrogorra's previous disuse.

Krieger was clad only in his boxing trunks, along with his shoes and socks. His trainer had removed his gloves and hand-wraps shortly after Krieger's brief encounter with Connolly. Krieger waited stoically as the doctor swabbed alcohol on a patch of skin on the fighter's left forearm. On a small cart beside the examination table, a syringe filled with a cloudy liquid waited to be used.

Von Dunkel tossed the swab into a trash can. Then he picked up the syringe and gave its plunger a gently push. A drop of liquid appeared at the end of the needle. Krieger did not look at the syringe.

"You did very well against this 'Cro-Magnon,' Wolf," the doctor said. "As I knew you would. If that *Neger* Jackson had seen what you did, his people would never allow him to get into the ring with you."

"How is Connolly, *Herr Doktor*?" Krieger asked.

"You broke his jaw, and he has a concussion. We will treat him here, at the camp, until after the fight. He will be well-compensated for his discomfort."

Krieger nodded. He did not flinch when the doctor jabbed the needle into the alcohol-numbed patch of skin. Nor did he join Von Dunkel in watching the cloudy liquid disappear from the barrel of the syringe. He remained impassive as Von Dunkel pulled the needle out.

Even so, Von Dunkel detected a flicker of negative emotion in the boxer's eyes. The doctor laid a hand on one of Krieger's broad shoulders, and gave the hard muscle beneath the skin a squeeze that approximated fatherly affection.

"I know how you feel about the *Starkenflessig*, Wolf," Von Dunkel said. "I know you believe you could defeat the *Neger* without it. But nothing can be left to chance – not as it was at the Olympics."

Both men scowled at the bitter memory of the Berlin Summer Games – an intended triumph of the Reich turned into a mockery by the black American athletes that ran and leaped like trained beasts, humiliating the Germans in almost every track and field event in which the *Negers* were entered.

Krieger's capture of a gold medal in the boxing competition was one of the rare bright spots in the Olympics' showcase events. But Krieger had not faced any black opponents during his march to the top of the podium. As well, Jackhammer Jackson had turned pro two years before the Games. There were many who believed that Jackson would have beaten Krieger had they fought in the Olympics. Those same people were certain that the Negro would prevail now.

"The *Schwartzers* have thick skulls, like apes," said Von Dunkel. "Their nerve endings are duller than ours, and are thus slower to register pain. They are closer to the primordial than we are – which is a hindrance to developing a civilization, but an asset in a brutish sport like prizefighting."

"Whites have defeated blacks in the ring before," said Krieger.

"*Ja*, of course," Von Dunkel retorted with a touch of asperity. "And I believe you could beat this Jackhammer without the *Starkenflessig*. But this time, we cannot leave anything to chance. In a few days, the eyes of the world will be focused on the 'Fight of the Century.' You *must* win, Wolf! For the Führer! For the Reich!"

"For the Führer. For the Reich," Krieger repeated.

"If I could mass-produce the *Starkenflessig*, the Reich would already rule the world," Von Dunkel said. "Alas, I cannot. I can only make a limited amount – for you, for this one great purpose. And, just recently, for *Der Tod*. Your imminent victory, Wolf, will mark the beginning of the Fatherland's vengeance for what was done to us after the Great War ended."

"*Jawohl!*" Krieger said, showing greater enthusiasm.

With cat-like grace, the boxer rose from the table and departed the room. Von Dunkel wrapped the syringe in tissue-paper and discarded it in the wastebasket. The benign expression faded from his face. He had another conversation on his agenda for the day. And this one would not be so pleasant.

❈ ❈ ❈

The doctor sat in a different office now – the one that had served as headquarters for Balrogorra's warden. Whatever way the warden might have furnished the office, stark efficiency now prevailed. A gunmetal-gray desk occupied the center of the room. Behind it was the chair in which Von Dunkel sat. There was no other furniture in the office – no chair for *Der Tod*, who stood at rigid attention while Von Dunkel professed to ignore him.

Papers were piled high on the surface of the desk. Most of them were newspaper clippings about the fight, in English and German. Others were dispatches from Germany. Still others were sheets covered with notes in German, written in a crabbed but precise hand.

Von Dunkel was writing now. The scratching of his pen was the only sound in the room. *Der Tod* made no attempt to read the writing upside-down. He continued to stand stolidly, eyes staring straight ahead at nothing.

Finally, Von Dunkel stopped writing and looked up at *Der Tod*.

"As you know, I am not fond of failure," the doctor said. "Yet you have failed not just once – but twice."

Der Tod's only response was a brief nod. He could not disagree with Von Dunkel's assessment. And he knew better than to attempt to excuse the botched robbery of the *Neger* woman's party, and the subsequent loss of the person who had organized the debacle.

"What have you learned of this Damballa?" Von Dunkel demanded, abruptly changing the subject.

"He is like a wraith, *Herr Doktor*," *Der Tod* replied. "He appears and disappears at will. He dresses in black. No one has seen his face. He uses dusts and powders that appear to be magical in nature ..."

"Not magic!" the doctor interrupted. "Science! I analyzed the powder that was on the faces of the men you brought back from the warehouse. It is made from an adhesive chemical combined with some kind of vegetal matter that I cannot identify with the equipment I have here. Remove from your mind any thought that this is some supernatural being. Damballa is a man – a very clever man."

"*Ja* ... clever," *Der Tod* agreed.

"Damballa could be a major threat to us," Von Dunkel said. "He must not be allowed to interfere with the coming victory of our Wolf. You, *Tod*, can atone for your previous incompetence by eliminating Damballa before he has the chance to do any more damage to our cause."

"Consider it done, *Herr Doktor!* The *Schwartzer* will die!"

"How do you know Damballa is a *Schwartzer?*"

The question hung in the air as *Der Tod* opened his mouth, then closed it again, before finally replying.

"He only helps the *Negers*," the big man said. "What else could he be but a *Neger* himself?"

"You are not thinking, *Tod*. The clever strategies ... the scientific expertise ... the quick decision-making ... nothing of this is within the limited capacities of a *Schwartzer's* mentality."

Von Dunkel paused to emphasize his point.

"The one who calls himself Damballa is a white man, *Tod*," the doctor said, jabbing a finger in the air for emphasis. "He is like the foolish John Brown, who died trying to free the *Negers* from their natural state of slavery. I am absolutely certain of that."

"*Ja*," *Der Tod* agreed after a period of deep cogitation. "I can see what you are saying, *Herr Doktor*."

"Then go. There is no time to lose."

Der Tod clicked his heels and shot out a stiff-armed Nazi salute.

"Heil Hitler!" he shouted.

"Heil Hitler," Von Dunkel returned. His own salute was not as crisp as that of his underling, who pretended not to notice.

Without another word, *Der Tod* turned on his heel and left his superior's office. Von Dunkel relaxed in his chair then. In the doctor's mind, *Der Tod's* blunders were not as disastrous as the doctor had made them out to be, though there was no need for *Der Tod* to know that. The failure of the *Neger* gang to make off with the money and jewelry from the pretentious black woman's party was annoying, of course, but also incidental. The robbery had still struck a spark of fear in the *Schwartzers* who so ineptly aped the ways of their betters in high white society.

And the snatching of the black gang leader had not done much harm, either. It had, at least, given Von Dunkel a better idea of Damballa's capabilities. He saw nothing that *Der Tod*, forewarned as he now was, could not overcome.

"Defeat for Damballa and Jackson," he said aloud. "Glory for the Reich."

Then he went back to his writing.

CHAPTER TEN

CHUM'S LATE-NIGHT STROLL

Chum Williams walked alone down the night-shrouded street. The street was in Harlem, but a long way from Sugar Row, in more ways than one. It was the Darkside – a place where most dreams had long-since died, and even the slightest hopes were just barely hanging on. Tenements grudgingly passed down from the white migrants of Europe to black refugees from the American South rose in ragged ranks against encroaching gloom.

Streetlamps were few on this row where sugar was hard to find. The illumination those lamps provided was pale, fitful, random. People with night errands to do moved carefully amid plains of darkness and islands of light. Tension born of an unholy alliance between desperate days and diminishing dollars gripped the Darkside like a cadaverous hand, squeezing slowly and inexorably. The only sure things here were death and blackness – and that was a truism Chum knew all too well.

In the semi-darkness, and with the peak of his cap pulled low on his forehead, Chum was certain he would not be recognized. Nobody would be fool enough to get all up in his face and spot his scar. As the trainer of the heavyweight champion of the world Chum was well-known in his own right. Even so, Jackhammer and the Salt-and-Pepper Twins were the main focus of attention, and that suited Chum just fine.

A tough man in and out of the ring, Chum knew how to carry himself in a way that quickly discouraged any interest he might have attracted from the occasional group of young bloods who were up to no good. Still, Chum kept one eye on the people he passed, and the other on the recesses in front of the shabby buildings, looking for the one that matched the description of the place he had been told to seek. Yet they all looked so much alike. ...

Chum had listened closely to what Jackhammer had told him about his locker room conversation with Damballa, a.k.a. "Kid Ebony." He understood Jackhammer's decision to put his trust in whatever the caped man was up to. But Chum was older than the champion, and had seen more of the misery and madness of the world, and therefore had a more skeptical viewpoint. Chum needed to know more about Damballa – and he would find out in his own way.

During his long-past days as a fighter and latter time as a trainer, Chum had cultivated contacts and cronies in many cities. Some of those acquaintances were aboveboard; others were so deep into the underworld that even the shadiest denizens of the fight game shunned them.

Chum had called in several debts from the past – and most likely turned some old friends into new enemies – to obtain the information he needed so quickly. He didn't care. The stakes were too high for anybody's hurt feelings to matter.

So intent was Chum on finding the recess he was looking for that his attention to other occupants of the sidewalk began to wane. A sudden jolt from a minor collision ended that lapse of consciousness.

"Watch where you goin', bub!" a harsh voice growled.

Chum stumbled for a moment. Regaining his balance, he looked up into the scowling face of a dark-skinned man who was considerably taller and heavier than the trainer.

"How 'bout you do the same ... bub," Chum retorted, without raising his voice.

The other man's scowl deepened. Then he looked more closely at Chum's half-shadowed face, and the way the smaller man's hand hung close to his coat pocket, as though a gun or knife might be within close reach.

"Forget you!" the big man grunted. Then he continued down the sidewalk, his shoulders swaying from side to side in a bully's swagger.

Chum scanned the sidewalk to determine whether any other unpleasant encounters were imminent. He didn't see anyone close to him. He turned his gaze back to the tenements – and then he saw it.

Four steps down ... the top of the door in the shape of a half moon ... no number ... a round, red eye in the center of the entablature ...

"Hmph," Chum snorted. "Motherjumper bumps me right where I was supposed to go. Some coincidence, huh?"

Despite that misgiving, the trainer walked down the four steps and knocked four times on the door under the red eye.

"Come in," a woman's voice said.

After a moment's hesitation, Chum turned the doorknob, opened the door, and entered the place of which he had been told. He did not see the crimson eye blink shut as he went in.

❊ ❊ ❊

A large touring car moved slowly down the nondescript street. Automobiles of this quality were rarely seen in this part of the city, and when one did appear, the Darkside denizens generally regarded it as prey. This machine, however, exuded an air of menace that marked it as a transporter of predators. No one attempted to stop the long, low-slung vehicle as it prowled forward, bright headlights glaring like a pair of searching eyes.

Black, hulking shapes crowded the interior of the car. A smaller form hunched in the back seat. The others' faces had been darkened with burnt cork, for the purpose of camouflage. The naturally dark skin of the small man in the back needed no such disguise. Although one of his companions – who looked and behaved more like captors – sat between him and the car's back door, he was still able to peer through the window. He perused the tenement fronts as though his life depended on finding what he so desperately sought.

And it did.

❊ ❊ ❊

Chum blinked against the dim light inside his destination. He was standing in a large room that looked smaller because of the many counters and cabinets that were situated in an apparently haphazard maze, and the strange, shadowy objects that hung on the walls.

The light came from bulbs covered by large globes that dampened the illumination. As Chum's eyes adjusted to the light, he recognized some of the items displayed on the counters: skulls of birds and small animals; leg-bones and ribs of larger beasts; cloth and leather pouches with long drawstrings; vials and bottles filled with murky liquids in which eyes, tongues, and other body parts floated. ...

Chum knew then that he was in a *gri-gri* shop. He had seen one before in New Orleans. This one was different, though. The one in New Orleans didn't have masks hanging on its walls, as did this one. Some of the masks bore distorted features with human and animal characteristics; others looked as though they were modeled from the faces of real men and women.

Chum's eyes narrowed in a skepticism that was second nature to him. He didn't hold with any of that voodoo-hoodoo stuff. But he was hardly a Holy Roller, either. He believed that people were going to do what they were going to do, and thought God ought to be smart enough to figure it all out in the end.

He looked around for the owner of the voice that had beckoned him inside. He saw no one.

"Anybody here?" he called out.

"Yes."

The voice came from his right. He turned quickly in that direction, hand not far from his coat pocket. And his eyes widened at what he saw.

A tall woman had appeared, seemingly out of nowhere. Chum had not heard any footsteps or other sounds that would have heralded her approach. The otherwise wan light in the shop brightened considerably around the woman, delineating her much more clearly than the objects on display.

The woman was clad in an odd combination of garments. A *pagne* – a tight, brightly colored, wraparound skirt – hung from her waist to her ankles. The patterns woven into the cloth resembled none that Chum had ever seen before, though the sight of them stirred something very much like a distant memory in his mind.

Atop the *pagne*, the woman wore a starched white blouse that would have been fashionable during the decade before the turn of the century. Its ruffled front reached to her neck, and its long sleeves covered her arms to the wrists. A long necklace made from cowrie-shells with a small wooden snake dangling from its bottom, along with beaded bangles at her wrists and an ivory brooch at her throat, constituted her only jewelry.

A *gele* – a head-wrap of the same material as the *pagne* – rose from the woman's head, adding to her not-inconsiderable height. Tightly twisted braids of white hair hung beneath the *gele*. That hair color, along with deep lines that cut across the woman's forehead and the sides of her eyes and mouth, were the only indications of her advanced age.

As well, she held a long walking stick in her right hand, even though her posture was as erect as that of a soldier standing at attention. The stick was hewn from black wood. Semi-abstract images of people and animals had been carved across its entire length. In contrast, the surface of its top – a sphere about the size of a baseball – was smooth.

Only the woman's face and hands were left uncovered by her garb. The skin that showed was the darkest Chum had ever seen. It was pure African black, a shade rarely seen among American Negroes after centuries of admixture with whites and Indians. It was a complexion that usually prompted cruel taunts from the mouths of colored and white alike.

But not this time.

"I know who you are, Isaac Washington," the woman said in a voice with a fluid accent. "And I know why you are here."

Chum's hands twitched reflexively.

"How you know that name?" he demanded. "Chum Williams" was the name Isaac Washington had adopted after some brushes with the law during his tumultuous youth had made it expedient to discard a name that had been scrawled in a family Bible on the day he was born. That Bible was long gone ... nothing but ashes since the house that had held it burned to the ground years ago. The cries of the night riders still echoed in his ears. ...

"I know many things," the woman responded cryptically.

"Yeah, well, there's googobs of things I damn sure don't know," Chum/ Isaac said gruffly as he strove to calm his jolted nerves. "For one thing, I don't know who the hell *you* is."

"My name is Mamadou," the woman said.

Chum nodded. "That's who my, uh, friends told me I find here. They told me you was the one to see if I wanted to talk to Damballa."

"Your friends were right."

"Can you take me to him?"

"No need," another voice – male – said.

Chum whirled in the direction from which the new voice came. A patch of darkness detached itself from a wall and glided toward him, as though it were floating. It was human in shape, with a cloak swirling behind it. The shadow from a hood obscured the features of the apparition.

Chum was a hard, tough man. But all he could do was stare speechlessly as the shadowy shape reached up and pulled back the hood of the cloak in a single, abrupt motion.

For the face that motion revealed was white.

❈ ❈ ❈

The black man imprisoned in the touring car gave a sudden start, as though he had been stung by a bee. The big men crowding him reacted immediately.

"Do you see it?" one of them demanded.

"Uh-huh," the black man replied. He pointed toward a recessed doorway that looked no different from any of the others.

"Are you sure that is the one, *Schwartzer*?"

"Sure's I'll ever be, Boss."

The car stopped. A moment later, its doors clicked open. Six large, dark-clothed men with blackened faces piled out of the vehicle – three from the front seat, three from the back. The ones in the back left their informant behind, having bound and gagged him quickly and efficiently.

The black man knew he was a goner, even though he was still breathing. The Germans had promised him some hefty scratch – money – if he could lead them to the lair of Damballa. He was almost 100 percent certain he had done so.

But now, he knew he had been duped. If he were wrong about the doorway he had pointed out, the Germans would come back and punish him, then let him live long enough to try to correct his error. Then they would kill him. If he were right – they would kill him anyway.

He hadn't thought that would be the case. He had made himself believe that the Germans really would give him more scratch than he'd ever dreamed of, just to lead them to that hoodoo-man, Damballa. The way they'd been talking as the car went down the street disabused him of that notion.

Moans muffled by his gag, the black man fought to loosen his bonds. Futility greeted his frenzied efforts.

Then a sudden thought pierced his consciousness like a spike of ice. *What if the Germans turned out to be no match for Damballa? What if Damballa learns who it was that brought them here?*

With greater urgency, the black man resumed his struggle against the unyielding bonds.

CHAPTER ELEVEN

BATTLE IN THE *GRI-GRI* SHOP

"**W**hat the – " Chum choked out as he stared wide-eyed at the pale, Caucasian-featured visage that appeared to be floating inexplicably above Damballa's black-cloaked body.

The trainer's eyes grew even wider as Damballa's right hand reached upward. His fingers clutched hard at the skin beneath his hairline ... and quickly pulled downward, apparently peeling away his epidermis to the accompaniment of a slight sucking sound.

What Damballa's action revealed was not dripping red flesh, however. It was another layer of skin, this one natural. The color was several shades lighter than that of Mamadou, but still very dark. With his other hand, Damballa pulled a lank-haired, light-colored wig from his head.

Chum's eyes narrowed as he peered closely at the features now revealed. He half-expected Damballa to remove yet another mask. But the cloaked man's hands did not move again.

Even in the fitful light of the shop, and even though the last time he had seen this face, it had been partially obscured by sparring headgear, Chum knew who he was looking at.

"Kid Ebony," the trainer muttered almost inaudibly.

"One of my many guises," said Damballa. Like Mamadou, he spoke with an unfamiliar accent, though his foreign intonation was far less obvious than that of the woman.

Damballa's features were more African than Negro American, though the mark of the continent was somewhat less pronounced on his face than on that of Mamadou. The hair that the wig had concealed was

56

"This helped me to fit in,"

close-cropped, with no sheen of the pomade that was fashionable among colored men. Damballa's eyes were black as midnight, yet they exuded a luminosity that drew Chum's gaze. …

Chum shook his head and took a backward step, as though he were ready to turn and walk out of the shop. Damballa disarmed him with a smile, a flash of white in the darkness of his face.

"I knew Jackhammer would eventually tell you about the talk he and I had in the locker room after our sparring session," Damballa said. "I knew you would try to find me. And even though some associates of mine helped you along the way, I am impressed that you succeeded."

"Yeah, well … Jackhammer say you was talkin' about some trouble that might be happenin' with the fight. I figured if that's true, I need to know about it."

"Jackhammer is fortunate to have a friend as loyal as you obviously are, Mr. Williams."

"That ain't neither here or there, *Mister* Kid Ebony Damballa," Chum said with asperity. "I ain't come to this here hoodoo-place to chit-chat. I come here to protect my fighter. Now, what you know, man?"

"Not much – yet," Damballa admitted. "I'm still searching. Earlier today, I was out at Krieger's camp, with the protesters."

He lifted the white mask he still held in his hand. It hung like a rag, only this rag had a face.

"This helped me to fit in," he said with a touch of humor. "I was looking for a way to get into the camp later."

"What you think you gon' find there?" Chum demanded. "Other than punchin' bags and boxin' gloves?"

"Well – "

At that moment, Mamadou, who had remained silent save for a snort at Chum's reference to the shop as a "hoodoo-place," hissed a single word.

"Danger!"

❀ ❀ ❀

Six formidable figures barreled across the sidewalk and down the steps that led to the door of the *gri-gri* shop. Two of them carried a long, thick metal bar that they intended to use as a ram. The others drew their weapons – deadly Luger automatic handguns.

So intent were the men on breaking open the doorway that none of them noticed the round, crimson eye that suddenly blinked wide open in the entablature above their heads. …

❀ ❀ ❀

Scarlet light suddenly bathed the interior of the shop. The lurid glow lasted only for a moment. But that moment provided sufficient time for Damballa and Mamadou to leap into action.

Cloak swirling, Damballa jumped in front of Chum. Mamadou, moving with an alacrity that belied her age, sprinted to the shop's main counter. Behind the counter, she bent and reached downward.

A moment later, the door crashed open and a group of dark-faced, dark-clad figures piled inside. Immediately spotting Damballa, they charged toward him, dropping their battering ram and squeezing the triggers of their guns.

None of the shots struck flesh. Amid the pounding of the intruders' feet on the floor, no one heard the soft click of the lever Mamadou pulled behind the counter. The effect of that action was immediate.

Narrow slots opened in the floor. From those apertures, long, sharp-pointed spikes of steel shot upward with the swiftness of a cobra's strike.

Some of the spikes struck nothing but air. Others embedded their points into feet, legs, groins. The intruders who had been pierced howled in agony as they went down, landing on other spikes that jutted like teeth in a gigantic jaw. Sheer reflex caused the intruders' arms to jerk upward, and the bullets they managed to fire burrowed into the ceiling.

None of the spikes hit Damballa, Mamadou, or Chum. As Damballa and Mamadou knew, the three of them were standing far from the area in which the shop's defenses lay hidden.

Three of the intruders were down, writhing on the steel-studded floor and bleeding profusely from their nether regions. The other three had managed to jump aside before the spikes could reach their flesh.

"*Verdammt!*" the biggest of the survivors cursed. Then he and another man who was almost as large pointed their Lugers at Damballa.

❊ ❊ ❊

The man who was tied up in the car had long since ceased his senseless flailing. He knew it wasn't doing him any good. Wasting energy like that wouldn't help him. He needed to *think*. …

Car like this ought to have rugs on the floor, he mused desperately. *This one don't. Cheap-ass Germans. … So if there's nothing but metal on the floor, maybe there's a sharp edge stickin' up. …*

He began to twist his bound body, this time slowly and with purpose. He resembled an earthworm wriggling, but going nowhere. If he had seen someone else in a predicament like his, he would surely have laughed. But he was the one tied up, so it wasn't funny at all.

I'd give all the scratch them Germans promised me if I could find an edge, the man thought. *Just an edge, that's all … just an edge. …*

❀ ❀ ❀

Damballa moved with lightning speed across the short distance that separated him from the surviving Germans. With unerring accuracy, he hurled two small, glittering, globular objects at his foes. The objects shattered upon contact with the intruders' gun hands.

A fluid clear as water splashed onto blackened flesh. It wasn't water, though. It seared the intruders' skin like acid, causing them to yelp in pain and surprise – and drop their weapons.

Damballa had moved away from Chum, so for the first time, the Germans realized there was a third adversary in the shop. The smaller of the intruders pulled a blackjack from his coat pocket and charged toward Chum, believing that the much-smaller man would go down easily.

The biggest of the intruders had no time to retrieve his gun or reach for the sap in his pocket, for Damballa was upon him like a dark storm. Fists and feet thudded into the German's face and body. But he did not fall. Instead, he planted his feet and swung a blow that sent Damballa staggering backward.

He is like a bear, this one, Damballa thought. *But I am like a panther. …*

Then the huge intruder spotted his automatic, which was lying a short distance away. Damballa saw it, too. Instantly, both men raced toward the weapon – the intruder out of necessity, and Damballa because he had no gun on him, having thought that one would not be necessary in the *gri-gri* shop.

❀ ❀ ❀

Chum's pockets weren't empty of weapons. Even as the shadowy shape of the intruder rushed toward him, Chum pulled out a long, sharp dagger. Its gleaming blade beckoned to his assailant, who stopped in his tracks as though he had collided with an unseen wall.

"Come and get it, baby," Chum said in a low, crooning, chilling tone. "Come to Papa. …"

The German wished he had taken the time to retrieve his Luger. Still, even armed with the dagger the *Schwartzer* was only half the intruder's size. With the pain in his hand acting as a goad, the German advanced cautiously, swinging his blackjack in wide arcs before him.

Chum smiled.

❀ ❀ ❀

Damballa's foot reached the gun a split-second before the German's hand could grasp the weapon. The gun clanged as it struck the forest of waist-high spikes.

Cursing vehemently, the German rolled away from the spikes before Damballa's foot could strike again. With an agility amazing for someone of his massive size, the German sprang to his feet and reached for the flapping end of Damballa's cloak. His intention was clear – he meant to seize the garment and use it to pull Damballa off-balance.

Just before the big man's hands could close on the cloth, Damballa whirled. His motion flipped the hem of his cloak upward, brushing against the German's eyes and momentarily obscuring his vision. When the black cloth dropped away, the big man saw something else in front of his eyes an instant before he felt it.

It was Damballa's right fist, at the end of a spear-straight punch delivered with the speed and accuracy Jack Johnson's boxing lessons had imparted. The blow landed precisely on the bridge of the big man's nose, directly between his eyes. Its crunching impact betokened the breaking of bone.

The intruder's head snapped back as though he had been hit by a bullet instead of a fist. He staggered, shuddered, wobbled – but did not fall. With an inarticulate roar of rage and pain, the German reached again for Damballa's cloak. This time, he was able to seize the garment. And he pulled it in a savage, twisting motion that yanked Damballa off his feet.

❀ ❀ ❀

With an evil grin on his blackened face, the third intruder who had evaded the spikes advanced on Mamadou. The old woman faced him without fear. Unobtrusively, she touched another lever. This one was located at the spherical top of her walking-stick. If the intruder heard the soft *snicking* sound that followed, he ignored it.

The German reached for Mamadou. He did not believe that the woman could swing her stick with enough force to harm him. That assumption proved to be decidedly incorrect.

Quick as a striking cobra, the knobbed head of Mamadou's stick struck one of the German's hands. A bark of pain followed the crack of the impact.

In a fluid motion, Mamadou's hands reversed the ends of the stick. From its bottom, a smaller version of the spikes that had shot up from the floor glittered wickedly in the dim illumination.

Before the intruder could react beyond widening his eyes in sudden shock, Mamadou thrust her stick forward. The tip of the spike tore through the German's clothing and pierced his heart.

❁ ❁ ❁

A move he had learned from someone other than Jack Johnson flowed through Damballa's entire body as his feet left the ground. Damballa knew he had to free his cloak before the items hidden in its interior pouches became damaged – items that the swiftness of the intruders' attack had not allowed him time to deploy. Now Damballa somersaulted, while at the same time jabbing the stiffened fingers of his left hand into the German's throat.

The intruder gagged in agony, and his hands involuntarily relaxed their grip enough to enable Damballa to pull his cloak free without tearing it. Damballa then landed on his feet, in a crouched position with his knees almost touching the floor. From that vantage, the cloaked man looked up in time to see the intruder's huge fists swinging down at him like a pair of sledgehammers.

Damballa seized both of the German's wrists and pulled forward, adding to his foe's momentum. Then Damballa rolled backward, positioning his feet on the abdomen of the intruder, and straightened his bent legs.

As the German flipped upward, Damballa released his hold on his attacker's wrists. The German's body flew in a high arc. His curses abruptly turned into a bellow of pain as he landed on the sharp tips of spikes like the ones that had impaled his luckless henchmen.

❁ ❁ ❁

Chum and his opponent had reached a deadly impasse. Each of their weapons provided a perimeter the other could not penetrate. The German's reach was longer, but his blackjack was not as dangerous as the blade of Chum's dagger.

The combatants circled each other warily, cold-eyed … waiting for the slightest stumble, the most minimal of miscues. …

Suddenly, the intruder stiffened, as though he had been struck from behind. That moment of stillness was all Chum needed. His blade whipped forward in a flashing arc, almost too quick for the eye to catch. A moment later, a sheet of blood cascaded from the German's throat. His blackjack dropped from loosened fingers and hit the floor with a loud thump.

As the German followed his weapon to the floor, another man was revealed, standing behind him. It was a burly black man. One of his hands massaged the knuckles of the other.

Chum stared at the newcomer. A wordless exclamation escaped his lips as he suddenly realized that he knew who this man was. It was the one who had bumped into him outside the *gri-gri* shop.

The man grinned as he saw that Chum had recognized him.

"Pleased to meet you again, Mr. Williams," the man said pleasantly. "I am called Kojo."

"It is all right, Chum," Damballa said from behind him. "Kojo is a friend of ours."

Chum's blood-dripping dagger remained in his hand.

"Will somebody please tell me what in the hell's goin' on around here?" he demanded.

"I will tell you everything," said Damballa. "But we've got a lot of work to do first."

Chum considered those words for a moment. Then he bent and carefully wiped his dagger on the clothing of the dead German. After he was satisfied that the blade was clean, he replaced it in his coat pocket.

"Where this 'we' mess come from?" he muttered.

❊ ❊ ❊

The touring car was empty. Raggedly severed ropes lay like dead snakes on the floor in front of the back seat. A torn gag covered some of the strands. From the floor, a tiny piece of metal protruded – a minuscule flaw in the vehicle's manufacture. Flecks of blood speckled the fragment and the floor.

The man who had been imprisoned in the car had found his edge. ...

CHAPTER TWELVE

DIRE DREAMS

Slavering, fang-filled mouth agape, the Beast loped across a stark, snow-covered landscape. The only sounds to be heard were the swift padding of the Beast's rushing feet, and the low growls that issued from deep within its chest. Clusters of shrub-like plants with leafless black barbs for limbs were all that broke the monotony of the flat, white landscape. Dark-gray clouds raced across a dim-lit sky, as though they were on a pursuit similar to that of the Beast far below. …

Far ahead, the beast could see its prey as black dots scuttling desperately across the snow. The distance between the dots and the Beast was slowly diminishing. The chase had been long. But the muscles beneath the shaggy hide of the Beast pumped tirelessly, inexorably, relentlessly. …

The Beast uttered a sound that was half-howl, half-roar, which burned like fire in his throat. Echoing across the snow, the cry caused the dots ahead to falter momentarily in their flight. Then they redoubled their speed, widening the gap between themselves and their pursuer. …

But that respite proved to be fleeting. With another chilling outcry, the Beast redoubled its speed. Yet for all its size and power, the Beast's paws made only a scant impression on the snow, and the sound of its passage remained subtle as a whisper. And again, the space between predator and prey diminished. …

Now the Beast remained silent as the dots grew in size and began to reveal details: long, gangling legs; lean, lithe bodies; small heads with features that were not yet distinguishable.

Those heads kept turning back to gauge how much closer the Beast had come. When they saw that their pursuer was gaining, their desperation widened the gap. But those periods of respite became briefer as the Beast drew closer. ...

Hunger was not the reason for the Beast's pursuit. Its compulsion to catch and kill its prey flowed deeper than any need to fill its stomach. Hatred was the fuel that urged the Beast onward. It desired nothing more than to seize its prey in its taloned paws and sink its teeth deep into helpless flesh. ...

There were three of them: one large, another slightly smaller, the third less than half the size of the others ... a male, its mate, and their offspring. ...

The male was the one the Beast wanted. The others were of no consequence. The male was the one that had to be brought down. Red death was the only thing that mattered. ...

No longer did the prey gain momentary advantages in distance. The Beast was moving more swiftly than ever. It could see the prey clearly now. The ungainly limbs of the creatures flailed awkwardly. Their flanks heaved in exhaustion. Their faces – more distinct now – displayed stark terror as their bloodshot eyes rolled. ...

A being other than the Beast might have paused at the sight of those visages. Half-human, half-beast, the creatures' faces jutted forward beneath large browbones. Large, square teeth protruded between thick, pendulous lips. Dog-like noses dominated their snouts. The hairless skin that stretched tightly across their bony bodies was black as pitch. ...

The male dropped back, hoping to protect its mate and progeny. Although fear still shone in its eyes, the prey-creature bared its sharp teeth and lashed out with the claws at the end of its forelimbs ...

With contemptuous ease, the Beast struck aside the prey-creature's claws. Then the head of the Beast darted forward. Fanged jaws closed on the prey-creature's throat, and then the coppery taste of fresh blood filled the predator's mouth. ...

Even as the prey-creature uttered a gurgling death-cry, the Beast opened its jaws, lifted its head, and hurled a triumphant howl-roar upward to the leaden sky. ...

❈ ❈ ❈

Jolted awake from a fitful slumber, Wolfgang Krieger abruptly sat up in his bed as though he had just suffered an electric shock. He could still feel the tension from an outcry in his throat, though the echo of its sound was gone.

"*Gott in Himmel,*" Krieger muttered as he peeled perspiration-soaked sheets away from his bare chest and swung his legs over the side of his bed.

Damned dreams, he thought as he pressed the palms of his hands against his forehead. He knew others had heard his outcry. The first time the Dream of the Beast had occurred, his bellowing roars had brought *Herr Doktor* and others rushing into his room, panic written plainly on their faces. After *Herr Doktor* had shooed the others out, Krieger had told him about the Dream of the Beast. When the boxer had finished his tale, Herr Doktor had … smiled.

"This is a mere side-effect of the *Starkenflessig*, Wolf," Von Dunkel had said. "In your mind, you are symbolizing what you will do to the *Neger* Jackhammer once you get into the ring with him."

"But I will be fighting Jackhammer with my fists, not my teeth," Krieger had said.

Herr Doktor had laughed.

"Your strength and skill, not the dream, will guide you in the fight," *Herr Doktor* reassured.

The dream had occurred every night since the *Starkenflessig* injections had begun. No longer did Krieger's bestial outcries cause anyone to come to his door … not since Von Dunkel told everyone that the roars were the war-chants of a champion, nothing more.

Krieger slammed his right fist into his left palm. The blow, which sounded like a pistol shot, should have been painful. All Krieger felt, however, was a slight stinging sensation.

He lay back down on his bed. Sleep would come eventually, and he would welcome it because he only endured the Dream of the Beast once a night. But sleep would not come just yet. Not while he was remembering – not the dream, but events that had occurred less than a year before now. …

※ ※ ※

Krieger stepped back from the embrace of his fiancée, Ilse Neusel. He could not believe what she had just said. She repeated it.

"I cannot go to America with you, Wolf."

They were in his dressing room at the Olympic Stadium in Berlin. Several hours before, Krieger had won the European heavyweight championship, scoring a brutal knockout over the Italian giant, Ugo Dippolito. That victory guaranteed Wolf a shot at Jackhammer Jackson's world title.

A celebratory fete awaited, with a dazzling guest list that included the Führer himself. But Ilse had insisted on speaking alone with Krieger before they attended the gala event.

Krieger shook his head in disbelief. He was clad in a black tuxedo specially tailored to fit his heroic proportions. The hulking Italian had not been able to hit Krieger hard enough to cut or bruise the German's face, or even to muss his hair. But the words Ilse had just spoken carried greater impact than any punch he had ever absorbed in the ring.

They had planned to go together to America for the title fight. Of course, Ilse would not be allowed to see much of Wolf at the training camp. But her glorious presence at ringside would be a feather in the cap of the Reich. And, after Krieger's inevitable defeat of the *Schwartzer*, he and Ilse would be wed in a ceremony that would outshine any royal nuptials the crowned heads of Europe could produce.

Ilse looked up at him. A youthful, petite, blonde dressed in a clinging, ivory-colored evening gown and an ermine shawl draped over her bare shoulders, she seemed childlike in comparison to Krieger's size. She was, however, a champion in her own right. In the 1936 Winter Olympics at Garmisch-Partenkirchen, she had won the gold medal in figureskating, defeating a popular Norwegian rival.

When they met during an event that honored Germany's champions from both the Winter and Summer Games, the attraction between Wolf and Ilse was instant and obvious. Soon, they became known as *Die Goldenen Paar* – "The Golden Couple."

Other than Wolf's training camps, they had spent as much time together as their schedules – and propriety – allowed. Their coming sojourn in America promised to be their most exciting experience since the Olympics.

And now, *this*. …

"Why?" Krieger demanded.

Ilse's face, the piquant beauty of which had adorned even more propaganda posters than that of her fiancé, showed regret – and a touch of fear. Tears shone in her large blue eyes.

"The Führer has determined that my presence is more valuable here in Germany, rather than the United States, Wolf," she said in a near whisper.

A frown furrowed Krieger's forehead. Well did he understand why the Führer would want to separate him from Ilse.

The *Starkenflessig*. …

Ever since *Herr Doktor* von Dunkel had first proposed the use of his secret concoction to enhance Krieger's already formidable physical prowess, the boxer had steadfastly resisted the notion. Krieger was certain he could overcome the *Schwartzer* without the physician-turned-scientist's dubious assistance.

But Von Dunkel had the ear of the Führer – as did more than a few pseudo-scientists and mystic mountebanks with hare-brained schemes ranging from the creation of an army of automatons to a quest for Odin's Spear. Von Dunkel, though eccentric, was no crackpot, however. He was a legitimate researcher, holding doctoral degrees in medicine, biology, and chemistry from the finest universities in Germany and Austria. When he spoke, the Führer was not the only one who listened. Not even Von Dunkel's bitter rival, Mengele, could gainsay him, despite Mengele's higher official status.

The Führer had acceded to Von Dunkel's reasoning regarding the use of the *Starkenflessig*. Krieger had continued to resist. But now, with Ilse to be effectively held hostage in the Fatherland, Krieger had no choice but to comply with *Herr Doktor's* scheme.

Wolf had previously told Ilse about the *Starkenflessig*; they kept no secrets from each other. Tears rolled down her cheeks as she looked at him now.

"I'm sorry, Wolf," she said plaintively, as though she had done something wrong.

The big man gathered her in his muscular arms and held her gently as she shook with sobs.

"Do not worry, *Liebling*," he said. "It is not your fault."

As he continued to comfort her, Ilse heard him say something else in a mutter almost too low for her to hear.

"*Schwein.*"

She did not know whether he was referring to Von Dunkel, or Hitler – or both.

❊ ❊ ❊

Now, as he lay in his training camp bed, Wolfgang Krieger struggled to quell the emotions that roiled within him. He feared for Ilse. He had received letters from her, and he was familiar enough with her handwriting to feel confident they were genuine. But the language was stilted, and the sentiments she expressed were shallow.

Those factors, in themselves, told him that Ilse continued to live under a threat that would be carried out if he did not continue to cooperate with Von Dunkel. Yet with that dire thought, and memory of the Dream of the Beast lingering in his mind, Krieger still managed to fall asleep.

He dreamed of Ilse, and he would whisper her name several times before he woke in the morning.

❊ ❊ ❊

Von Dunkel slept in an austere chamber that that had been the office of one of the prison's lesser officials. He lay so still that only the slight rise and fall of the bedclothes provided an indication that he was alive.

Whatever *Herr Doktor* was dreaming about now, it put a smile on his face.

CHAPTER THIRTEEN

'WHO ARE YOU ... REALLY?'

Chum sat stolidly on the passenger side of the touring car's front seat. Damballa was driving. The crime-fighter's face was like a silhouette, except for the glitter of his eyes, which flashed whenever the automobile passed beneath a street light. Chum turned his head and looked past the blanket-covered pile of corpses in the back seat – three of the Germans who had invaded the *gri-gri* shop. The others were stuffed in the car's ample trunk.

When he had helped Damballa load the bodies into the vehicle, Chum had wondered at the lack of interest from the Darkside denizens. He saw no one on the sidewalks, only a few people's shadows appeared in the lit windows of the tenements. And those shadows did not linger long.

"Guess folks 'round here don't wanna mess with you," Chum had commented.

"They know me," was the only response Damballa provided.

Chum was still thinking about that comment as he eyed the pair of headlights that followed a short distance behind the touring car. Those lights didn't alarm him; he knew they belonged to Damballa's own vehicle. Kojo was driving it. Mamadou had stayed behind "to take care of things," as she succinctly put it.

"So where we dumpin' the stiffs?" Chum asked, looking again at Damballa.

"We are not going to 'dump' them," Damballa replied.

More silence passed as the two cars rolled farther away from the city, traveling now over roads flanked by trees rather than structures. Finally, Chum asked the question that had occupied the forefront of his mind since Jackhammer had told him the true identity of "Kid Ebony."

"Who are you … really?" the trainer inquired.

Damballa gave him a penetrating stare, which seemed almost palpable within the dark confines of the car. Then the cloaked man returned his attention to the road.

Chum didn't think Damballa was going to reply. And that was fine with Chum. After all, the old trainer harbored some secrets even Jackhammer didn't know. …

Damballa spoke then.

"Have you ever heard of Reverend Walter Horace Shropshire?" he asked.

The name sounded familiar to Chum, but he couldn't immediately place it. Then, as he thought back further, memory lit a spark in his mind.

"Yeah," he said. "He use to go on them church missions to Africa. Didn't they use to call him 'The Colored Livingstone?' "

"Among other things," Damballa said. "He was many things to many people. And he was my father."

The touring car's motor purred as Chum digested that revelation. Another memory occurred to him then. He was reluctant to speak of it. But he was always one to finish what he started, either in or out of the boxing ring.

"I heard Shropshire had a daughter," the trainer said. "Never heard nothin' about no son."

"My mother was not his wife," said Damballa.

The story that followed those words riveted Chum's attention until the touring car reached Damballa's intended destination.

❋❋❋

The Followers of the Good Shepherd society had unleashed a storm of controversy among its fellow Christian organizations when it announced during the 1890s its intention to send American Negro clergymen to do missionary work in the heart of the Congo Free State. It was not the ironic misnomer of the territory – which was actually a private fiefdom of Belgium's King Leopold II – that stirred unease in Christian-outreach circles. It was the notion of sending colored ministers abroad when they were of much better use in keeping their people at home docile and cooperative.

And then there was the matter of placing Negroes in charge of overseas operations – a circumstance that raised the hackles of many prominent donors to the Followers of the Good Shepherd.

The FGS board of trustees worked hard to reassure the skeptics, vowing that each of the black missionaries would work under the supervision and mentorship of a white minister. That provision did not satisfy all the doubting benefactors. Those who were not convinced redirected their donations. But enough remained onsite to ensure that the missions to Africa could be financed without compromising the other endeavors of the FGS.

The most prominent of the colored missionaries was Walter Horace Shropshire, the Virginia-born son of a former slave. With his wife, Esther, and white supervisor, Rev. John Lipton, Shropshire was sent to aid and convert the Bakosi people, who lived in one of the most remote areas of the Congo region.

After an initial period of distrust, during which they were perceived as "black white people" in league with "true white people" such as the Belgians and Lipton, the Shropshires earned the Bakosis' trust. Walter's practical knowledge of agriculture, hunting, and mechanics, complemented by his mesmerizing performances in the pulpit, along with Esther's skills as a nurse, did much to allay the Bakosis' misgivings about them. Lipton also won acceptance, but to a lesser extent.

Although Lipton was nominally in charge of the mission, he soon deferred to his colleague in most matters. For Lipton was able to acknowledge Shropshire's merits without feeling any threat to his own position on the color hierarchy – a hierarchy Lipton rejected, though it was considered gospel in some quarters of the FGS.

Lipton was the one who sent dispatches and progress reports to the FGS headquarters in Pennsylvania. The Shropshires, however, were the ones truly in charge of the mission, and Lipton never developed any resentment of that reality.

Shropshire learned much about both the Bakosi and the region in which they lived. Swiftly seeing through the conventional wisdom that viewed Africans as nothing more than irredeemable savages, he came to appreciate the language, arts and character of the Bakosi. He began to wonder whether they had once been far greater than they were now. Something in their sculptures, and the way their dwellings were constructed, suggested a remnant of the grandeur of ancient times ... perhaps of Carthage, or even Egypt.

In the meantime, the missionary learned things about the Congo Free State ... disquieting things.

Rubber was to the Congo what gold had been to California and Alaska.

It was a commodity that could put plenty of money in the pockets of entrepreneurs, if it could be extracted quickly and cheaply from the trees that harbored it.

King Leopold was the biggest entrepreneur of all. His private holdings in the Free State included millions of rubber trees. And the people of the region, demoralized as they were by the centuries of warfare and ravaged by the slave trade, provided a deep pool of forced laborers.

As Shropshire's awareness of the Belgians' depredations grew, so did his outrage. He began to send dispatches under his own name to FGS headquarters, with the blessing and support of Lipton. The indifferent responses he received from the society's leaders angered him yet further. Instead of "staying in his place," as headquarters tartly advised him to do, he sent articles and photographs to major newspapers on both sides of the Atlantic.

The subsequent publication of the information he had gathered transformed Shropshire from an obscure Negro clergyman to a personage of international renown – the "Colored Livingstone," the black race's answer to the Scottish medical missionary who had died not long after being famously located by the explorer Henry Morton Stanley.

Shropshire's fame shielded him from the wrath of the FGS establishment, which was beginning to question the wisdom of its decision to send black missionaries to Africa. A wave of resentment over the possible undermining of white rule on the Dark Continent countered the sympathy for the oppressed Africans that Shropshire's revelations had engendered.

As Shropshire continued to write his articles, he embarked on a well-attended lecture tour through the United States and Britain. He negotiated a tenuous tightrope, beneath which his enemies in the FGS and the Belgian agents and their black proxies who sought to eliminate him waited eagerly for the slightest misstep.

Throughout this peril, three people remained steadfastly loyal to Shropshire: his wife, Esther; his colleague, Reverend Lipton – and an enigmatic Bakosi woman named Mamadou.

Of unknown age and without formal rank in the Bakosi hierarchy, Mamadou was nonetheless a person of influence not only in her own tribe, but also in much of the surrounding region. Her acceptance of the outlanders' presence had aided in the establishment of the mission, which had encountered some resistance when its pastors had first arrived.

Though Mamadou declined to convert to Christianity, she did not

"In that place, which was old before the Egyptians built their pyramids ... I was raised to adolescence."

discourage others from doing so – including her three daughters, who became very helpful to Esther Shropshire. In conversations with Reverend Shropshire, Mamadou implied that she had access to a core of knowledge that was far older than the books of the Bible. She revealed only hints of that lore to Shropshire. Yet she was not loath to learn as much as she could about the expertise of the whites – especially in medicine.

For a time, Shropshire was able to sure-footedly negotiate his tightrope, cultivating the friends of his cause and keeping its – and his – enemies at bay. Then Esther became pregnant – and at the same time fell ill as a result of one of the tropical diseases the missionaries had previously managed to avoid. Shropshire then made the difficult decision to send Esther back to the United States, out of reach of the Congo's pestilences.

With a heavy heart, Shropshire watched a steamboat carry Esther away on the great Congo River. Several months later, his heart grew heavier still when he heard the news that Esther had died in childbirth. Their daughter, whom Esther had with her last breath named Amelia, would be cared for by Esther's family, for Walter had only a few known kinfolk.

Shropshire chose to continue his work among the Bakosi. But another blow fell when Reverend Lipton also succumbed to disease.

Even as they arranged for the burial of Lipton in his Indiana hometown, the FDS officials set long-awaited contingency plans into motion. Another white minister, Reverend Obadiah Helmsford, was sent to take control of the Bakosi mission.

Helmsford possessed nothing of his predecessor's racial enlightenment. From the moment he stepped off the steamboat, he imposed his authority like a yoke upon Shropshire and the rest of the mission's staff. The policies and procedures Shropshire had initiated were summarily overturned, with no dissent countenanced. Helmsford treated Shropshire like a servant rather than a fellow man of the cloth. For the sake of the Bakosi, whom he had long-since come to regard as his own people, Shropshire suffered silently and did the best he could under difficult circumstances.

Then, abruptly, the FGS recalled Shropshire. Despite the ensuing clamor in the newspapers and amid religious and philanthropic circles, the FGS provided no rationale for its drastic measure. And Shropshire himself remained tight-lipped, retiring to the ministry of a small colored church in North Carolina and trying to be a good father to his daughter.

Although Shropshire's fame faded, innuendo remained … whispers that he had become involved with a native woman even before his wife had become pregnant. That accusation was never proven. Questions to

Shropshire and the FGS encountered an impenetrable wall of silence. Fueled by the lack of information, the rumors multiplied over the years. It was said, for example, that Shropshire had left behind a child by the Bakosi woman. ...

CHAPTER FOURTEEN

FURTHER REVELATIONS

"I am that child," said Damballa as the touring car, with its grisly burden, continued its journey through the night.

If that disclosure came as a surprise to Chum, he didn't show it.

"Is Mamadou your mother?" the trainer asked.

Damballa shook his head. In the darkness of the car's interior, Chum could barely see the motion.

"No. Mamadou is my grandmother. My mother's name was Kaloya. She was one of the daughters Mamadou sent to the mission."

"You say 'was,'" Chum commented after a short silence.

"Like the mother of the sister I have never met, Kaloya died not long after I was born. But it was not childbirth that killed her."

Damballa became quiet again. Similar silences had not interrupted his previous narration. Chum respected the other man's memories of loss.

Lord knows, I got plenty of my own, the trainer thought.

"After my father was forced out, Helmsford turned the mission from a beacon of hope to a pit of despair," Damballa said. "Instead of joining the mission, the people of the region shunned it. And the ones who were already part of the flock turned away from what my father taught them. It was their respect and love for him that had converted them. Helmsford's bigotry undid everything my father and Reverend Lipton had accomplished.

"Then the Belgians came."

Another silence. Chum could well anticipate what Damballa would say next.

"Only my father's reputation had prevented King Leopold's lackeys from attacking the mission much earlier. Because they knew what was coming, the people there who were not Bakosi deserted. The Bakosi stayed – not out of any loyalty to Helmsford, but because there were preparations they needed to carry out.

"But their time ran out. The mission was assailed by a predatory tribe called the Jumuku, with the connivance of Belgian agents. Some of the Bakosi managed to escape. Most did not. Mamadou has told me that my mother threw me toward her a moment before a Jumuku spear took her life. Mamadou caught me and escaped into the forest along with only a fraction of the Bakosi.

"Helmsford was burned alive in the mission house. The Jumuku did not devour his remains, if that is what you are thinking."

"Weren't thinkin' that at all," Chum lied.

"The Bakosi went deep into the forest," Damballa continued, "along secret paths they still knew, even though many generations had passed since those paths had last been used. They were going to an ancient place, forgotten by all save the Bakosi. It was the place where the ancient ancestors of the Bakosi had dwelled – and from which they had been driven by a people very much like the Belgians.

"After many perils that led to more deaths, the last of Bakosi reached their ancestral home. It had long since been deserted, for the conquerors had not been able to thrive in a place they had stolen by deception. Stone ruins surrounded a lake too perfectly circular to be natural. Some of the towers rose higher than the trees; others lay fallen and shattered.

"In that place, which was old before the Egyptians built their pyramids, the Bakosi reclaimed their time-lost heritage. In that place, I was raised to adolescence."

"How you get from that place to this one?" Chum inquired.

"When I reached 14 rains – the age at which a Bakosi boy becomes a man – my grandmother gave me a letter that my father had left for me, to be opened only after I had passed through all the puberty rites. Mamadou had taught me to read, for books were part of what the Bakosi had carried away from the mission.

"In the letter, my father expressed regret that he could not be part of my life because of the circumstances of my birth. He encouraged me to learn all I could of the ways of the blacks and the ways of the whites, and to use that knowledge for the betterment of all people – but especially people of African descent, for they were most in need of help. He promised that if I ever came to him in America, he would accept me as his son, no matter what anyone might think of me – or him."

"I heard that Reverend Shropshire passed years ago," said Chum. "You ever get the chance to meet him?"

"No."

That word ended the conversation for a time. The headlights of the touring car stabbed forward, leading the way to Damballa's unknown destination. Several miles passed before the cloaked man spoke again.

"After my father's letter was read, the remnants of the Bakosi gathered in council amid the ruins of their ancestors' civilization. I told them I wanted to honor my father's wishes ... to combine the knowledge I had gathered from my mother's people and combine it with the science that has served the whites so well.

"Having made that decision, I knew – and the Bakosi knew – that I was to leave the ancestral land, never to return.

"It was a difficult parting, for the Bakosi had loved my father and honored me as his son. Mamadou decided to join me, for I was still young even in the wake of my rites. So did a few others, such as Kojo. We took with us some of the valuables left behind by the Bakosis' ancestors – treasure that had been hidden from the avaricious conquerors. It provided us the wherewithal to escape from the Congo under the noses of the Belgians, and buy my way into Europe in the guise of 'exiled African royalty.'"

"They swallowed that line?" Chum asked incredulously. "Who they think you was, Haile Selassie?"

Damballa chuckled at Chum's mention of the Abyssinian monarch who had been deposed by the Italians.

"Something like that," the cloaked man said.

"It is said that people do not care about the color of one's money, Chum," Damballa continued. "But you and I know they do care about the color of the hand that is holding it."

"Ain't that the truth."

"Indeed. I remember one professor in Germany who would not allow me to enter his classroom, even though I had paid my tuition like any other student. I was able to get into other classrooms, though. I studied chemistry, physics, and biology at several European universities – including some German ones. I studied other subjects as well ... things that are not taught behind ivy-covered walls.

"I had read with interest about the American guardians of liberty and justice who operate beyond the strictures of the law. People like The Shadow, Doc Savage, Captain Hazzard, Jim Anthony ... and I became convinced that our people needed such a defender as well. A champion like your Jackhammer, but outside the boxing ring. A champion for my father's people and, eventually, my mother's.

"And so I learned various methods of armed and unarmed combat from masters of their respective arts. ..."

"Yeah," Chum interjected. "Jackhammer told me about you and Jack Johnson."

"You do not much like Johnson, do you?"

"Let's just say I never seen eye-to-eye with the man. Got to admit, though, he taught you good."

"As did the others. At any rate, by the time I finished my studies, I was able to combine the modern knowledge I had acquired at the universities with the erudition of the ancient Bakosi, which lives on in Mamadou. The time had come to discard the persona of the 'African prince' and acquire another identity – the identity of Damballa."

"Why that name, instead of 'Doc Negro,' or somethin'?" Chum asked.

The cloaked man flashed a brief smile.

"Damballa is but one name of the most important deity in Africa – the serpent god, the bringer of wisdom and its accompanying woe. It is the name recognized by practitioners of what you call 'voodoo' or 'hoodoo,' which is the many-times-removed vestige of what the ancient Bakosi knew."

"Hmpf," Chum snorted.

Silence followed as the trainer ruminated over the astounding tale Damballa had told. He could not think of any reason for Damballa to lie to him. Still, something wasn't right. Finally, Chum gave voice to his misgivings.

"You been tellin' me stuff you wouldn't want most folks to know," he said. "There's lots of stuff about me I don't want nobody to know, neither. But somehow, your Grandma know my real name. That tell me y'all been studyin' me before you stepped foot in the trainin' camp.

"Now, we *both* know stuff that puts us over a barrel with each other. And what you been tellin' me's got somethin' to do with the Krieger fight. People got killed tonight. ... I ask you straight out, Damballa – is Jackhammer's life in danger? Should we call off the fight?"

"Yes to the first, no to the second."

"Huh?"

"As you well know, Chum, the life of any man who climbs into the ring to fight is in danger. And I am certain that the Nazis are up to something that will give their man an advantage. I intend to find out what that is, and put a stop to it.

"But you must not call off the Krieger fight, Chum. There is far too much at stake. This is a chance to undo the long aftermath of the Johnson-Jeffries fight. I know you are old enough to remember what happened when Johnson humiliated the Great White Hope."

"Yeah," said Chum. "Some of that 'what' happened to me. White folks went plumb crazy when Jeffries went down. It was kill or be killed. Weren't nobody gon' kill *this* baby."

Deliberately or by chance, Chum's hand brushed against the scar on his face.

"I know," Damballa said quietly. He did not need to say more. They both knew the secret Chum had buried with his birth name.

"It's different this time, Chum," Damballa continued. "Unlike the fight between Johnson and Jeffries, this one is about more than simply black against white. This time it is, literally, good against evil. And this time, the black man goes in as the representative of good. If the fight is called off, the Nazis will say that Jackhammer is afraid of their Wolf. And far too many people will believe that to be true. Good would lose then. *We* would lose."

"I understand that, Damballa," Chum said. "But if these 'Ratzis' is tryin' to pull a fast one – "

"I am here to make certain that they do not," said Damballa. "Whatever I learn, you and Jackhammer will learn. If I advise you to do something that may seem unusual, please trust me and do it. Kojo will be your contact."

"Hmpf. Hope he learn to watch where he goin'."

Damballa chuckled. Then he slowed the car and brought it to a stop. In the vehicle behind, Kojo did the same.

"This is close enough … and far enough," said Damballa.

"What you talkin' about?

"You will see. Come on. I need your help," Damballa said as he opened the door on his side of the car.

❊ ❊ ❊

It was well past midnight when Chum returned to Compton Lakes. He was exhausted. This had been the most eventful night he had ever experienced in his hardscrabble life, and he was no longer a spring chicken. And for the first time in that life, he was placing his fate in the hands of someone else. …

Chum knew he had only a few hours left to get some sleep, for the camp's routine began at the crack of dawn, when Jackhammer would do his morning run. He needed to get rid of his clothes, though. There was bound to be some blood on them.

Chum sighed as he opened the door to his room and stepped inside. So much to think about … so damn much to *worry* about while he was trying to get Jackhammer ready for the biggest boxing match the world had ever seen. Bigger than Johnson-Jeffries, because there wasn't any radio in those days.

Chum flipped the switch of his light.

And he froze in mid-motion as illumination filled the room.

Someone was sitting on Chum's bed.

It was Jackhammer, clad in pajamas.

"Where you been, Chum?" the champion asked, his deadpan expression never wavering.

CHAPTER FIFTEEN

BLOOD WILL TELL

Von Dunkel kept his concern hidden beneath an icy mask. *Der Tod* and his men should have returned last night. Now the day had passed well into morning, yet there was still no sign of the big man and his picked underlings.

Der Tod had been excited when he spoke to Von Dunkel about the lead he had come across concerning the whereabouts of Damballa.

"His neck is in our noose, *Herr Doktor*," *Der Tod* had enthused. "This night, he will belong to the Reich!"

Von Dunkel had merely nodded and sent *Der Tod* on his way. The doctor was beginning to question the wisdom of injecting *Der Tod* with the *Starkenflessig*. Von Dunkel had hoped to be able to duplicate the marvelous effects the compound had initiated in Krieger. *Der Tod*, whose loyalty did not need to be compelled as it had been in the case of the boxer, was an ideal subject for further research into the *Starkenflessig's* attributes.

In the short term, the experiment had proven successful. *Der Tod's* physical prowess had increased, though not to the same extent as Krieger's. But *Der Tod's* behavior became more erratic, and his judgment questionable. Consequences such as these had not occurred in Krieger. Perhaps the *Starkenflessig* affected different people in different ways – some of which might not prove to be of benefit to the Reich ... or to Von Dunkel.

But if *Der Tod* could eliminate this Damballa, even as Krieger would soon defeat Jackhammer Jackson in the ring, then Von Dunkel's concerns about expanded use of the *Starkenflessig* would be allayed.

Der Tod had not returned, however. And Von Dunkel's concerns rose with each moment of the big man's absence.

Finally, the doctor summoned an underling named Oskar Schutz.

"Find *Der Tod*," Von Dunkel commanded. "Take as many men as you need."

"*Jawohl!*" Schutz, a medium-sized, nondescript man, acknowledged.

The wait for the answer to the mystery of *Der Tod's* disappearance proved to be far shorter than Von Dunkel had anticipated. Less than half an hour passed before Schutz returned. The underling's face was ashen, as though he had just seen something that was incredibly ghastly and shocking.

"Well?" Von Dunkel demanded. "You have found him so soon?"

"*Ja, Herr Doktor,*" Schutz replied in a shaky tone.

"Where is he, then?" Von Dunkel barked impatiently.

"You ... need to see for yourself, *Herr Doktor.*"

"*Ach!*" Von Dunkel grumbled as he rose from his chair and followed the underling out of the office. A moment later, they were in one of the training camp's cars.

Few words were exchanged as Schutz drove Von Dunkel a surprisingly short distance from Balrogorra. Other cars were parked away from the road. Von Dunkel could see yet another vehicle beyond those – a vehicle he recognized as the touring car *Der Tod* and his men had taken the night before.

But he did not see *Der Tod*.

Von Dunkel and Schutz got out of their car and approached the other men, all of whom shared the underling's shaken demeanor. The doctor saw that the door of the touring car hung open.

"We did not touch anything after we opened the door, *Herr Doktor,*" Schutz said.

Von Dunkel pushed unceremoniously through the others, and peered past the car door. As he recoiled in consternation at what he saw, his head nearly bumped into the roof of the vehicle.

Der Tod and his five henchmen were seated in the car – three in the front and three in the back. Their heads slumped forward, as though the men were dozing. But there was no indication that any of them were breathing.

Blackened faces displayed the slackness of death. Blood congealed in clumps and patches across the clothing of the corpses. Gore stuck to the seats of the car. The weapons *Der Tod* and his men had carried were gone.

A word had been scrawled across the dashboard of the car – a word written in German blood.

That word was: *Damballa*.

❖ ❖ ❖

Not all the cells of the prison-turned-training-camp were empty. In the weak illumination cast by the few light bulbs that shone in the hall ceiling, large, humped, motionless shapes could be seen in several of the cages that were meant to confine criminals. Stalks of metal stood beside each shape. Plastic tubing snaked between the shapes and the containers that hung like fruit from the metal stalks.

A musty odor permeated the range of cells, as did a slight sough of sound reminiscent of the rustling of dry leaves in a slight breeze. But there was no wind in these dank confines.

Von Dunkel stood in front of one of the cells. His posture was ramrod-straight, and his hands were folded behind his back. Though his eyes regarded the lumpish shape in the cell, his mind roved elsewhere.

He was thinking of the fight, only a few days away now. The fight would prove to be a triumph for both Wolf and himself. And, of course, for the Reich.

But he was also thinking of *Der Tod* and the others, their gore-soaked corpses propped like mannequins in the touring car. He was thinking of the name that had been written in blood. …

And for the first time in years, fear crept into the thoughts of *Herr Doktor* Claus von Dunkel.

❖ ❖ ❖

When Detective Errol Bynoe and a squad of four uniformed police officers entered Mamadou's *gri-gri* shop, the crimson eye above the door did not open. For the arrival of the law signaled neither danger nor disaster to the shop's contents – or its owner.

Mamadou stood behind the main counter as though she had been expecting her visitors. Her carved stick leaned against the side of the counter. Her demeanor was unsmiling, but not unpleasant, as she greeted the police.

"Good morning, Detective Bynoe," she said. "What can I do for you and your colleagues?"

Bynoe had not met Mamadou before. But he was not surprised that she knew who he was. Colored police detectives were not exactly commonplace, after all. And a great deal of publicity had accompanied his ascension to his post. His picture had been in the papers.

"We have received reports of a … disturbance here last night, Miss Mamadou," Bynoe said. "We've come to investigate those reports."

A lift of the eyebrows on Mamadou's ebony face greeted those words.

"As you can see, Detective, nothing is 'disturbed' here."

"Do you mind if we take a look around, anyway?" Bynoe asked.

"Go ahead."

Bynoe nodded toward the four uniformed officers – all of them big, dark-skinned, no-nonsense types; the kind of officers that were able to command respect in the Darkside. All four men began to look around the shop. Mamadou remained behind the counter. Her hands rested on its top, nowhere near the lever that would release the rows of lethal spikes.

Of the deadly battle that had occurred during the previous night, no sign remained. The damaged front door had been replaced. And Mamadou had cleared every speck of blood from the shop's floor, walls, and artifacts. She had patched the holes made by the intruders' bullets with material that blended perfectly with the wood. Artifacts that had been damaged in the fray were removed and replaced by others, so that no conspicuous-looking gaps were present.

Though their inspection was thorough, the police did not touch many of the objects they observed. None of them was particularly superstitious, though Bynoe remembered tales of *obeah*-magic from his native Virgin Islands. The investigators were more interested in what might be on the objects: specks of blood, bits of cloth, a smudge that might yield a fingerprint.

They found nothing.

When the search ended, Bynoe turned his attention back to Mamadou, who was staring ahead imperturbably. Bynoe found himself comparing her to Madame Pomp, with whom he had spoken a few days before.

A pair of colored queens, these two, the detective thought. *But Delia Pomphrey was scared when I talked to her. I don't think this lady has been afraid a day in her life.*

"There doesn't seem to be anything wrong here, ma'am," he said. "So, why do you suppose somebody told us there was?"

"Perhaps that 'somebody' is the only one who can answer that question, Detective," Mamadou replied.

Her tone was neither insolent nor dismissive. Even so, Bynoe knew he would gain nothing from prolonging his visit.

"Thank you for your cooperation, Miss Mamadou," he said.

Mamadou nodded.

Bynoe's gaze strayed to the snake-shaped pendant on Mamadou's bosom. For the first time, he noticed the crimson jewels that were its eyes … eyes that seemed to be staring at him.

"Let's go, men." Bynoe said to the uniforms.

With that, the lawmen departed from the shop. Outside, the pair of officers assigned to protect the two squad cars from the attention of the bolder Darkside denizens relaxed their guard. All the lawmen entered the vehicles. After Bynoe reported to headquarters on the newfangled two-way radio that turned people's voices into the squawking of seagulls, the cars drove away.

❃ ❃ ❃

Inside the shop, Mamadou waited until she could be certain that the police were gone, and had left no one behind to conduct surveillance. The eye above the door remained closed, and the sounds outside were muted.

Satisfied, Mamadou took up her stick and walked away from the door and past the main counter. She headed for the back wall. She carried the stick instead of using it as an aid for walking.

With the bottom end of the stick – its wicked spike hidden – she touched the eye-hole of a particularly grotesque-looking mask on the wall. Silently, the section on which the mask hung swung outward.

Damballa stood in the revealed opening. He had heard everything that passed between Bynoe and Mamadou.

"I do not think he suspects anything," Mamadou said.

"I believe you are right," Damballa agreed. "But when all this is over, we are going to have to find another place. This one is becoming too well-known."

Mamadou nodded. They were speaking in Kibakosi, the language Mamadou had taught her grandson, along with English.

"Come now," said Damballa. "There is something you need to see."

Mamadou followed Damballa into the darkness. A moment later, the wall swung shut, and the mask stared outward.

❃ ❃ ❃

Darkness reigned in the catacombs beneath the city block on which the *gri-gri* shop was located. But Mamadou and Damballa did not need light to navigate the subterranean labyrinth of tunnels known only to the two of them. Though neither of them could see in the pitch-blackness, senses they had nurtured in another, even darker, place led them unerringly to their destination.

When they arrived, Damballa's finger flicked a switch. The lights that came on emitted a soft luminescence, like sunlight diffused by a high canopy of leaves in a dense forest.

The illumination revealed a room that was in many ways similar to the shop above. But instead of artifacts and vials and bottles of unknown liquids, the counters and laboratory tables here were covered with chemistry apparatus: test tubes, Bunsen burners, flasks, ring stands, and equipment for other disciplines as well.

The walls held shelves laden with glass containers filled with powders of various hues and consistencies. As well, thin cylinders made from wood and quills lined part of one wall like an assemblage of small but deadly weapons – an impression heightened by the darts that were included in the collection.

Doorways indicated other components of the underground complex: living quarters and a kitchen redolent of the lingering aromas of exotic cooking.

Only one African artifact could be seen in the sanctum: a mask carved in a style more realistic than usual. The face depicted was tranquil, with closed eyes and lips parted in a slight smile. Thick strands of raffia hung from the edges of the mask, giving the impression of hair and a beard.

The mask was a portrait of Walter Horace Shropshire, carved by a master Bakosi craftsman in honor of the man-from-afar who had been such a friend to that beleaguered people.

Damballa led Mamadou to one of several microscopes on one of the laboratory tables. A red blotch could be seen on the slide beneath its powerful lens.

"This is blood from the German who was so difficult to bring down," Damballa said.

Mamadou needed no invitation to sit on the stool in front of the microscope and peer through the eyepiece. She stared for a long moment at the fluid captured between the slide and the cover slip. Then she looked up at Damballa with a look of deep concern on her face.

"Now we know, Mamadou," Damballa said.

Mamadou nodded solemnly.

CHAPTER SIXTEEN

NIGHT WORK

Shimmy-boy Moore knew he was being followed. Worse, he knew his pursuer wanted him to be aware of that fact. The glimpses he had caught of a dark shape ducking out of sight behind corners and slipping into empty doorways communicated an ominous message: the split-seconds of lingering in view could only be by design.

The dark shape wanted to be seen. And it was drawing closer with each of Shimmy-boy's sightings.

A singular ability to wriggle out of all kinds of tight spots had earned Shimmy-boy his street name. He didn't think he had ever been in a worse predicament than being tied up in the back seat of the Germans' car a couple of nights ago. He had still gotten out of that one, though.

But now, he suspected he might be in his worst fix yet, even though his arms and legs were free and he could go wherever he wanted.

No, he thought. *Not where I want to go, but where this cat back there wants me to be. ...*

Shimmy-boy cursed his decision to remain for a time before getting out of the city. He didn't know how long he would be gone. But it would, at the very least, be until after the big fight. By then, whether their man won or lost, the Germans would go back to where they came from, and Shimmy-boy would be in the clear.

He didn't know whether the fight had anything to do with that hoodoo-man, Damballa, he had fingered for the Germans. He didn't much care, either. All he wanted was the scratch ... but he wasn't all that upset that he didn't get it, because he knew what would have happened if those Germans had come back before he got away.

Why it take 'em so long, Shimmy-boy wondered, not for the first time since his escape. He'd heard shots fired, and assumed that anyone inside the place the Germans had broken into had to be dead. Yet the Germans hadn't come back, and that gave Shimmy-boy the time he needed to find – and use – his edge.

Lay low in the Darkside … come out at night … catch the first thing smokin' out of one of those dingy little train stations hardly anybody used … head for Philadelphia, or maybe Baltimore. That was Shimmy-boy's plan.

Eventually, he would come back to the city that was so nice they had to name it twice. In no other place could he pull off his petty hustles – selling information here, dope there, sometimes both at once – for a decent amount of scratch, although nothing like the pile of it those Germans had promised.

But when he left his hideaway earlier this night, he quickly found that he was being tailed.

Shimmy-boy's half-glimpsed pursuer was doing more than simply following him. Shimmy-boy was being herded like a sheep. He had long since left the Darkside behind. But he wasn't on his way to any remote train station. Instead, his nemesis had forced him to scurry into a part of the city that made the Darkside, Hell's Kitchen, and other notorious crime-beds look like Park Avenue.

This place was so derelict that even its name didn't matter anymore. Its buildings were on the decline when the stock market crash of '29 hit, and the hard times that followed rang its death-knell. Now, its only inhabitants were rats, along with the lowest of two-legged lowlifes.

Shimmy-boy felt that he was out of his element.

He looked behind him again – and saw nothing. Not even the flicker of movement that signaled the presence of his pursuer.

When Shimmy-boy first became aware that he was being followed, he knew that the barely glimpsed figure was either one of the Germans, or Damballa. He did not know how Damballa could have survived an encounter with the six Germans, had the cloaked man indeed been inside the hoodoo-place.

Then again, the Germans had not come back.

Find Mamadou, and you find Damballa … that's what some drunk snitch had whispered in his ear in a dingy Darkside bar. That tip made sense to Shimmy-boy. One hoodoo leading to another, although he had never before seen any reason to connect the mysterious old woman with the even more mysterious cloaked man.

He happened to know where Mamadou's shop was. Easy scratch. …

Shimmy-boy stopped momentarily as he scanned the gloom for any sign of movement. He saw none. He turned, planning to wend his way out of this rat-hole that was not only godforsaken, but cast aside by the devil as well.

He was in front of one of the taller abandoned structures lining the street. As he began to move away from it, a sudden instinct warned him of danger from above. Before he could react further, a thin loop settled over his shoulders, then around his chest and arms. He had time to utter only a single outcry before he was yanked upward like a fish on a line.

❖ ❖ ❖

At the *gri-gri* shop, the eye above the doorway remained closed. The shop itself was shrouded in darkness. It would not be open for business again. But that did not mean the depths below the building in which it was located were devoid of activity.

Mamadou was hard at work, despite the lateness of the hour. She sat on the stool in front of the microscope at which Damballa had shown her what was in the big German's blood. That slide remained under the lens. Mamadou continually adjusted the magnification and scribbled notes on a pad next to the microscope.

Although Mamadou had adopted the guise of a servant while with her grandson during his studies in Europe, she had learned along with him. Of course, she could not attend his classes. But she read the same books he did. And sometimes, the questions Damballa asked in the classroom were actually Mamadou's.

Thus, as Mamadou perused the German's blood, she did so with an understanding of modern science that was not that much less than that of Damballa. She wrote her observations in English. But the language in which she occasionally muttered to herself was an ancient one, older than Kibakosi.

CHAPTER SEVENTEEN

UP ON THE ROOF

Shimmy-boy barely had time to blink as he was hauled onto a sagging rooftop and dragged across its rough surface. Then, as he opened his mouth to cry out again, he heard a single word, spoken barely above a whisper:

"Silence."

Shimmy-boy's mouth closed with an audible click of teeth. Something in that ominous voice told him that his life depended upon acceding to the will of its owner. He was certain he knew who the speaker was – and it could not be one of the Germans. He knew how their accent sounded, and it wasn't like this.

Oh, Jesus, Shimmy-boy thought, invoking a name he seldom thought about.

The thin rope – which uncomfortably reminded him of the bonds from which he had freed himself in the Germans' car – jerked, pulling him a few inches forward and scraping off a bit more of his skin.

"Stand up," the voice commanded.

Although the limited use of his arms caused him difficulty, Shimmy-boy rose awkwardly to his feet. He could not move backward ... the taut rope curtailed that option. And he had no desire to go forward ... not toward the shape that loomed in the darkness at the other end of the rope.

He could barely distinguish the shape's outline against the surrounding shadows. A cloaked form, with one hand holding the end of the tether, and the other an object Shimmy-boy could not identify.

The low-toned voice spoke again.

"I am Damballa. You will answer the questions I put to you – or you will die. Do you understand?"

"I understand, Boss."

"I understand, too, Shimmy-boy. I understand that those Germans promised to pay you to find me, but they went back on their word. Severed ropes and a torn gag in the back of their car told me that. Now, how did you know where to lead the Germans?"

How he know my name? Shimmy-boy wondered. He knew it was not a good idea to ask. Best to stick to the topic at hand.

"I heard Chum Williams was goin' around askin' about how to find you, Boss. So I figure if I talk to who Williams was talkin' to, I find out what he find out. Sure enough, I find the cat told Williams where to go. Cat so drunk off the scratch Williams give him, he tell me, too."

"What was this cat's name?"

"Don't know his real name, but on the street they call him 'Do-Nasty.' You can guess why."

"Did he say I would be at the *gri-gri* shop?"

"Naw, Boss. He just say 'find Mamadou, and you find Damballa.'"

Damballa fell silent. If this lowlife was telling the truth, then he and Mamadou were only partially compromised. The secret of his sanctum remained intact; nobody knew what lay under the shop. It was no surprise to him some people thought there was a link between him and Mamadou, but those thoughts had only been rumors, and rumors were a dime a dozen in the Darkside.

This time, though, the rumor could have cost Mamadou her life, not to mention that of Chum Williams. That thought nearly caused Damballa to seize Shimmy-boy and hurl him from the rooftop.

But there was still some use in this lowlife. Therefore, the cloaked man forestalled his impulse.

"Where can I find this Do-Nasty?" Damballa asked.

"I could tell you, Boss, but it wouldn't do you no good. I tell him I give him some of my scratch for what he tell me. But I ain't givin' up nothin', and there ain't no need for him to be around to tell somebody what I was askin'. Soon's Do-Nasty tell me what I want to know, I take him in a alley and get rid of him."

"Just like the Germans decided to get rid of you."

"You right about that, Boss."

Again, Damballa let silence fall. He stepped closer to Shimmy-boy, who tensed instinctively to flee, even though he knew he had nowhere to go but down a long way – without an elevator.

"Do not move," Damballa said, anticipating Shimmy-boy's impulse.

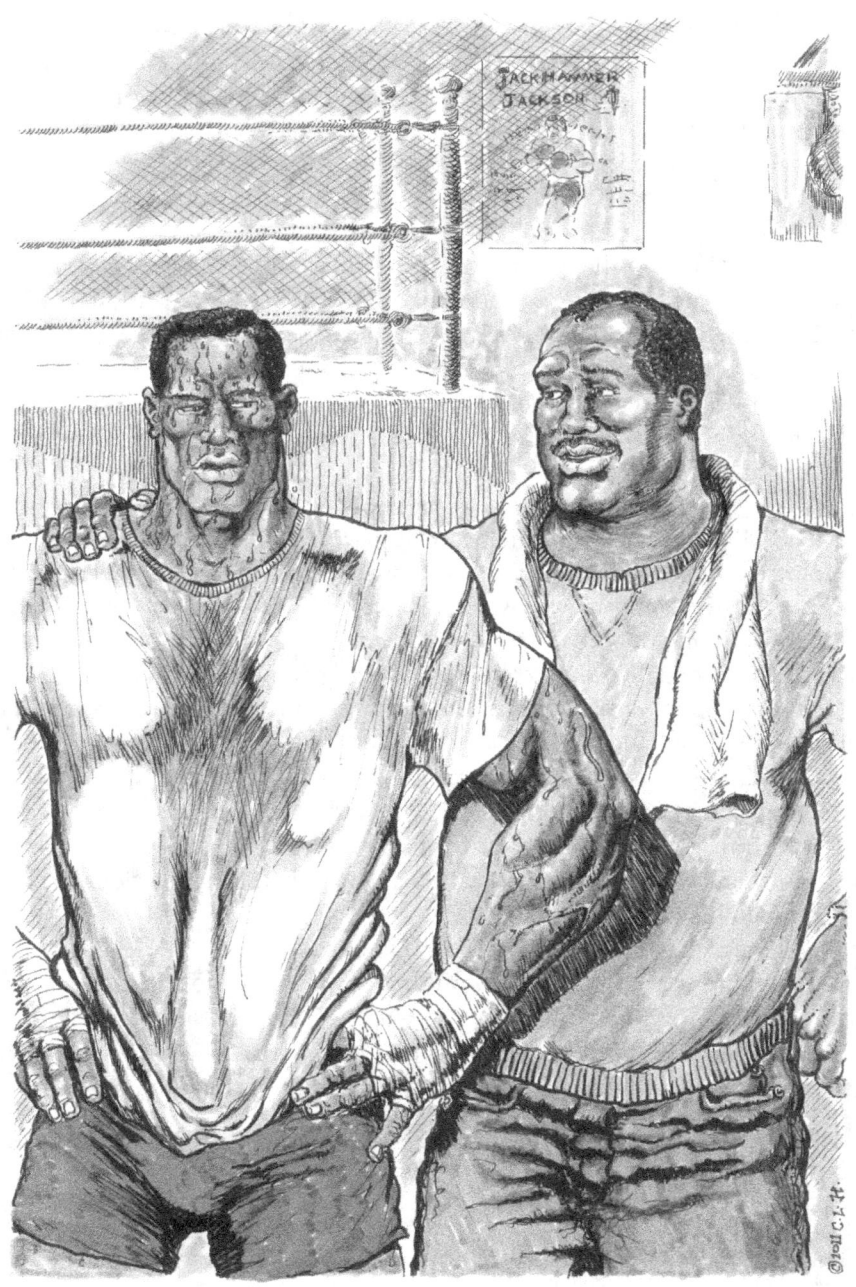

"What's wrong, man? You lookin' like your dog just died, or somethin'."

"Ain't goin' nowhere, Boss," said Shimmy-boy.

I hope, he added silently.

"One more thing," Damballa said. "Did the Germans ever talk about the fight that is coming up?"

"Oh, yeah. They was always goin' on about how they boy was gonna kick Jackhammer's black ass. I didn't pay 'em no mind –"

Before he could finish speaking, Shimmy-boy heard a slight *whooshing* sound in front of his face. He hadn't seen Damballa move his hand upward. He felt tiny particles strike his skin. Then he smelled them. He inhaled involuntarily – and collapsed.

Damballa caught him.

❀ ❀ ❀

Detective Bynoe was working late in his "second office" – a cheap, one-room apartment he rented in Harlem so he could be closer to the action. Had he been married, he most likely would have been hen pecked over the many late hours he spent in this place. But he had remained a bachelor, so women and men alike admired him for "working twice as hard to get half as much," as the old saying went.

The only furnishings in the room were an old-but-functional desk, a couple of chairs, and a cot pushed against a wall. A pot on a hotplate was redolent with the smell of coffee. Bynoe's service revolver lay within easy reach on his desk.

A knock sounded at the door. Bynoe lifted his gaze from the papers he had been studying. He did not reach for his revolver as he rose from his chair, for his visitor could only be another member of the NYPD. No one else knew about his "second office."

"Who is it," the detective asked after he reached the door and put his hand on the knob.

"Officer Chancy, sir," replied the person on the other side of the door.

Bynoe unlocked the door and swung it open. Chancy, one of the officers who had accompanied Bynoe to the *gri-gri* shop, stood close to the door. Another of those officers, a fellow Virgin Islander named Stridiron, stood a few feet behind Chancy. Bynoe could tell there was someone between the policemen, but he couldn't see who it was.

Then Chancy stepped aside to reveal the man he and Stridiron had brought to Bynoe. The detective immediately recognized the man's slight stature and pinched features.

"Well, well, well," the detective said in a bemused tone. "If it isn't Shimmy-boy Moore."

Bynoe had thrown this particular lowlife in jail before, but Shimmy-boy just kept on turning up on the streets, perpetrating his petty crimes – and sometimes big ones.

As he looked more closely at Shimmy-boy, Bynoe's breath drew inward in a slight hiss. For the normally walnut-colored skin of Shimmy-boy's face was coated with a fine-grained gray powder that froze his features into a mask-like grimace. The detective had seen this rictus on several other faces during recent days.

Then Shimmy-boy spoke.

"Bynoe ... Damballa ... danger."

Shimmy-boy's eyes stared vacantly. His voice sounded as though it were coming from beyond the grave.

"We found him on a sidewalk in the Darkside," Chancy said. "What he just said now is all we could get out of him."

"So we brought him to you, sir," said Stridiron.

"You did the right thing," said Bynoe. "Usher my 'guest' inside, please. Chancy, you'll stay here. Stridiron, you can go back to your duties. Good work, both of you."

Both uniformed officers nodded. Stridiron walked away and Chancy took Shimmy-boy by the arm and led him into the room.

"I hope you've got something more to tell me, Shimmy-boy," Bynoe said.

Shimmy-boy did.

CHAPTER EIGHTEEN

THAT WHICH IS HIDDEN

A persistent, drum-like rhythm echoed through the gym as Jackhammer Jackson pounded the heavy bag. The man who was holding the large cylinder from the other end was big enough to keep it steady. But he could still feel the impact of Jackhammer's heavy punches through the rags and sand that filled the bag.

Someone always anchored the heavy bag when Jackhammer worked out on it, for the champion had a proclivity for knocking them off the heavy chains that suspended them from the ceiling. The man behind the bag this day was Frankie Gittens, an old friend of Jackhammer's from Chicago.

Even though he was bigger than Jackhammer, Frankie didn't have enough talent for boxing even to serve as a sparring partner. His role in the camp was to anchor the heavy bag, and lighten Jackhammer's mood whenever the champion fell into a brooding frame of mind.

Jackhammer was in one of those moods today. Usually, Frankie could keep his buddy loose with a string of witticisms along the lines of, "Can't you hit no harder'n that, Junie? You gon' have that German laughin' at your ass."

Frankie was one of the few people who could call Jackhammer by his childhood nickname and get away with it. Any other time, Jackhammer would chuckle, then hit the bag harder. On this day, he hit the bag harder – but didn't crack a smile. And that worried Frankie.

Finally, Frankie stepped back.

"That's enough, Junie," he said. "You done wore me *and* the bag out."

Jackhammer stopped punching. His expression still did not change.

Freddie stepped around the bag and put a beefy hand on his friend's shoulder, which was covered by a sweat-soaked training camp T-shirt.

"What's wrong, man?" Frankie asked. "You lookin' like your dog just died, or somethin'."

A ghost of a smile appeared on Jackhammer's face. They both knew Jackhammer didn't much like dogs, and could barely tolerate the yapping, nipping toy poodle his fiancée Lola insisted on keeping.

"I know one damn dog I wish would drop the hell dead," said Jackhammer.

Frankie laughed hard. Jackhammer joined him, but only for a moment. Frankie looked at him, a serious expression replacing the merriment on the round, dark moon of his face.

"I know somethin' on your mind, man," he said. "Wan' talk about it?"

Jackhammer knew he could not say anything to Frankie about the long talk the champion had with Chum the night before. The strain of the events at the *gri-gri* shop and the time he had spent telling the tale to Jackhammer had weighed on Chum, and the old trainer was sleeping in this day.

Jackhammer's personal discipline was sufficient to enable him to train unsupervised for at least one day, even this close to the Krieger fight. And it was sufficient, he knew, to ensure that he could keep his mouth shut about Damballa. He knew, as well, that Frankie could never keep quiet about something like this, no matter how hard he might try.

Jackhammer didn't want to lie to his friend, though. So he told Frankie a small fraction of the truth.

"It's the fight, man," Jackhammer said. "Now, don't be getting' the idea that I'm worried about the German. I ain't takin' the man lightly, understand. But I sure as hell ain't scared of him."

"If it ain't the German, then what is it?" Frankie asked.

"All the other people," Jackhammer said with a slight frown. "Some people been pullin' for me right from the time I start boxin'. Some people thought I was just another nigger before I become champ, and now they all for me. Some people think it's not gonna be just two men in the ring when I fight Krieger, but two different countries – two different ways of thinkin'."

He paused and shook his head. A rueful smile crossed his lips.

"Even the President told me he want me to whup that German's Nazi ass," he continued. "Course, he didn't use them exact words, but I sure knew what the man was sayin'."

Jackhammer looked directly into Frankie's eyes then.

"Weighs on me sometimes, man," the champion said. "What if that German catch me with a lucky punch, or somethin'? Lot of folks be let down if that happen."

"Well, look at it this way, old buddy," said Frankie. "Least you ain't Jack Johnson. Whole world ain't lookin' to see you get *your* ass beat."

Jackhammer laughed, and Frankie joined him.

"C'mon, Champ," Frankie said when their hilarity died down. "Let's go hit the speed bag."

"Where you get this 'let's' stuff, man?" Jackhammer demanded, still grinning. "You know you ain't never hit that speed bag but once – and then it hit you back!"

Both men laughed again, and they headed toward the small, teardrop-shaped bag that had absorbed countless rapid-fire punches. Both men felt relieved – each for his own reasons.

✺ ✺ ✺

A pair of city police cars rolled along the road to Balrogorra. They went past the spot where the touring car stuffed with corpses had been. But of course the car and its contents had been moved elsewhere, eliminated from detection by visitors such as the ones who now approached. It was early in the morning; the protesters had not yet arrived.

One of the cars was filled with black enforcers of the law; the other with their white counterparts. Detective Bynoe was in the car that carried the Negroes. A white detective named Carter Dodson was in the other vehicle. The separation was part of the strategy the two men had worked out before leaving headquarters.

Dodson was one of the few white friends Bynoe had made in the police force. They had been in the same class during the department's detective-training course, and had developed a mutual respect. Unlike such ersatz "friends of the Negro" as the writer Kurt van Vallen, Dodson did not come across as condescending or patronizing. He regarded Bynoe as a fellow law enforcer – no more, no less.

When they reached the front gate of Balrogorra, the police cars halted side by side. Almost simultaneously, the doors of the cars flew open, and three officers got out of each of them. The cars' drivers remained seated behind their steering wheels.

Bynoe and Dodson exchanged a brief nod. Dodson was tall and

athletic-looking, with a face that seemed more suitable for an actor playing a detective on the silver screen than a real-life crime-solver. More than one miscreant had come to regret believing that the impression Dodson projected corresponded with the reality of the man.

Both squads marched up to the front gate – Bynoe and Dodson side by side, with their uniformed officers behind them. Dodson was carrying a notebook; Bynoe was empty-handed. The pair of camp guards in the towers stared silently at the unexpected guests.

Oskar Schutz approached the interior side of the gate and eyed the lawmen without speaking. His gaze flicked dismissively over Bynoe, then settled on Dodson.

"*Ja?*" the German asked. "How may I help you?"

"Police," Dodson said curtly. "I am Detective Dodson, and this is Detective Bynoe. We would like to speak with ..."

At that point, he made a show of consulting his notebook, then looking up again.

"*Herr* Hans Wimmer, please."

"With regard to what?"

"That is between us and *Herr* Wimmer, sir."

"Do you have a warrant?"

"We are only here to speak with *Herr* Wimmer, not arrest him," Dodson said. "Unless, of course, there is a reason for us to return with a warrant, *Herr* ... sorry, I didn't catch your name."

"Schutz. Oskar Schutz. Very well, you may enter."

At a signal from Schutz, one of the tower guards pulled a lever, and the gates swung inward. Dodson and his companions stepped through first, followed by Bynoe and his men. Before Bynoe's foot could cross the entrance, Schutz held up his hand.

"Not them," the German said firmly.

"Why not?" Dodson demanded.

Schutz glared at Bynoe, then at Dodson. At any other time, the German would have simply stated that the polluting presence of *Schwartzers*, *Juden*, and other *Untermenschen* was not to be permitted in the camp. But the coming championship fight, with its racial implications, made matters more ... complicated. He did not answer the detective's question.

Dodson filled the silence.

"The questions we have for *Herr* Wimmer concern certain incidents that have occurred in Detective Bynoe's precinct. That's why he is here. If you deny him and the others entrance, *Herr* Schutz, we would find it necessary to obtain that search warrant after all."

Schutz's scowl deepened. Then, with a grudging gesture, he stood aside and allowed the Negro lawmen to enter.

"Easy, men," Bynoe said in a low tone as he sensed the tension rising in the officers behind him. He was not immune to the impression of foreboding that affected them. He felt as though he were entering enemy territory, even though war had not been declared.

Camp functionaries – uniformed and otherwise – paused in their tasks to stare at the contingent of lawmen Schutz was leading toward the main building. For the most part, the gazes reflected curiosity, which quickly turned to hostility at the sight of Bynoe and the two black uniformed officers. No one was impulsive or foolish enough make a move against them, however. An international incident was the last thing the Germans needed.

There was no sign of Wolfgang Krieger, even though the boxer was the reason for the camp's existence.

At a command Schutz called out in German, one of the uniformed men quick-marched ahead of the procession and disappeared into the building, presumably to inform Wimmer that visitors were coming. Then the police and Schutz entered.

The interior of the building looked sterile, as befitting the former function of the camp as a whole. Bynoe and Dodson were not the only ones who wondered why Krieger's handlers had chosen a former penitentiary for their training camp. As it was, the place was scheduled for demolition not long after the fight. But that mystery was of no concern to the police now. Besides, the Germans were paying handsomely for the use of the defunct prison, and their money was as good as anyone else's. At least it was now that the insane inflation of the previous decade had ended.

Schutz stopped at an office door that still bore the outline of the word "Warden" on its glass. He rapped on the wooden part of the door.

"*Hereingekommen,*" a voice inside said.

❖ ❖ ❖

In Damballa's sanctum, he and Mamadou worked intently at their laboratory tables. They peered into microscopes, mixed substances in flasks and test tubes, and wrote copious notes. Few words were exchanged; it was as though they could read each other's minds.

And the thoughts on those minds were troubled. ...

Finally, Damballa looked up from the slide he was studying. Mamadou did the same.

"It is worse than we thought," said Damballa.

Mamadou nodded.

"Do you think we can duplicate it?" Damballa asked.

"No. We do not have the ingredients. And I do not want to even think about what we would have to do to obtain them."

"Neither do I, Mamadou."

Damballa fell silent then, deep in thought. Mamadou waited. Finally, he gave her the gaze of determination she had seen in him since he was a small boy growing up without a father.

"There is only one alternative, then," he said.

"I agree," said Mamadou.

She went back to her test tubes. And Damballa went to another table, upon which a map of New York City and its surroundings was spread. It was a schematic of what lay beneath the streets and roads – a labyrinth far more complicated than the one that led to the sanctum.

CHAPTER NINETEEN

'MYSTERIOUS INQUIRIES'

Schutz opened the office door and stood aside to allow the lawmen to enter. He wrinkled his nose as the blacks walked past him.

"Police to see you, *Herr* Wimmer," Schutz said in English.

Wimmer was seated behind the desk that was really Von Dunkel's. The manager was not alone. Von Dunkel was there, too, sitting in a chair beside the desk. The chair was turned so that Von Dunkel, eschewing his previous secrecy, faced the visitors.

There were not enough chairs to accommodate everyone in the room. Without waiting to be invited, Dodson and Bynoe commandeered two of the available seats, directly in front of the Germans. The two pairs of uniformed officers took up positions at the sides of the door. Snorting in disapproval, Schutz departed and closed the door behind him.

All the men introduced themselves. No one shook hands. The Germans did not stand up.

"To what do we owe this visit from gentlemen of the law?" Wimmer asked.

"This is Detective Bynoe's case," Dodson replied. "He is the one who should tell you."

The eyes of the Germans turned to the black detective. Wimmer's showed curiosity; Von Dunkel's, undisguised disdain.

"There have been reports of Germans in Harlem, asking unusual questions," Bynoe said. "We wonder whether or not you know anything about that."

The eyes of both Wimmer and Von Dunkel widened in surprise.

❀ ❀ ❀

Bynoe suppressed a smile at the two Germans' reaction to his statement. He knew it was not the words that had startled the pair. It was the fact that he had spoken them in German, a language he had learned during his studies at the Academy of the West Indies. Although his Caribbean accent was unavoidable, his vocabulary was impeccable.

"It would be more ... comfortable to conduct this conversation in English," Wimmer finally said.

"Understood, sir," said Bynoe.

"I am curious," said Wimmer. "What was so unusual about the questions these Germans are supposed to have asked?"

"One would think they would be asking about the upcoming fight between Jackson and Krieger," said Bynoe. "But they didn't. They were asking about a man called Damballa. Now, I'm not saying that those questions have any connection with this camp. However, you may be able to help us find out who the questioners are."

"Damballa," Wimmer said, steepling his fingers. "We have heard of him. But he has nothing to do with the fight. There is no reason for anyone from here to be asking any questions about him. Besides, there are many Germans here in New York right now. They came over to see the fight."

"Yes, and, like you, they are welcome visitors. According to our information, though, the ones who asked about Damballa were offering money for any information about him. Big money. Also, even though they were not wearing uniforms, we were told that the questioners had a military bearing. Unusual, don't you think?"

Until now, Von Dunkel had remained silent. Wimmer had introduced him as a "consultant," without saying anything more about the reason the doctor was involved with the interview. For the first time, Von Dunkel spoke – pointedly, not to Bynoe, but to Dodson.

"We have nothing to do with any mysterious inquiries in the Negro quarter of your city, Detective," the doctor said. "No one here knows anything about that. You are wasting your time – and ours."

"We are following all our leads, sir," said Dodson. "There is no waste of time involved. Your cooperation would be greatly appreciated."

"We know that several high-ranking officers in the *Wehrmacht* are in town to see the fight," said Bynoe. "However, it is obvious that some of the men in this camp look to be in the military, even though their uniforms are not regulation. That is part of why we are here for this interview."

"Then this interview is over," said Von Dunkel, who still refused to look at Bynoe. "We have already told you we have no knowledge of these mystery men. We have nothing more to say."

Bynoe and Dodson noticed that Von Dunkel appeared to be speaking for both himself and Wimmer. Strange, both lawmen thought. Usually, it was the fighter's manager and trainer who would be in charge of a camp, not some "consultant."

The detectives knew they were not going to get anything more out of the Germans. It was time to leave.

"Thank you for your time, sir," Dodson said to Wimmer. The detective did not look at Von Dunkel.

Wimmer simply nodded. Von Dunkel stared straight ahead, not looking at either of the detectives.

Without further ceremony, Dodson and Bynoe rose and departed from the office, along with the four uniformed officers. On the other side of the door, Schutz stood waiting to escort the Americans out of the building.

As they followed Schutz, the detectives exchanged a glance, and an unspoken conclusion passed between them.

They're hiding something, both men thought. And they were determined to find out what it was.

❄ ❄ ❄

"Do you think they know more than they are saying?" Wimmer asked nervously after the police were gone.

"*Nein*," said Von Dunkel. "If they did, they would have come with a search warrant, and many more officers."

They had exchanged chairs, and now Von Dunkel sat in his usual position behind the desk, while Wimmer occupied the subordinate's seat.

"It is this Damballa who is our primary concern, not the American police, who are foolish enough to include *Negers* in their ranks. We do not know what *Der Tod* may have told Damballa before Damballa killed him."

Von Dunkel frowned. Wimmer looked nervous. Wimmer, along with Krieger and his trainer, Franz Kohlbrecher, knew the secret of the *Starkenflessig*, and what was kept in the cells. Others in the camp had only a vague awareness of what was going on, and that was the way Von Dunkel wanted it.

"I should never have given the *Starkenflessig* to *Der Tod*," Von Dunkel said. "At least I know now that it should be reserved for the best of our kind, like our Wolf."

Wimmer did not say anything. In this camp, Von Dunkel was the Führer, and his moods were more volatile even than those of the Führer in Berlin.

"The question is," von Dunkel said slowly, "what does Damballa know?"

CHAPTER TWENTY

WORD ON THE STREET

As the day of the big fight rapidly approached, rumors buzzed through Harlem like a swarm of hornets. Some were based on fact; others spun out of thin air. No one could tell which was which.

Madame Pomp's place damn near got robbed, but Damballa stopped it. ...

Some shady characters been disappearin', and Damballa's behind it. ...

Them Germans been pokin' around, askin' questions about Damballa. ...

Don't see no Germans around here no more. ...

People sayin' somebody done got to Jackhammer, and he gon' throw the fight. ...

Naw, Damballa ain't gon' let that happen. ...

Ain't heard nothin' about Damballa since that night at Madame Pomp's place, though. ...

Never mind. Damballa watchin' out for us, and for Jackhammer, too. ...

Jackhammer gon' win. He got God and Damballa on his side. ...

Yeah, well, if Jackhammer lose, it gonna be hell on us. ...

Jackhammer ain't gon' lose. ...

How you know?

The talk continued. Bets were laid. Liquor poured like a flooding river from Sugar Row to the Darkside, and back again. Crime dropped considerably, as attention focused on the coming fight, and all its ramifications: black against white, yes, but also the Stars and Stripes against the Swastika. Tenuous alliances formed, and Jackhammer's name was emblematic of a moment that was hopeful, but most likely fleeting.

Damballa's name, on the other hand, was emblematic of … something else.

❀ ❀ ❀

The *gri-gri* shop was empty. Nothing was on either the counters or the shelves. All the artifacts and other items had been taken elsewhere. Shadows shrouded the space in which a vicious battle had been fought, and copious blood spilled. The crimson eye over the outside of the door remained closed.

Although the replacement door looked as though it were made of wood like its two predecessors, it was actually cast from steel, disguised by paint to conceal its true nature. It was also barred from within, and even its jambs were now made from metal. Anyone who sought to break into the shop, as the Germans had done – and the police still might – would find the task difficult, if not impossible.

And in the end, such a venture would prove futile, given that the shop was bare and the device that opened the way to the underground sanctum was concealed, even though the mask that had hidden it before was gone.

The people of the Darkside wondered what had happened to Mamadou. Word of the Germans' attack on the shop, and of the subsequent visit by Detective Bynoe and his Black Bulls – the street name for Negro police officers – had spread rapidly through the area. So did news of the apparent absence of the shop's proprietor.

To the extent that was possible in a place rife with crime and degradation, Mamadou's shop had in a short time become something of an institution – a small island of stability amid a swirl of often-lethal chaos. When she had first established the business, some of the Darksiders had tried to rob it outright. Others had attempted to impose an involuntary "protection" regime. The consequences those wrong doers had suffered discouraged any further attempts at unlawful interference with the operation of the shop.

For it quickly became known that the place was already under protection … the protection of Damballa.

Even though the Darksiders were not aware of the true relationship between Damballa and Mamadou, the cloaked man had made it painfully apparent that the shop was off-limits to the neighborhood's usual brand of depredation. And those who wanted to hold on to their lives knew enough to heed Damballa's word, which was the closest thing to law in the forsaken Darkside.

Now the shop was shuttered, and no one knew where Mamadou was. If she were gone, did that mean Damballa was gone, too?

That question weighed on the minds of many in the Darkside, as well as people from elsewhere who had regularly bought items from the shop. For now, however, curiosity about Mamadou and Damballa took second place to feverish anticipation of the Jackson-Krieger bout. Even the most disruptive Darksiders were caught up in the excitement.

After the fight was over, though, more attention would be paid to what now lay behind the recessed door beneath the quiescent crimson eye.

❀ ❀ ❀

"Thank you so much for agreeing to see me, Delia," Lola Thorne said as she took a sip of tea.

"No trouble at all, dear," said Madame Pomp.

The two women were sitting on a couch in one of the many parlors in the Pomp Palace. The damage done during the attempted robbery had long since been cleaned up and repaired, but Delia continued to avoid the salon in which the rudely interrupted party had taken place. Being in there strained her nerves, and she wasn't about to display any weakness to anyone – including her glamorous guest.

Lola was dressed in a pearl-gray suit, complete with veiled hat. Not to be outmatched, Delia wore a shimmering turquoise caftan with a matching turban that made her look like a queen from the *Arabian Nights*.

As she sipped the tea that had been poured from the sterling silver service on the mahogany table in front of them, Delia eyed her guest over the rim of her cup. She was surprised – and intrigued – at the anxiety in Lola's voice when the singer-actress had telephoned her to ask to visit. Now, it was time to end the obligatory small talk and cut to the chase.

"What can I do for you, Lola?" she asked.

Lola looked away for a moment. Then her eyes met Delia's in a steady, sincere gaze.

"It's not so much me," she replied. "It's Jackhammer."

Delia raised her eyebrows. Lola put her cup back on its saucer, then folded her hands and twisted them in a nervous gesture.

"Something's bothering him," The younger woman said. "He's trying to hide it from me – you know how men are."

Delia smiled.

"Indeed I do," she said, her tone saying far more than those three words conveyed.

Lola smiled in return before continuing.

"Even though Chum and the Salt-and-Pepper Twins haven't let me see Jackhammer for weeks now, I still talk to him on the telephone. And I can tell his mind is on something other than the fight, and our wedding. I need to find out what it is – for his sake as well as mine."

"And you think I can help you?"

"I know you can, Delia. This is your town, not mine. You have a lot of influence here. I don't. If something's going on with the fight … well, you know what could happen."

Delia's thoughts raced. She had heard some things. And she remembered her conversations with Detective Bynoe and Damballa. Beyond that, she believed that the robbery attempt involved more than just Bullets Jones' desire to get back at her for imagined slights back in New Orleans.

She placed her teacup on its saucer, then clasped Lola's hands in her own and gave them a reassuring squeeze.

"I think you may have exaggerated my influence, dear," she said. "Still, I'll see what I can do."

"Thank you," Lola breathed, relief showing in her eyes.

TWENTY-ONE

PREPARATIONS

Damballa and Mamadou were in the deepest chamber of their underground complex. Unlike the laboratory, this space contained no scientific equipment. The only furnishing in the small chamber was a large, cube-shaped altar made from hardened clay, with demonic-looking faces jutting from all four of its sides. Other, less-ominous visages were carved into the chamber's walls. The motif of the carvings was African, but different from the artifacts displayed in most museums.

Dozens of pale candles provided wavering illumination for the otherwise-shadowy space. Strings of smoke wafted toward vent slits that were cut between the reliefs on the walls.

The only sound in the chamber was the slow, steady pulse of a drum. The rhythm resembled the beating of a heart. Mamadou was the drummer. Her only garment was a black *pareu*. Dozens of strands made from beads, bones, and bits of wood and metal covered her bosom.

Candlelight picked out the bony ridges of her bare back as her palms struck the skin of the drum in front of her. She had dispensed with her head wrap, and the unbound white plaits of her hair lent her a Medusa-like appearance as she bobbed her head in time with the beating of the drum, and chanted in the ancient language only she, her daughters, and Damballa knew.

Damballa wore only a strip of leopard-skin that concealed his loins. White stripes that resembled bones had been painted on his skin, including daubs that gave his face the semblance of a skull.

He eschewed other ornamentation. His bare feet tapped the chamber's floor in consonance with Mamadou's drumbeat. His voice echoed

Mamadou's chant. In gradual increments, he moved closer to the altar, and to the thing that rested on its flat surface.

The occupant of the altar was a gigantic, coiled serpent that was larger than any known python or boa constrictor. Scales of gray, white and black stretched in a mosaic of patterns across the serpent's mighty frame. It lay so still that it could have been mistaken for an incredibly detailed sculpture. But the way its crimson, forked tongue darted in and out of its mouth in synch with the drumbeats belied that impression.

This was M'satha, the last of the god-serpents that had been central to the Bakosis' religion since the time before their ancestors had built their lost city. M'satha was one of the "others" that had accompanied Damballa and Mamadou on their journey out of Africa, and the ancient serpent now lived beneath the modern metropolis, unseen and unknown.

Other snakes, much smaller than M'satha, crawled in front of the altar. These serpents were known as the Silent Ones.

As Damballa approached, the Silent Ones made way for him. M'satha's head rose slowly, until the serpent gazed eye to eye with the painted man. Only inches away from the altar, Damballa stopped. Mamadou's beat did not waver.

Then the chant changed. Only one person's voice could be heard now: Damballa's. Mamadou confined herself to the beating of the drum. She kept her gaze fixed firmly on Damballa and M'satha.

Damballa's feet stopped moving. Even though he stood ramrod-stiff, he showed no sign of trepidation as M'satha uncoiled and slid toward him. As Damballa continued to chant, the gigantic serpent encircled his lean, muscular frame like a huge, mottled ribbon.

The serpent's weight surpassed Damballa's. But Damballa did not falter. As it was, he did not bear M'satha's full weight. By the time M'satha's head reached the level of Damballa's, two-thirds of the serpent's length remained on the altar.

Now Damballa relaxed in the serpent's embrace. He stopped chanting. And Mamadou's drumbeats ceased. Damballa looked into M'satha's eyes. As always, he recognized the intelligence that looked back at him from that slit-pupiled gaze – a consciousness that was not human, yet still far above that of an ordinary reptile.

Damballa closed his eyes. A moment later, he felt the feathery touch of M'satha's tongue against his forehead, his eyes, his nose, and his lips. When he opened his eyes again, he saw M'satha gazing at him. Then the huge serpent gently disengaged its coils and slid out of the chamber, pausing only to touch the face of Mamadou with its flickering tongue.

Damballa turned and looked at Mamadou, who had risen to her feet. "Now I am ready," he said.

Mamadou nodded.

❁ ❁ ❁

The Beast tore into the male prey-animal. Fangs punched deep into black, rubbery flesh. Talons ripped deep, parallel grooves that quickly brimmed with blood. The terrified shrieks of the prey-animal echoed across the featureless landscape. Although the prey-animal struggled to break free, its feeble efforts had little effect other than to increase the fury of the ravening Beast. ...

Eventually, the prey-animal stopped moving, and its outcries ceased. The Beast's wrath did not end, though. Instead of devouring its fallen quarry, the Beast continued its attack – crunching bones in its powerful jaws, and severing limbs and hurling them across the blood-spattered snow. Then it obliterated the features of the prey-animal's repulsive face. ...

The Beast did not awaken. Instead, it continued to rend the shredded carcass and scream its defiance and dominance to the gray sky. ...

❁ ❁ ❁

Von Dunkel tugged the hypodermic out of Krieger's forearm. Immediately, the sedative the doctor had shot into the fighter took effect. The snarl on Krieger's face subsided; the ominous growls he was uttering ended; the powerful muscles of his arms and shoulders unclenched; and his breathing became that of normal slumber rather than the ragged, desperate gasps that had alarmed Von Dunkel and the others who had hurried into Krieger's room when the fighter's nightly outcries became louder and more bestial than usual.

The four burly men who had held Krieger's thrashing limbs released their grips and rose shakily to their feet. They sighed in relief as they regarded the disarranged sheets and askew position of the bed. Holding Krieger still enough to allow Von Dunkel to administer the sedative had proven to be a difficult task. It was like wrestling a bear or a gorilla. They were glad when the doctor was able to inject the contents of the syringe into the crazed boxer's arm.

Restraints similar to those used at insane asylums secured Krieger to his bed. Never before had he experienced more than one of his Beast-dreams per night. But Von Dunkel was not taking any chances. Not with so much at stake, and so close to occurring.

"He should be fine now," the doctor said. "But just as a precaution, I want at least two of you to remain here with Wolf until the morning. You can take shifts. If he has another … episode, let me know at once. The restraints should hold him, but I still want to know if his behavior is repeated."

"*Ja, Herr Doktor*," said one of the men, speaking for himself and the others, who presumably shared the apprehension that lay beneath his tone.

One other person was in the room: Franz Kohlbrecher, Krieger's trainer. As the four henchmen decided which pair would take the first shift, Kohlbrecher spoke.

"May I have a word with you, *Herr Doktor?*" he asked. "In private?"

Von Dunkel gave Kohlbrecher a cold look, followed by a curt nod.

❀ ❀ ❀

The two men exchanged few words as they walked to Von Dunkel's office. Von Dunkel opened the door and flicked on the light. He took his customary seat behind the desk. Kohlbrecher sat in one of the other chairs. Von Dunkel waited for the trainer to say what was on his mind.

"What are you doing to my fighter?" Kohlbrecher finally demanded.

Von Dunkel gave him a flat, hard stare. Kohlbrecher returned the look. The trainer's face bore the marks of his previous time in the ring. He did not scare easily; not even in Germany's current climate of fear.

"*Your* fighter?" the doctor said with a touch of incredulity. "You mean you actually believe Wolf is still *your* fighter?"

Kohlbrecher struggled to suppress an outward display of a resentment he did not want the doctor to have the satisfaction of seeing.

Well did Kohlbrecher remember the day a ragged young giant, not yet out of his teenage years, had wandered into the trainer's gym in Munich not long after the National Socialists came into power. Kohlbrecher soon learned that Wolfgang Krieger's parents were dead, and the young man was destitute.

Aside from Krieger's physique, which promised to be formidable once his lanky frame filled out, there was a glint of determination in his eyes that Kohlbrecher instantly recognized. For a similar spark had glimmered in Kohlbrecher's own eyes in the time when he had been a promising young middleweight.

A knee injury had ended Kohlbrecher's professional career almost as soon as it began. Although bitterly disappointed, Kohlbrecher had re-channeled his passion for the sport to the trainer's role. He had nurtured many young fighters who had varying degrees of talent. But none of them possessed the will and potential skill Kohlbrecher had seen in Wolfgang Krieger.

Under Kohlbrecher's tutelage, Krieger rose quickly in the amateur ranks, culminating with his Olympic gold medal. A professional career beckoned – and so did the Party. Almost as soon as the gold medal was hung around Krieger's neck, the party seized the young fighter's managerial reins from Kohlbrecher and handed them to Wimmer, who had the strong Nazi connections Kohlbrecher lacked.

Kohlbrecher was allowed to stay on as trainer. But he had no say in determining who Krieger fought, or when. Because he thought of Wolf as the son he'd never had, Kohlbrecher accepted his reduced role. Even so, Von Dunkel's words cut deeply.

"Very well, *Herr Doktor*," Kohlbrecher grated. "The Reich's fighter. The question remains: what is this concoction of yours doing to Wolf?"

"It is making him the greatest, most dangerous fighting man that ever lived," Von Dunkel replied. "It is making him a fighter who will chew the *Neger* up and spit him out, piece by piece, for the glory of the Reich."

"But at what price, *Herr Doktor*? At what point will whatever it is that is disturbing Wolf's dreams affect his performance in the ring? Or – much worse – his overall health, both mental and physical?"

"I have every confidence in my methods."

"Well, I do not! Not anymore. Wolf's well-being may be in jeopardy. I cannot allow the fight to go on until we learn more about *all* the effects of your *Starkenflessig*."

"What makes you think you can prevent the fight from occurring?" Von Dunkel asked in a deceptively soft tone.

"Contrary to what you may believe, *Herr Doktor*, you are *not* the highest authority in the Reich. I will go – as the Americans say – over your head."

With disdain etched plainly on his features, the trainer rose to leave the room. Von Dunkel's next words halted him in mid-motion.

"And what will the 'higher authority' do when I tell them who – and what – you truly are, Kohlbrecher?"

Ashen-faced, Kohlbrecher slid back into his seat. Eyes wide in sudden panic, he tried to speak. His mouth opened and closed several times before words finally came out.

"How ... how did you find out?"

The doctor gave him a feral grin.

"I assume the fight is on, then?" he asked.

Kohlbrecher could only nod miserably.

CHAPTER TWENTY-TWO

FROM BELOW TO ABOVE

A single ray of light lanced through the stygian darkness inside a long, twisting sewer tunnel. Behind the light came a blot of blackness even darker than the shadows of the tunnel. The sounds of soft splashes accompanied the progress of the light and its holder. The splashes were caused by a pair of booted feet stepping cautiously through the stream that flowed at the sewer's bottom.

Damballa's was the hand that held the source of the illumination: a slender black flashlight with an adjustable beam. At the moment, the light shone at its widest range, so that it could show as much as possible of what lay ahead. By manipulating a set of shutters on the lens, Damballa could turn the beam into a line of light no wider than a pencil.

Even though he had never before been in this foul-smelling place, Damballa knew where he was going. He had committed his map of the sewer-tunnels to memory. He had also perused a schematic of the former prison that served as Krieger's training camp, and he knew where Balrogorra and the tunnel he was following intersected.

Originally, Damballa had intended to use a white-face disguise to infiltrate the camp and obtain what he sought. Circumstances had forced him to discard that plan. But Damballa never relied on a sole strategy. He always made sure that alternatives were available.

Damballa knew his destination was not far away. Yet he continued to step carefully. He had no desire to slip and fall into the noisome mire that sloshed beneath his feet.

Suddenly, Damballa stopped short, and the splashes of his feet ceased. But he could hear other splashes behind him. Many splashes. ...

❉ ❉ ❉

Franz Kohlbrecher tossed and turned fitfully in his narrow bed. His sweat-soaked pajamas clung clammily to his skin. He could not sleep. He wondered whether he would ever sleep again.

How did Von Dunkel find out? Kohlbrecher asked himself for the hundredth time. *How?*

Kohlbrecher's family had meticulously guarded its secret for three generations. At first, it had been simply a matter of convenience. But when the Führer and his legion of thugs came into power five years ago, it became a matter of dire necessity ... a matter of survival.

For Kohlbrecher, the maternal grandmother who had died long before he was born had been only a name ... a *changed* name, according to his mother, who had told him the truth when he was old enough to understand that knowledge and secrecy could exist at the same time.

The change – and the need to conceal its existence – had been born of a love that transcended the strictures of its time. Currently, concealment took precedence. Even though he was certain that no one knew, Kohlbrecher had not become careless and complacent, as had certain unfortunate others.

Yet that fiend Von Dunkel found out, Kohlbrecher thought in a combination of fury and fear.

How?

How, indeed, had *Herr Doktor* discovered that, according to the Reich's racial hygiene laws, Franz Kohlbrecher was a Jew?

❈ ❈ ❈

Damballa turned and shined his flashlight toward the sounds that were following him. He saw ripples in the shallow water. He also saw snouts, whiskers, and many pairs of beady, malevolent eyes. The owners of those eyes swam more quickly toward him now.

Damned rats, Damballa cursed as he identified his pursuers. The sewers were the rodents' domain, and the loathsome creatures had grown huge gorging on the bounty of the underground. They disliked intruders, and they had their own ways of dealing with them.

Damballa did not move as the rat-horde approached. He kept the beam of his flashlight focused on them as they abandoned all pretense of stealth. The rodents did not squeal, but their intent was plain as they bared their sharp incisors and surged forward in a lethal wave.

Still, Damballa made no move to flee or defend himself.

Abruptly, the rat in the vanguard of the mass vanished – pulled downward by *something* beneath the rancid surface of the water. The water thrashed, and the other rats stopped in sudden confusion. Then other rats disappeared from view, and the ray from Damballa's flashlight revealed traces of crimson on the surface.

Enraged and bewildered, the rats began to turn on each other, and they were no longer silent as they fought. The bodies of the ones that had been pulled underwater floated motionlessly to the surface, where they were devoured by their maddened pack mates.

Damballa's flashlight followed a series of subtle ripples that moved away from the melee, and toward – then past – him. Unlike the wake of the rodents, these ripples were sinuous, and the bodies that made them remained unseen as they continued to move in the direction Damballa was taking.

"Thank you, my friends," Damballa whispered softly as he resumed his underground journey. Behind him, the rats continued their chaotic warfare against each other.

❋ ❋ ❋

Von Dunkel lay awake in his bed. He was not sweating. He seldom had reason to perspire.

He was thinking about Kohlbrecher. The thoughts were not pleasant. Von Dunkel had not wanted so soon to reveal that he knew the trainer's secret. Later, when Krieger was heavyweight champion of the world and the Reich in its full ascendance as the world's overlord, Von Dunkel would set Party investigators on Kohlbrecher's trail – and that would be the end of him.

But Kohlbrecher had dared to threaten to interfere with the doctor's plans. For that, the trainer would not have long to live after the fight was over. With the *Starkenflessig* in full effect, and the championship won, Krieger would no longer require the services of a trainer.

With that gratifying thought in mind, Von Dunkel fell asleep. As usual, his slumber was untroubled. Had he known who was coming to the training camp, he would not have closed his eyes so readily.

❋ ❋ ❋

Black-gloved fingers clutched the large grate at the end of the corridor between the two rows of prison cells. Slowly, with a minimum of sound, the grate rose and a hooded head appeared. The hands laid the grate onto the concrete floor, and Damballa emerged from a tight-fitting shaft.

The rodents did not squeal, but their intent was plain as they bared their sharp incisors and surged forward in a lethal wave.

A rope was tied around Damballa's waist, its length reaching down into the shaft. Damballa pulled the rope upward. Its end was tied to a large sack made of black cloth. The sack wriggled slightly as Damballa laid it beside the grate.

Damballa was about to untie the top of the sack when the smell hit him – an odor far different from the stench of the sewer. It was a dank, musty aroma that was familiar to the cloaked man – and not entirely unanticipated.

A frown formed on his face at this concrete confirmation of his – and Mamadou's – suspicions.

Untying the rope from his waist, Damballa left the bag closed. He looked toward the cells, and saw that some of them were occupied. Only one of several lightbulbs in the ceiling was lit. The wan illumination showed only humped, silent shapes, along with thin stalks of metal festooned with plastic tubing.

Damballa walked to the nearest cell that had an occupant. There was no trail of wet footprints behind him, for he had left his boots at the bottom of the shaft. He now wore soft-soled shoes that enabled him to move silently and untraceably.

When he reached the bars of the cell, Damballa directed the beam of his flashlight inside. He had a good idea of what the light would reveal. Even so, he was forced to muster a strong measure of discipline to prevent himself from recoiling in shock at the sight that greeted his gaze.

A lion sprawled limply on the floor of the cell. The beast was emaciated, with ribs pressing beneath its tawny hide. Its once-powerful limbs had been reduced to mere fur-covered bones. Were it not for the intravenous tubing attached to a sac of nutrient fluid, the lion would have been mistaken for dead. As it was, the beast was barely clinging to life.

Damballa had seen intravenous-feeding arrangements before, though under vastly different circumstances – in places of healing, not horror. Of greater significance to him was a second tube that was attached to a spot on the lion's skull from which its mane had been shaven away.

The second tube did not reach upward. Instead, it was directed downward, into a jar about the size of a soda bottle. Fluid trickled from the lion's brain into the jar. The process was so slow that Damballa could count the seconds that passed between each drip.

Damballa inspected several other cells, and found the same arrangement in each, though different beasts were imprisoned. Bears, tigers, leopards, wolves, more lions … all unconscious, all alive only because of liquid nutrient, while in turn giving up fluid from the same part of their brains.

Lips pressed together in an expression of disgust, Damballa returned to the bag beside the grate.

With Mamadou's help, he had been able to determine the source of the anomalies in the big German's blood. But Damballa had not anticipated that the process responsible for those anomalies was continuing.

Quickly, Damballa untied the top of the sack and pulled it open. Four supple shapes wriggled out of their cloth confines. They were gray-scaled snakes, like the ones in the ritual chamber, smaller kin to M'satha's species. They were two to two-and-a-half feet in length – a sufficient size to pull creatures like rats underwater and kill them.

Damballa picked up the sack and folded it into a small square, which he in turn slipped into a pouch inside his cloak. He concealed his rope as well, rolling it into a tight, compact ball before placing it in another pouch. Then he looked at the four serpents – the Silent Ones.

The cloth of the sack had dried the serpents' scales. Thus, like Damballa, they would leave no tell-tale trail on the floor. Their tongues flicked incessantly as they looked up at their master. Damballa signaled with his hands, and the Silent Ones slid toward the doorway of the cellblock. They paid no heed to the quiescent occupants of the cells-turned-cages.

The Silent Ones had been thoroughly trained by Mamadou and Damballa. Having tasted the tainted blood of the German, the serpents would be able to trace the anomalies to their source.

Damballa had memorized the layout of Balrogorra, but a room-to-room search would be far too time-consuming, even though he could have logically eliminated many locations. The senses of the Silent Ones, however, would lead him unerringly to the right destination.

With a final look toward the imprisoned predators, Damballa followed the Silent Ones out of the cellblock and into the outside corridor. The four serpents moved forward without hesitation.

CHAPTER TWENTY-THREE

THE *STARKENFLESSIG*

Two members of Von Dunkel's paramilitary kept watch over Krieger. The boxer had already undergone his nightly battle with the Beast Dream, and *Herr Doktor* had used a stronger-than usual sedative to calm him. As a precautionary measure, Krieger was strapped to his bed.

Even so, the minders watched him warily. To enable themselves to remain alert during their vigil, they had slept through the previous day. Thus far, nothing had happened that would have required them to disturb *Herr Doktor's* slumber – which they were, at any rate, loath to do.

From time to time, however, Krieger would writhe briefly in his bonds, as though he were unconsciously attempting to free himself. Sometimes he uttered words, either singly or in brief phrases, never complete sentences. Most of what he said made no sense to his minders.

One word did, though: *Ilse.*

It was when Krieger began to growl that the hair on the back of his minders' necks stood on end.

❄ ❄ ❄

Damballa trailed the Silent Ones down an unlit corridor. The Silent Ones moved confidently. Damballa was certain they were now close to their destination.

As a precaution, Damballa refrained from using his flashlight. Unlike the stygian blackness of the sewer tunnel, the corridor was not dark enough to prevent him from seeing the shadowy shapes of the Silent Ones.

Thus far, Damballa had not encountered any interference. Nor had he expected to, for the Germans had no reason to suspect that an intruder would attempt to gain entrance to Balragorra through the sewer grate. Damballa hoped that his luck would hold.

The Silent Ones stopped at an ominous-looking metal door. Then they waited for Damballa. When he reached the door, Damballa tried the knob. It was locked – as Damballa had anticipated.

A cold, mirthless smile crossed Damballa's lips as he watched the tails of the Silent Ones disappear through the scant space at the bottom of the slab of steel that comprised the doorway. This place was not where he would have initially expected the Germans to have stored their fiendish concoction. He stood still and silent, in contemplation of what he beheld.

Were Damballa searching without the aid of the Silent Ones, the warden's office and the prison's former medical dispensary would have been the obvious first of his choices. But the place to which the Silent Ones had led him was not so obvious, even though Damballa realized that it was, indeed, appropriate in a macabre, diabolical manner.

Damballa did not need the detailed knowledge he had absorbed about the prison to be aware of what lay behind the metal door. This room had once been Balrogorra's execution chamber.

❖ ❖ ❖

Oskar Schutz abandoned his attempt to sleep. It was, he knew, useless. Too many uncomfortable thoughts crowded into his mind: dire doubts, niggling worries, persistent fears. ...

He was glad that the fight was only a few days away. The passage of more time would only mean more opportunity for some unfathomable disaster to crash down upon the Germans like an avalanche in the Alps. As it was, matters could still go horribly wrong even in the short time remaining before Krieger and Jackson would finally face each other in the ring.

Schutz had argued vehemently against the instigation of the robbery attempt at Delia Pomphrey's pre-fight fete. At the time, Schutz believed the theft would only be an unnecessary distraction and could create an unwelcome link between the Germans and the Negro underworld.

But Von Dunkel's megalomania equaled that of the Führer himself. Sometimes, Schutz wondered whether *Herr Doktor* might actually believe himself to be *more* than equal to Hitler. ...

At any rate, Von Dunkel had summarily dismissed Schutz's misgivings. As a result, Von Dunkel's intended corrective to the laughable *Schwartzer* "elite" who dared to aspire to rise from their natural lowly station had brought the German contingent to the attention of the murderous monster known as Damballa – an entirely unforeseen development.

This Damballa had handled six of Von Dunkel's paramilitary as easily as he had the bumbling *Schwartzers* who had botched the Pomphrey robbery. He had slain *Der Tod*, who was nearly as formidable as Krieger himself. What else might this wraith of darkness be capable of doing?

With that thought in mind, Schutz removed his sleepwear and donned his black uniform. He made certain his Luger was loaded before placing it into the holster at his side.

He knew a personal patrol at this time of night was unnecessary, and Von Dunkel would consider him a weak-kneed, un-Aryan fool for doing so. The guard towers at the entrance to the camp were manned day and night. No one without permission or authorization could possibly enter the premises without being seen, stopped, and dealt with.

If nothing else, though, a patrol would ease Schutz's and perhaps enable him to get a few hours' sleep.

"Better to be safe," he muttered to himself as he left his room.

✻ ✻ ✻

What better place could these monsters have chosen? Damballa thought as he reached into his cloak and extracted a set of lockpicks. With the thin beam of his flashlight guiding his movements, the cloaked man worked quickly and efficiently, taking his time even though haste may have seemed necessary. A few moments later, a slight click rewarded his efforts.

Slowly, he eased the door open. Its hinges squealed softly. The sound was of no concern to Damballa, for the execution chamber was located far from the areas the Germans were using as living and training headquarters. Besides, who could be awake to hear anything?

Damballa carefully closed the door behind him. He heard no indication that the lock had automatically clicked back into place. That was good; he wanted to depart quickly once he found what he sought.

His cloak swirled as he shone his flashlight in the direction the Silent Ones were taking. He paused momentarily when his light showed him the shape of the chamber's electric chair, which retained its air of menace even after years of disuse.

✻ ✻ ✻

Schutz chided himself as he surveyed the corridors of Balrogorra. Flashlight shining, he had passed quickly through the wing that held the sleeping quarters. There was no reason to believe anything suspicious would turn up there. Even Krieger's room was quiet. Schutz suppressed a quiver as he remembered the sounds Krieger made during his dream-terrors.

Schutz's unease increased as he considered how much the boxer had changed since he and the others in the entourage had arrived in New York. Before, Krieger had been approachable, if not overly friendly. Now, his demeanor reminded Schutz of the Doberman dogs utilized for police and military duty back home: fierce, unapproachable, deadly. ...

Now Schutz headed toward the less frequented parts of the complex. He had no real need to patrol those areas. His sojourns there, however, provided him an opportunity to think, and to reassure himself that his position in Von Dunkel's hierarchy – and in the new order as a whole – remained secure.

This time, he decided he did not have much to worry about. *Der Tod's* multiple failures were Von Dunkel's responsibility, not Schutz's. Never once had Schutz given a direct order to *Der Tod*. And Schutz had handled the situation with the visit from the police as well as could be expected. He could not very well have kept the lawmen out, even though some of them were *Negers*. The encounter was unpleasant, but also unavoidable.

He had only two more locations to go to before his mind could be completely at ease: the cellblocks and the execution chamber. Schutz had never been inside either place, for Von Dunkel had declared them off-limits to everyone other than himself. Although Schutz had a good idea of what each place held, he kept his thoughts on that matter strictly to himself.

That, Schutz well knew, was the most practical way to stay on the good side of *Herr Doktor*.

He walked quickly past the cellblock area. Its door was closed; that was all he needed to know.

When he approached the execution chamber, Schutz slowed his steps. This place had disquieted him since the time he had first seen its huge metal door. Despite the brightness of his flashlight's beam, the shadows seemed darker and denser here. It was as though they were moving, reaching out. ...

Suddenly, Schutz stopped in his tracks.

Had he just heard something behind the door? He could not be sure.

The rational part of his mind attempted to reassure him that he had heard nothing. But it would be best to make certain of that.

Besides, he thought he could detect the hint of an unusual odor. ...

He headed toward the door.

❖ ❖ ❖

Damballa allowed himself only a sidelong glance at the electric chair as he passed it. Then he looked ahead to the end of his flashlight's beam. There, he saw the four Silent Ones coiled beneath a cabinet on the far wall of the chamber.

He guessed that the cabinet had once contained the few medical supplies that were relevant to the procedures involved in carrying out an execution. Now, as the Silent Ones indicated, there was something far less ordinary behind the cabinet's doors.

Bending to one knee, Damballa touched each of the serpents in turn. The contact conveyed a message: *Well done.* It was through touch and visual signals that Damballa and Mamadou communicated with the Silent Ones and M'satha for, like all the serpent kind, they were unable to hear.

Then Damballa rose and attempted to open the cabinet. It was, as he expected, locked. He reached into his cloak and extracted a lockpick significantly smaller than the one he had used to open the entrance door. This time, his efforts were rewarded much more quickly.

Returning the lockpick to its place in his cloak, Damballa opened the door of the cabinet. In his flashlight's beam, he saw several rows of vials that contained a cloudy fluid. Damballa had not seen this liquid before. But he knew what it was. And he knew its creator.

If this concoction could be synthesized, the Nazis would have an army second to none, Damballa mused. *Otherwise, they would need to capture and drain countless predator animals. Then again, I would not put even a monstrous deed such as that past* him. ...

Casting that disturbing thought aside, Damballa extracted a glass container of water from his cloak. He unscrewed the lid of the container and dropped a small amount of powder into the water. He had anticipated that the fluid he sought would be less than clear.

He compared the subsequent murkiness of the water to that of the fluid in the vials. When he was satisfied with their similarity, he laid the water-container on the floor and pulled a handful of empty vials from another pouch in his cloak.

Then he took five vials from the cabinet and poured their contents into his empty ones. Having completed that task, he stoppered the ones he had filled and put them into his cloak. Then he refilled the ones he had emptied with the counterfeit fluid he had just produced. His rock-steady hands did not spill a single drop.

Again, Damballa shone his light on the cabinet. There were empty spaces at the top and bottom. The spaces at the bottom had once held the vials Von Dunkel had already used. The spaces at the top were where the five Damballa had emptied and refilled were held.

Damballa replaced those vials. He had reasoned that the vials were being taken from the bottom as they were used for their nefarious purpose. He did not believe that all of them would be used before the fight, and his ruse would thus remain undetected long enough to serve his objective. His only concern was the continuous draining of the wretched beasts confined in the cellblock – which indicated that a constant supply of their fluids was needed.

He already knew that at least one of the Germans besides Krieger had been using the fluid. Perhaps there were others, in an expanded experiment. ...

A sudden hiss from the Silent Ones claimed Damballa's attention. He looked down, and saw that the four serpents had uncoiled and were headed toward the door. Their sensitivity to vibrations had detected what Damballa's own keen senses had not. Someone was coming.

Then Damballa heard the sound of footsteps approaching from the other side of the door.

CHAPTER TWENTY-FOUR

THE VOICE

Schutz tried the handle of the execution chamber door. It was unlocked. ...
Beads of sweat popped out on the German's brow. *How can this be?* he thought uneasily.

Herr Doktor was the only one who possessed a key to this room. Was *Herr Doktor* in there now, at this ungodly hour? If so, he would certainly not wish to be disturbed in whatever he was doing.

On the other hand, if this were some unfathomable breach of the camp's security, it warranted immediate action, *Herr Doktor* notwithstanding.

Besides, there was that strange hint of an odor – something faint, but foul. The smell was more pronounced here.

For a moment, Schutz considered going back to see whether Von Dunkel was in his quarters, rather than on the other side of the metal door. Then he discarded that idea. If *Herr Doktor* was in the place where the *Starkenflessig* was stored, Schutz would receive a severe tongue-lashing for his intrusion.

If it were someone else. ...

Schutz pushed the door open, laid his hand on the butt of his Luger, and stepped into the chamber. His flashlight showed nothing unusual; only the electric chair and the cabinet at the far wall.

Yet the odor he had noticed was even more detectable than before. It smelled like a sewer. And why was the door unlocked in the first place?

Slowly, the German advanced through the chamber. His light probed the empty spaces where chairs for the prison officials and other witnesses to the executions had been placed.

As he passed by the electric chair, the only sound Schutz could hear was the click of his shoes against the stone floor. Then he thought he heard some sort of rustle near his feet. When he looked down, he caught a flicker of movement. Or was it simply the product of sudden, uncharacteristic nervousness?

Suddenly, he heard a slight swish. As he turned to seek its source, he saw a shape of blackness rise ghost-like from the back of the electric chair. Before Schutz could cry out or unholster his Luger, a fine, stinging powder struck his face ... and he knew no more.

❊ ❊ ❊

When Schutz regained consciousness, he found himself sitting on the edge of his bed. He looked down at himself and was startled to realize that he was wearing his black uniform, complete with Luger, in the middle of the night. Or, at least, he *thought* it was the middle of the night.

Schutz looked around his room. His vision blurred, then snapped back into clear focus. He saw his rumpled pajamas lying in a heap on the floor, and he wondered why they were there, and why his hand was resting on his holstered automatic as though he were about to draw it.

His face stung, as though someone had slapped him. He closed his eyes and rubbed his fingers through his close-cropped hair. Fragments of visions flashed against the black screen of his closed eyelids. Elusive memories flitted like motes through his mind.

A door ... a chamber ... blackness rising ... his legs folding bonelessly as he collapsed. ...

"*Gott in Himmel,*" he muttered as he opened his eyes and shook his head. "Something is wrong with me. I must go and see *Herr Doktor.*"

No. ...

The voice was only a whisper in his skull. Yet its tone was as compelling as a shouted command.

You saw ... nothing. You know ... nothing. You did not leave this room on this night.

Again Schutz shook his head, as though the insistent suggestions could be shed like droplets of water from a wet dog's hide. Yet the voice in his mind continued relentlessly. He laid his hands against the sides of his head and pushed hard, as if he could squeeze out the unwelcome voice he could only half-remember, and wanted to forget.

Finally, Schutz succumbed to the thoughts that were not his own. Almost mechanically, he stripped off his uniform, folded it, and laid it in its usual place. He donned a spare pair of pajamas, and stuffed the ones he had been wearing before into his laundry bag. As he reclined on his bed, the voice in his head became soothing rather than stressful.

Sleep, it whispered almost inaudibly. *You know nothing ... nothing. ...*

And the slumber that had eluded Oskar Schutz earlier this night embraced him at last and drew him into a place where he did not dream, and he did not remember his impromptu patrol of Balrogorra's dark and silent halls.

❊ ❊ ❊

Damballa carefully pulled the grate in the cellblock floor into place as he began his descent back into the shaft that connected the prison's drain with the main sewer tunnel. He made certain that the grate was aligned exactly the way it had been when he first saw it. Nothing could be seen to be amiss when the Germans commenced their morning routine.

Regret pricked at Damballa's conscience when he thought of the drugged, drained predators lying helplessly in cages that had once held convicts. He knew the animals were dying slowly. Damballa wished he could have dispatched them all, putting an end to the prolongation of the creatures' misery.

But that deed of mercy would have alerted the Germans to his intrusion, and proof of his presence was the last thing Damballa wanted.

Accordingly, he had not left any of his usual mementos this time. He had not scrawled his name on any surface; he had relocked the door of the execution chamber; he had removed every speck of the hypnotic powder from the face of the black-clad German who had come so close to discovering his presence; he had made certain the German would return to his room without arousing suspicion.

His only concern was that the German might possess sufficient strength of will to resist the post hypnotic suggestions he had planted in the other man's mind. Then he dismissed that misgiving. Unquestioning obedience was, after all, the principal coin of the Third Reich's realm.

Soundlessly, Damballa descended the metal ladder. He did not need his flashlight to guide his descent. The sack containing the Silent Ones rested securely against his back. The five vials of *Starkenflessig* were stored securely inside his cloak. So was his rope.

When his feet touched water, Damballa turned on his flashlight. His boots were where he had left them. No contingent of sewer rats confronted him this time. The Silent Ones had taught a deadly lesson that the loathsome denizens of the tunnel would not soon forget.

Damballa opened the sack, and the Silent Ones slid into the water and disappeared beneath its surface. The beam of the cloaked man's flashlight led him back the way he had come.

He took no satisfaction in the successful completion of a mission that would have been unthinkable for anyone else. For he was well aware there was more – much more – to come.

CHAPTER TWENTY-FIVE

PRELIMINARIES PROCEED

"**A**ny progress to report, gentlemen?" Commissioner Wheelwright said in a tone that was deceptively calm.

Detectives Bynoe and Dodson exchanged a quick, uncomfortable glance. They were seated in front of the commissioner's desk. Wheelwright sat patiently, waiting for a reply.

"Not much, sir," Bynoe finally replied, speaking for both himself and his colleague.

"Care to elaborate?"

"We've run thorough investigations in the Darkside and other unsavory sections of Harlem, sir," Bynoe reported. "There's been no suspicious activity since the disturbance at the voodoo shop. And … the shop itself appears to have been closed."

"What do you make of that?"

Bynoe hesitated a moment before replying.

"It's probably for the best, sir. There's never been any evidence of wrongdoing in that place, but I never liked the way it stirred up ignorant superstitions that should have been abandoned long ago."

"You're probably right, Bynoe," the commissioner said. Then he turned his attention to Dodson.

"What about the Germans?" Wheelwright asked.

"Their attitude was to be expected, sir. But we were not able to discern anything that would give us reason to ask for a search warrant."

"I see," Wheelwright said, steepling his fingers. "Thus far, gentlemen, I have heard only negatives from you: 'no clues,' 'no leads,' 'nothing to justify a warrant.' It sounds more like, 'not anything.' Now, tell me this:

Have either of you uncovered anything that even remotely represents progress on this file?"

Dodson and Bynoe exchanged another look. Dodson gave a slight, almost imperceptible nod.

"There is … something," Bynoe said. "Something that may seem irrelevant, but it's all we've got so far."

"Please enlighten me."

Dodson was the one who explained, as this line of investigation had been his idea.

"Since we weren't finding anything anywhere else, I thought we might go down to the docks and take a look at the ships that brought Krieger and his people here. It was just a hunch. Even so, we needed to be as thorough as possible, considering the circumstances."

"What did you find?"

"In one of the empty cargo holds, I saw a few tufts of something that looked like hair from an animal. I asked the crew about it, but they claimed ignorance. I took a sample of the hairs to our laboratory for analysis. They haven't come up with an answer as yet."

Wheelwright turned to Bynoe.

"What did you see?" the commissioner asked.

"Nothing," Bynoe replied in a flat tone. "They wouldn't let me on the ship. I didn't think the matter was worth seeking a search warrant, as they were willing to allow Detective Dodson on board. He showed me the hairs he found. I agree with him that they look like animal fur of some kind."

The commissioner winced in acknowledgement of yet another in the endless parade of racial slights Bynoe endured. Wheelwright had heard about the dispute at the training camp as well. Not for the first time, Wheelwright wondered whether he had done Bynoe all that much of a favor by promoting him to detective. He decided, as always, that Bynoe would have to be the one to decide how much abuse he was willing to endure to hold on to his position.

"It's a small clue, as you say," the commissioner declared. "But even the smallest of clues can sometimes break a case. Do you think we can do anything with this?"

"Depending on the lab results, we could possibly ask for a warrant to search the training camp on the grounds of illegal importation of animals," Bynoe replied. "Of course, that would just be an excuse for a thorough search of the place. Detective Dodson and I both got the impression that the Germans are hiding something. Whether or not that has anything to do with animals, or the upcoming fight, I do not know. But I think we need to find out."

Wheelwright considered Bynoe's words. Given the immense import of the Jackson-Krieger fight, and the delicate state of diplomatic relations between Germany and the United States, a few hairs that may or may not have come from some unknown animal seemed to be scant reason to disrupt a long-anticipated event.

Even so, Wheelwright had learned to respect Bynoe's hunches, as well as those of Dodson. Though Dodson was a good detective, Bynoe had the potential to become an exceptional investigator. If Bynoe thought something unusual was going on at Krieger's camp, Wheelwright was willing to accommodate him.

But would a judge be willing to issue a warrant on such tentative grounds, even at the request of the commissioner? There was only one way to find out.

"I'll try to get you a warrant if the lab results justify the request," Wheelwright said. "But there's no guarantee that I will succeed."

The two detectives nodded in agreement. They knew they could not ask for anything more of either Commissioner Wheelwright or whatever judge he happened to consult.

❖ ❖ ❖

Delia Pomphrey sat behind the ornate desk that dominated her study. A frown crossed her features as she lifted her hand from the telephone receiver she had just replaced in its cradle.

"Another dead end," she said to herself.

True to her word, Madame Pomp had done her best to seek information that would either confirm or deny Lola Thorne's misgivings. Thus far, Delia had learned nothing. And she was not accustomed to failure.

Not now, at least. In earlier times, before her success in the cosmetics industry, frustration and disappointment had greeted her every morning, along with the rise of the sun.

The robbery attempt had unnerved her more than she was willing to admit, even to herself. And she was not the only one for whom that was the case. Only a few of her guests that night had contacted her again. Lola was the only one who had visited the Pomp Palace. It was as though Delia's friends now associated her with the terror that had held them in an icy grip before Damballa intervened.

She couldn't really blame her social set for what amounted to a tacit, but still obvious, form of snubbing. She was honest enough to understand that she would have behaved the same way, had the criminals' incursion happened at some other person's event.

Delia was wondering who to call next in her quest to aid Lola when her telephone rang, startling her out of her reverie.

"Hello," she said after picking up the receiver.

"Hello, Madame Pomphrey," a whispery voice intoned.

Delia almost dropped the receiver. She recognized that voice, for she had heard it recently, late one night. ...

"Damballa," she breathed.

"You have been making certain inquiries, Madame Pomphrey," Damballa said. "Why are you doing so?"

Delia's breathing quickened. *Perhaps he has the information I seek*, she thought. *He seems to know everything else.* In terse sentences, she told him about Lola's fears and her own efforts to help Jackhammer's fiancée. Damballa listened without interrupting her narrative.

"I understand why you are trying to help Miss Thorne," Damballa said when Delia was done. "But your inquiries are interfering with some of my efforts. I want you to tell Miss Thorne that you have not learned anything that could be of aid to her. Leave the investigating to me."

Delia was loath to receive commands from anyone. But Damballa had saved her from a great loss and possibly greater harm. So for him, she made an exception.

"Very well, Damballa. I will do as you ask."

"Thank you, Madame Pomphrey."

The receiver went dead in Delia's ear. She held it for a while before putting it down. Then she picked it up again and placed a call to Lola Thorne.

❄ ❄ ❄

Damballa and Mamadou looked up from their microscopes as though an unspoken signal had passed between their minds. They had been studying samples of the pure *Starkenflessig*, which yielded answers to the questions that the anomalies in *Der Tod's* blood had raised.

Those answers were deeply disturbing, even though Damballa and Mamadou had anticipated the facts their investigation ultimately revealed. Although they had each encountered the uncanny and the unbelievable in Africa, Europe, and the United States, the sheer, unambivalent dreadfulness of what they saw in the murky liquid on the slide took them aback.

Damballa, who was clad in ordinary clothing and a white lab coat rather than his usual garb, shook his head in dismay.

"How could they?" he muttered as much to himself as to Mamadou.

"You know very well how they could," Mamadou retorted. "It would be just as well to ask how death and destruction came into the world."

Damballa fell silent. For as long as he could remember, he had heard accounts from Mamadou and other people of the Bakosi about the depredations the Belgians had inflicted long before he was born. For Mamadou, there was no difference between the Belgians and the Germans.

Through his own experiences since he had decided to become a crimefighter, Damballa's antipathy was only slightly less than that of his grandmother. He did, however, allow for exceptions to her insistence that no whites – and few blacks – were to be trusted.

He was able, for example, to spare a measure of sympathy for Wolfgang Krieger, the victim of the Germans' scientific machinations. Mamadou could not do the same. For her, the ultimate victim of the *Starkenflessig* was not Krieger. It was Jackhammer Jackson.

Damballa looked at the row of vials that lay on his laboratory table. The liquid they contained looked cloudy and inert. Yet knowing what it was, Damballa could well imagine that the fluid was mocking him, taunting him in a manner reminiscent of that of its maker.

And Damballa was certain that he could identify the one responsible for this damnable concoction. He knew of no other person who possessed the combination of evil and expertise necessary to have conceived and executed such a vile and overweening undertaking.

"We know what this fluid can do," Damballa said. "But we do not know how long Krieger was subjected to it while he was in Germany."

"Too long," Mamadou muttered tersely.

Damballa agreed with her. Now, some fateful decisions needed to be made. And he knew that he and Mamadou were not the only ones who needed to be involved in their making.

"There are people I need to speak with," he said.

Mamadou nodded.

CHAPTER TWENTY-SIX

THE PINEAL GLAND

Rumors ran rife through Jackhammer Jackson's training camp. Sparring partners, cooks, drivers and maintenance men contributed to the gossip. Jackhammer's brain trust was about to hold an unscheduled meeting in the gym. None of the big shots had said a word concerning what they needed to talk about so close to fight night. The hired help could only guess at what was happening. And none of their surmises came even close to the truth.

So they watched and whispered as the big cars rolled into Compton Lakes and disgorged their occupants. Few words were exchanged with the people who held open the car doors. Facial expressions told their own tale, though – a tale of perplexity and concern.

Even so, the grapevine soon became quiescent. Only after the big wheels came out of their meeting would tongues begin to wag again, in and out of the camp. If something was going on that would affect the fight, no lid would be tight enough to contain that news.

❈ ❈ ❈

"This had better be good," Arnie Ruland growled as an unlit cigar bobbed between his lips. "Time is money, and we can't be wasting either one this close to the big day."

"If Chum says it's important, it's important," said Joby Washington. "He's never steered us wrong before, has he? If he hadn't brought Jackhammer to us, where would we be now?"

Ruland grunted something unintelligible as the Salt-and-Pepper Twins

So they watched and whispered as the big cars rolled into Compton Lakes and disgorged their occupants.

walked toward the entrance to the gym. A third party accompanied them ... a short, slight, middle-aged man who could have been a swarthy-skinned white person or a light-skinned Negro. He was the latter. His suit was far more stylish than the ones Ruland and Washington wore, and a diamond stickpin glittered on his necktie.

This was Bob Brownlee, who was the primary financial backer of Jackhammer's career. The sources of his wealth were unknown, but rumored to be less than legal – numbers, and other rackets. Nothing had ever been proven against him, though, or even brought to court. His involvement with Jackhammer was as discreet as it was significant. This was the first time the financier had ever been to one of the champion's training camps.

But when Chum called, even Brownlee heeded.

"We shall learn what is going on in due time, gentlemen," Brownlee said in a smooth tone. "Just as soon as we step through that door."

Since neither of the Salt-and-Pepper Twins could disagree with that observation, the rest of the walk to the gym proceeded in silence. Washington was the one who pushed the door inward, for he had visited Compton Lakes far more often than Ruland. The others followed him inside – first Ruland, then Brownlee.

The illumination inside the gym was muted, for the windows were all shuttered against the sunlight, and some of the interior lights had not been turned on. The three men continued to a large room that served as an office.

When Washington opened the office door, he and the others saw four men sitting in chairs around a rectangular table. Several other chairs remained empty.

Jackhammer was there, clad in the training togs that were his usual daytime attire in camp. Chum was there, with an even grimmer than usual expression on his hard face. Frankie Gittens was there. His usually jovial demeanor was absent.

The fourth man was swathed in a hooded cloak that hid his features and appeared, uncannily, to extend the darkness that surrounded it.

Damballa. ...

❀ ❀ ❀

In Balrogorra, Wolfgang Krieger shadow-boxed in front of a mirror. He had stopped sparring. In the wake of what Wolf had done to Cro-Magnon Connolly, Kohlbrecher had decided that further sparring work was neither necessary nor desirable. Wimmer had managed to put a tight lid on the extent of the damage Krieger had inflicted on Connolly. If the same thing – or worse – happened to another sparmate, the manager might not prove as successful at concealing it.

Kruger's ungloved fists blurred as he practiced his combinations. Never before had Kohlbrecher seen such phenomenal speed, not even in fighters half Wolf's size. And each punch the fighter threw possessed the power to break men's bones and short-circuit their brains.

Sweat slid down Krieger's skin as he hurled his hands at his own image. Kohlbrecher noticed, not for the first time, that Krieger appeared to have grown since preparations for the Jackson fight had begun in earnest. The musculature that had earned Krieger the soubriquet "Aryan Adonis" had become thicker and more defined.

Ordinarily, such development would have alarmed Kohlbrecher, for a muscle-bound fighter was a vulnerable fighter. But that wasn't the case with Krieger. Already quick-handed for a man his size, Wolf was throwing punches faster than he ever had before. He was more nimble on his feet as well, and more elusive in his defensive maneuvers.

The Starkenflessig, Kohlbrecher thought resentfully. *The* verdammt Starkenflessig. …

The trainer looked at Krieger's face. What he saw alarmed him. Krieger's lips were drawn back from his teeth in a primal snarl. His eyes blazed beneath brow ridges that seemed to have become more prominent over the past weeks.

Then Kohlbrecher heard the beginning of a low growl forming deep in Krieger's throat. And the fighter's hands were moving dangerously closer to the glass of the mirror.

"Enough, Wolf!" Kohlbrecher said sharply.

Krieger's hands stopped moving. Slowly, he turned toward Kohlbrecher. The feral expression had not left the fighter's face. Growls continued to rumble in his throat. His hands opened and closed, seemingly not of their own volition.

Kohlbrecher loved his fighter as though he were his own son. But now, he was afraid of his protégé.

Then the trainer took a step backward as a sudden thought strobed through his mind: *Does Wolf know? Did that devil Von Dunkel tell him my secret?*

No, he decided. For now, it would not be to *Herr Doktor's* advantage to let anyone else know what lay buried in Kohlbrecher's ancestry.

Even so, it was obvious that Krieger was close to losing control of himself. Krieger knew he had to pull the fighter back from the brink.

"Wolf," Kohlbrecher said softly, his voice barely above the level of Krieger's growls.

Krieger glared at him. But the intensity of his growls diminished as he concentrated on Kohlbrecher.

"Wolf, I am sorry I got you into this," Kohlbrecher said. "I never meant for your boxing career to lead to this point."

Krieger's growls ceased as he prevailed in his battle to regain his calm, and to banish the Beast rage that smoldered within him – a task that was becoming more difficult every day. The glare of madness faded from his eyes, and he laid a hand on his trainer's shoulder.

"You do not need to apologize, Franz," the fighter said. "It is not your fault. We are all puppets now, and the madmen of the Reich are the ones who pull the strings."

Kohlbrecher nodded in forlorn acknowledgement. Then the two men walked silently out of the gym.

❀ ❀ ❀

"So, you're saying that the Germans are using some sort of weird liquid to turn Wolfgang Krieger into a ... superfighter?" Ruland asked, breaking the incredulous silence that had greeted Damballa's words of revelation.

"Yes," Damballa replied, paying no heed to the skepticism in Ruland's tone.

Although the hood of his cloak was down, Damballa had yet again altered his appearance. He had thickened his features, and his skin tone was now closer to sienna than ebony. Although Jackhammer and Chum had seen his true countenance, they had agreed not to reveal that fact.

"To be more specific, it is a combination of extracts from the limbic systems and pineal glands of powerful predatory species, such as lions and tigers," Damballa elaborated.

"Pineal gland?" Brownlee inquired. "Isn't that the so-called 'third eye,' buried deep in the brain?"

Damballa looked with interest at the financier, who returned the cloaked man's gaze without looking away, as most other men would.

"I was a medical student before circumstances forced me to go into another line of work," Brownlee said. "Please continue."

Damballa nodded.

"You are correct, Mr. Brownlee," he said. "Descartes called the pineal gland the 'seat of the soul.' But its true function has always been a mystery. However, a German scientist named Claus von Dunkel has discovered the way the gland works in predatory animals. And he has developed a way to transfer that function to human beings, in whom the pineal gland has become largely dormant."

"Von Dunkel?" Ruland said. "Isn't he that mystery man who's over at Krieger's camp now? Nobody knows what he's doing there, but I heard that he's Krieger's personal physician."

"He is that and more," Damballa said. A brief narrowing of his eyes was the only indication of the antipathy the German's very name elicited within him.

"What is this 'function' of the gland?" Washington prodded.

"When combined with hormones from the limbic system, which controls emotions and the autonomic nervous system, extract from the pineal stimulates muscle growth, and quickens the transmission of impulses in the nervous system. It also awakens latent predatory instincts."

"So you're telling us that less than two days from now, Jackhammer's going to be facing some kind of jacked-up man-beast instead of a normal human being?" Washington said, anger showing on his face.

"Yes," said Damballa.

"If what you're saying is true, Damballa, then we would have no choice other than to call off the fight," Brownlee said gravely.

"There is no 'if,' Mr. Brownlee," Damballa said imperturbably. "I have obtained samples of Von Dunkel's fluid, and have examined it thoroughly. My findings leave no doubt."

"And just how did you 'obtain' those samples?" Ruland demanded with a touch of belligerence.

"Man say he done it, he done it," Chum said laconically.

Then Jackhammer, who had remained silent thus far, spoke.

"Ain't nobody callin' off the fight," the champion declared.

❖ ❖ ❖

A small, elegant coupe wended its way impatiently through thick mid-afternoon New York traffic. The driver of the vehicle was determined to get out of the city as quickly as possible, but the traffic was proving to be a formidable impediment. Each red light seemed to last forever. The other drivers, in their slow-moving cars, taxis and trucks, were adversaries. The traffic cops, with their red faces and shrill whistles, were unwelcome intruders.

The coupe's driver fumed, but refrained from breaking any laws. Being pulled over and delayed would not be helpful – especially once the driver's identity was recognized. And the face that was shadowed by a wide-brimmed hat was, indeed, very well-known.

After what seemed an interminable crawl through myriad streets, the coupe finally exited the sprawling city and rolled along the open road. Although relieved now that the choking traffic had been left behind, the driver's expression didn't change. It remained grim – and angry.

The road the coupe traveled led to Compton Lakes. The driver of the coupe had never before been to the site of Jackhammer Jackson's training camp. The coupe barreled along as though the driver were making up for lost time.

CHAPTER TWENTY-SEVEN

THE CHOICE IS MADE

"**M**an, you gone crazy or what?" Frankie expostulated. "That German was gon' be a hard enough nut to crack even without this stuff Damballa's talkin' about. You better call this thing off, Junie. You can always say you got hurt while you was trainin."

Jackhammer shook his head.

"Naw, man," the champion said. "No matter what kind of excuse I came up with, it would look like I chumped out cause I was scared. I can't let our people down like that. I can't let America down like that."

"So you're willing to go up against some kind of human gorilla just to show you ain't scared?" Washington asked incredulously. "What the hell good is it gonna do for you to get your ass killed while the whole world listens to it happenin' on the radio?"

"And here I thought you had confidence in me, Joby," Jackhammer said with an unreadable expression.

To that, Washington could only open his mouth, then close it again without saying anything.

"Ordinarily, you would be right, Mr. Washington," said Damballa. "The field of combat would be dangerously uneven if Jackhammer were to fight an opponent with Krieger's ... enhancements."

"So what's not ordinary?" Ruland demanded.

"There is a way to level the field," said Damballa.

❊ ❊ ❊

The coupe came to a halt outside the entrance to Compton Lakes. The private security officers Brownlee had hired to guard the camp soon became embroiled in an intense discussion with the driver of the car. Voices rose. Tempers flared. Threats were exchanged.

Finally the security officers relented, for the driver was not one who could be easily deterred or dismissed. The coupe's engine roared as it accelerated past the befuddled guards. The driver only slowed the vehicle when it approached the gym. Then the coupe stopped.

When the driver got out and shut the vehicle's door, the few camp personnel who were in the vicinity stopped in their tracks and stared wide-eyed and gape-mouthed, as though they were witnessing an extraordinary phenomenon.

Paying no heed to the onlookers, the driver marched to the doors of the gym, pushed them open, and strode inside.

❈ ❈ ❈

"Are you saying what I think you're saying?" Brownlee demanded, staring hard at Damballa.

"That depends on what you think I am saying," Damballa replied calmly.

The disguise that altered the cloaked man's features could not conceal the deep intensity of his gaze. Brownlee was a hard and ruthless individual. Even so, he was the first to look away.

"I was able to obtain more than just a small sample of Von Dunkel's fluid," Damballa said. "I have a fairly sizable quantity of it. The Germans have no way of knowing it is gone; I left a substitute behind."

"How were you able to do that?" Washington asked.

"I have my ways."

Washington knew Damballa would not elaborate on that statement. He leaned back in his chair and waited for the cloaked man to continue.

"Here is my point: If Jackhammer were infused with a large quantity of this fluid, he could become sufficiently enhanced to offset Krieger's advantages," Damballa said. "As I mentioned before, we do not know how long the treatment has been applied to Krieger. However, a sizeable dosage to Jackhammer would bring their abilities closer to even, and Jackhammer would stand a greater chance for victory."

Silence followed those words. Brownlee shook his head and raked his hand across his brow, as though he were brushing away a spider web. Ruland slowly shook his head. Washington stared straight ahead. Frankie blinked rapidly, as though specks of dirt had gotten into his eyes. Only Damballa, Jackhammer and Chum remained calm.

"I can't believe we're having this conversation," Brownlee said. "It's like something out of one of those crazy pulp magazines."

"So am I, to some people," said Damballa. "But I am real enough, am I not?

"Granted, but what you've been saying is inconceivable," Brownlee retorted. "If it weren't for the fact that I wouldn't put anything past those goddamn Nazis, I'd've already called the cops – not to mention the men in white coats."

"That would not be advisable," said Damballa.

"This kind of talk getting us nowhere," said Ruland. "Either we believe Damballa, or we don't. And right now, I don't know whether I believe him or not."

"I believe him," said Chum.

The manager, the moneyman and Frankie all looked at the scar-faced trainer. His gaze was unwavering and his mouth was set in a grim line. Everyone knew he was the most practical-minded person in the room. Therefore, his words carried deep impact.

"I would trust my life to this man," Chum elaborated, nodding his head toward Damballa.

"Well, if that's good enough for you fellas, it's good enough for me," said Frankie.

Suddenly, the door to the room swung open and the driver of the coupe strode inside.

"It's not good enough for me!" Lola Thorne said sharply.

❊ ❊ ❊

The men in the room – even the stoic Chum – stared wide-eyed at Jackhammer's fiancée.

Hands on hips, she raked the room's occupants with her blazing eyes. She was clad in a pair of wide-legged slacks and an open-collared shirt. A wide-brimmed hat hung from one of her hands. Her face was devoid of makeup. And she looked better than most other women would in an evening gown and jewels.

"I *knew* something was going on that shouldn't be," Lola fumed. "I've been outside that door, listening to all this talk about shooting Jackhammer up with some crazy kind of dope."

Then she focused on Damballa.

"I appreciate the way you stopped that robbery at Delia Pomphrey's," she said. "But I'll be damned if I allow you to put that stuff in my man."

"It's too late, Miss Thorne," Damballa said imperturbably. "The process has already been implemented."

Gasps of shock greeted that announcement. Only Chum and Jackhammer had agreed before the meeting to be injected with the

Starkenflessig. Damballa had been about to reveal that information, but Lola's arrival had forestalled him.

"It's true, baby," Jackhammer said, looking directly at Lola. "The stuff's in me. And it's workin'."

❀ ❀ ❀

The Beast prowled through an endless savanna of golden grass, stretching beneath a cerulean sky and a bright saffron sun. Giant muscles rippled beneath the Beast's sleek, ebony-furred hide as it scanned the savanna for prey. Herds of horned grass-eaters fled as a hot breeze carried the scent of the Beast toward their quivering nostrils. ...

The Beast did not deign to pursue the horned ones. For its own nostrils had picked up the rank odor of a different breed of prey. ... a breed the Beast despised; a type of creature it stalked and slew at every opportunity. ...

Despite the huge dimensions of its taloned paws, the Beast moved soundlessly, creeping stealthily through the grass. Although the Beast could not yet seek the prey, its stink grew steadily stronger. The Beast struggled to suppress a growl that would have given away its presence. ...

Suddenly the breeze shifted, carrying the Beast's scent forward. Ahead of the beast, a pale shape leaped abruptly from its place of concealment, and began to flee. ...

The Beast opened a mouth armed with rows of wicked, hook-shaped fangs. The roar that issued from its throat reverberated across the plain. No lion could have matched that awesome thunder. It was a challenge, a warning. ... and an assertion of dominance ...

The prey-creature fled, leaping across the grass with prodigious, fear-fuelled speed. The Beast pursued, moving more quickly than imaginable, given its gargantuan bulk. ...

Inexorably, the Beast gained on the prey-creature. The Beast moved so rapidly that the blades of grass beneath its feet blended into a golden blur. The prey-creature continued its flight, even though it knew its chances for escape were virtually non-existent. It could have outraced any other animal that inhabited the endless savanna. But not the Beast. ...

Finally, sensing the inevitable, the prey-creature turned at bay. The prey-creature's body was long and lanky, with rope-like sinews writhing beneath a naked hide as white as the clouds that hung overhead. A crest of spiky yellow hair extended from the center of its skull to the base of its short tail. A pair of long, straight, sharp-pointed horns jutted forward above its eyes. The square teeth of a grass-eater protruded from its drawn-back lips. ...

Fear and defiance blazed in the prey-creature's blue eyes as it attempted to use its horns to impale the Beast. With a contemptuous swipe of its paw, the Beast knocked the horns aside, shattering one of them. Then the Beast's jaws closed on the prey-creature's throat, and blood spurted even as the victim's gurgling death-cry echoed in the Beast's ears. ...

❄ ❄ ❄

"That should be enough," Damballa said as he eased the needle of a syringe from Jackhammer's arm.

The cloaked man and Chum were standing at the side of Jackhammer's bed. Jackhammer was asleep. Moments earlier, however, his thrashings and outcries had thoroughly alarmed the other two men. Chum had watched warily while Damballa injected Jackhammer with a sedative.

Now Chum stared hard at Damballa.

"Did you know this was gon' happen to him?" the trainer demanded.

"Not specifically," Damballa replied. "But I knew there would be side-effects of some kind. I tried to prepare for the possibilities."

Chum grunted, and his gaze softened slightly. He thought back to the way the meeting in the office had ended ... unsatisfactorily. The Salt-and-Pepper Twins were clearly uncomfortable with what Jackhammer had allowed Damballa to do. Frankie had simply shaken his head and said, "Um, um, um." Lola had barely spoken to Jackhammer before departing, though she agreed not to say anything to anybody about Damballa's revelation.

Only the moneybags, Bob Brownlee, betrayed no response to the extraordinary disclosure, and the events that were about to unfold. Chum was beginning to think the rumors were true: Brownlee really did have ice water instead of blood flowing through his veins.

"You think this stuff'll wear off after the fight?" Chum asked.

"Hopefully," said Damballa. "I do not know enough about the fluid to be certain of that. However, Mamadou and I are working on something that should counter its effects."

"Glad to hear she in on it," said Chum.

Both men looked down at Jackhammer, who continued to slumber peacefully. There would be no more Beast Dreams for him this night. But the massive amount of *Starkenflessig* he had received was working changes that were not apparent from the outside.

CHAPTER TWENTY-EIGHT

TIME RUNS FAST

Detective Bynoe replaced the telephone receiver in its cradle. His eyes met those of Detective Dodson. They were in Bynoe's "second office." Dodson was, likely, the only white person within a twenty-block radius of the building. That didn't matter to him, though.

Not anymore. Not since the first time he'd come here.

Bynoe's expression did not change. But Dodson knew his partner well enough to guess what he was about to say.

"That was the commissioner. He says the judge won't issue us a warrant to search Balrogorra."

Bynoe paused. His eyes narrowed with a familiar anger that he struggled, as always, to suppress.

"The Commissioner said he's sorry … for all the damn good that does."

"I'm sorry, too," said Dodson. "Even though I know it doesn't do any damn good."

Dodson leaned back in his chair. Both detectives were in shirtsleeves, their automatics resting in shoulder holsters. Bynoe looked at Dodson.

"The judge might have granted the warrant if it had come from some other detective team," Bynoe said.

He had no need to elaborate. Granted, a few hairs and a hunch did not in themselves constitute a compelling case for a search warrant. However, both detectives knew that warrants had sometimes been granted on the basis of evidence even more tenuous than what they had found. But those requests had been made by other detectives, other teams.…

"I hear you," said Dodson. "But what's done is done. We have to move on."

Bynoe looked away. A slight grimace crossed his face. Then he looked at Dodson again.

"Even though we can't search Balrogorra, we can still keep an eye on the place," he said. "And we can still do our best to find out what the Germans are up to."

"*If* they're up to anything," said Dodson.

"You and I both know they are."

Dodson nodded slowly. Without further conversation, the detectives donned their suit jackets and left the room.

❖ ❖ ❖

Had Bynoe and Dodson been able to raid Balrogorra that day, they would have found nothing to confirm the suspicions raised by the tuft of hairs found on the ship. The cages in the cellblock were now empty. Their pitiful inhabitants had been dispatched with bullets to their skulls, and their remains buried well beyond the grounds of the former prison. The intravenous stands and fluid-collection vials had been disposed of in similar fashion.

With the fight occurring the next night, there was no need for further injections of the *Starkenflessig* into Krieger. The concoction had long since achieved its purpose. In the minds of the camp personnel, Krieger could not lose.

In the mind of Von Dunkel, though, a concern had recently taken root like an unwelcome weed. He was beginning to detect signs of another side effect of the *Starkenflessig* ... an effect that was far more worrisome than Krieger's nightmares and mood swings ... an effect that might have proved disastrous had the fight not been imminent.

Nothing can go wrong, Von Dunkel fervently convinced himself as he sat in his office and gazed at the unused vials of *Starkenflessig* he was about to stuff into a black satchel.

Nothing. ...

❖ ❖ ❖

Lola Thorne reached for the telephone, then took her hand away. She had already done this more than once. A frown crossed her face as she found fault with her own indecision.

She wanted to call Jackhammer and apologize for walking out on him in a huff, when she knew he needed her. What she had overheard, however, was more than she could handle. That, and what Jackhammer admitted he had done ... allowed himself to get shot up with some kind of hoodoo-juice on the say-so of Damballa.

Yet that same Damballa had prevented those hoodlums from stripping and humiliating her and the others at Madame Pomp's party. Surely he was trustworthy. Or was he? What if he were running some kind of game of his own? After all, nobody knew who he was or where he had come from.

Lola didn't know whether Jackhammer would even take her call. Their relationship was passionate, but also tempestuous. She and Jackhammer had always known that she would not have given him the time of day had he not become the most famous Negro in the world. And for all the love they had for each other, that unpleasant truth would occasionally rise unbidden and unexpected between them.

If Lola could not apologize directly, there was something else she could do for her man. When she left Compton Lakes, she had told Jackhammer's people that she would not breathe a word about what she had heard about the hoodoo-juice. And, being the foolish men that they were, they'd let her go.

A woman can always change her mind, she thought as she rose from the couch in her luxurious apartment, located in an area even tonier than Sugar Row.

She slipped out of her lounging robe and put on a suit similar to the one she had worn on her visit to Delia Pomphrey. Lola was getting ready to do something that would most likely end things between her and Jackhammer. But she didn't want to see him get hurt, or possibly killed, in the ring.

A telephone call would not be enough. She needed to do what she had to do in person. Things always worked out better when people could look at her.

Lola opened her front door – and gasped as she took a step backward. A large black man – bigger than Jackhammer – loomed in front of her. An equally dark-skinned woman stood at his side. She was considerably shorter, and much more round, than her companion.

The man stepped forward, forcing Lola to give him sufficient space to enter the apartment. The woman came in behind him, and closed the door.

"Who are you?" Lola demanded, trying not to show her fear. "What are you doing here?

The man, who was clad in the uniform of a janitor, smiled disarmingly.

So did the woman, who was dressed as a cleaning lady.

"My name is Kojo, Miss Thorne," he replied, speaking with an accent Lola could not place. "This is my wife, Mary. We are friends of Damballa's. He asked us to stay with you in order to make certain you keep your word about not doing anything to stop the fight."

Lola frowned as she regarded Kojo and Mary. Something in the demeanor of this couple told her that her wiles would not sway them from their purpose. She sighed in anger and frustration.

❊ ❊ ❊

In Atlanta, a crew of colored maintenance workers gathered for lunch in the basement of the building they were cleaning. As they wolfed down thick sandwiches pulled from metal lunchbuckets and slurped down coffee and other beverages, they talked about the fight, and how Jackhammer was going to make that German cat holler for his mama.

One of the men sat apart from the others. He stared vacantly as his jaws chomped mechanically on his sandwich. Instead of a lunchbox, he carried his food in a grease-stained paper bag. If he could hear what the other men were saying, he gave no indication. Nor did he pay any heed to the crumbs that slowly accumulated on his overalls.

The other members of the crew turned their attention to the loner. Nudges, winks and chuckles abounded as they rose from their seats and sauntered over to their co-worker – who did not acknowledge their arrival.

"Hey, Know-nothin'," one of the men said. "Who you think gon' win the fight tomorrow night?"

The loner swallowed the bit of sandwich he was chewing. He looked up. His eyes continued to convey their constant message: nobody's home.

Finally, he spoke.

"I don' know nothin' about it," he mumbled.

His co-workers' braying laughter echoed through the basement as they returned to their seats. He showed no reaction to their derision. Then again, he didn't respond to much of anything other than the foreman's commands, which was the reason that the crew kept him around to perform the tasks that were unpleasant even by their job's standards.

His nickname was inevitable, given his unvarying reply to most questions. But he was only being honest. For the clouds in his mind swirled so thickly that they obliterated nearly everything he had once known about the world – and himself.

He did not, for example, remember that he used to be known as "Bullets," and there was a time when these loudmouthed turkeys he worked with would have been scared to death of him.

He didn't know nothin' about it. ...

CHAPTER TWENTY-NINE

THE NIGHT BEFORE

From Sugar Row to the Darkside, Negro New York was hopping like a jitterbug on a hotplate in anticipation of the Fight of the Century. Every nightspot from Big's Paradise to the Boll Weevil Club to the Yovas Lounge was packed with people celebrating ahead of time. The Duke, the Count, the King, and a slew of other black bandleaders with pseudo-aristocratic monikers wailed to the full extent of their hearts and souls, as though the soaring notes of their horns could carry Jackhammer to victory. Dance floors throbbed as countless pairs of feet hoofed in time with the music.

Adventurous white folks joined long, dark lines to get into the "black-and-tan" clubs, which daringly welcomed an integrated clientele. The pre-fight partying extended to whites-only establishments as well, where revelers raised numerous toasts to a champion who would not have been allowed past the front door had he desired to join the festivities.

Not everyone in New York, or the nation as a whole for that matter, was hoping for a Jackhammer victory. For various reasons – some racial, some not – certain people preferred Wolfgang Krieger to the current champion. These people admired the progress the National Socialist government appeared to have made in Germany, as opposed to the way the Depression was refusing to release its hold on the United States.

On this night, the Krieger sympathizers kept to themselves. If the German won the fight, his American fans would emerge from the background and celebrate in a big way.

❀ ❀ ❀

Balrogorra looked as though it had returned to its previous state of abandonment. The training ring was no longer in the old prison yard. Only a few lights shone in the grim buildings. The guard towers, however, were still manned by black-clad Germans. And the front gates were closed.

In Krieger's room, a dim light delineated his sleeping form. He was strapped down with leather bands even thicker than the ones that had restrained him on previous nights. This time, though, he neither moaned nor moved. His chest rose and fell in a slow rhythm beneath the binding that crossed it.

Krieger was not alone in his room. Von Dunkel was there, monitoring Krieger closely. The doctor's lack of sleep showed on his face. Even so, his concentration did not falter.

Kohlbrecher and Wimmer were there as well. A frown of concern creased Kohlbrecher's brow, and he fidgeted in his seat. Wimmer also looked worried, although not to the same extent as the trainer.

Kohlbrecher broke the silence. He knew the sound of conversation would not disturb Krieger, who had been rendered virtually insensate by a powerful combination of sedatives.

"This mixing of the *Starkenflessig* and sleep aids worries me, *Herr Doktor*," the trainer said.

"And what medical school did you attend, Kohlbrecher?" Von Dunkel demanded in a sardonic tone.

Despite the damning knowledge Von Dunkel possessed, Kohlbrecher did not look away.

"What you are doing has not been done before – by any *Doktor*," Kohlbrecher pointed out.

Wimmer opened his mouth to say some placating words, for he knew that tensions were rising to a perilous level. At a look from Von Dunkel, Wimmer's words remained unspoken.

"Only one day remains," Von Dunkel said. "We need only to get Wolf through the weigh-in, and then the fight. The fight will be brief. If the *Neger* lasts as long as one minute, I will be surprised. By this time tomorrow night, Wolf will be the heavyweight champion of the world. On the next day, we will be on our ship, and gone from this country of money-mad fools.

"At that point, there will no longer be a need for either the *Starkenflessig* or the sedatives. I will do everything I can to undo the negative effects the drugs have had on Wolf. When we return to Germany, we will be hailed as heroes of the Reich.

"And then – "

Von Dunkel stopped speaking, as though he were preventing himself from saying something he did not want the others to hear.

Wimmer nodded in concurrence with what *Herr Doktor* said. So did

He looked over at Mamadou, and yet again he marveled at her ability to link the wisdom of the blacks with that of the whites.

Kohlbrecher. The three men continued their vigil over Krieger, who – mercifully – did not dream.

❀ ❀ ❀

In Compton Lakes, Jackhammer's slumber was less tranquil than Krieger's. Like Krieger, though, Jackhammer's body was confined by leather restraints. And two observers watched him with deep concern as his head whipped from side to side, and his teeth snapped, and low growls escaped his throat. He bucked and strained against the bonds that prevented him from leaping off the bed. Patches of sweat soaked through his sleepwear.

Finally, Jackhammer's struggles ceased. The snarling expression on his face relaxed. His breathing became regular. Soon he began to snore … lightly, but still audibly.

A look of relief crossed Chum's features. Jackhammer always snored – not loud enough to be annoying, but sufficient to make for humor in his training camps, mainly jokes about how it was Jackhammer who was snoring for a change, and not some luckless opponent.

Chum turned to the other person in the room: Damballa. The cloaked man's attention was focused on Jackhammer.

"You gon' give him any more of that stuff?" Chum asked.

Damballa shook his head.

"If I gave him any more of it, his body would become over-stimulated, and he could die of a heart attack. I have given him enough to allow him to stand a chance tomorrow. The rest is up to him."

Damballa was looking at Chum now. The trainer held the other man's gaze, then nodded.

"Can't ask for nothin' more'n that," Chum said. "If you gon' trust a man, then you trust him."

"He should be fine for the rest of the night," said Damballa. "Still, you should watch him, just to be certain. You can take shifts with Frankie."

"You ain't stayin'?"

"There are things I must do elsewhere."

"You gon' be at the fight?"

"Yes. But you will not recognize me."

Chum's gimlet gaze lingered on Damballa a moment longer.

"I don' know whether to thank you, or cuss your ass out," the trainer said.

"You can decide tomorrow," Damballa returned.

A moment later, he was gone.

❀ ❀ ❀

It was past midnight when Damballa returned to the depths of his sanctum. As he had expected, Mamadou was awake and working hard in the laboratory. A chaotic clutter of test tubes, vials and other equipment filled the room, in contrast with its usual state of neatness. But Damballa knew Mamadou was aware of the location of every item she needed.

She barely greeted him when he entered the laboratory. She was concentrating on the mixture of plant-powders and synthetic compounds she was preparing. If the lateness of the hour and the intensity of her work wearied her, she showed no sign.

Damballa removed his cloak, and carefully hung it in a closet that contained several such garments. Then, curling his fingers against his forehead, he peeled away the filmy substance that had altered his features. The mask hung eyeless and open-mouthed in his hand before he disposed of it in a nearby waste can.

He looked over at Mamadou, and yet again he marveled at her ability to link the wisdom of the blacks with that of the whites. Of course, he did the same. But she did it far more adroitly.

In a fair world, Mamadou would enjoy as much renown as a Marie Curie, he mused. *And in a fair world, wisdom and knowledge would be viewed as neither black nor white. …*

"How is it coming, Mamadou?" Damballa asked in the Bakosi tongue.

"As well as can be expected," she replied. "There will be no time to do a proper testing procedure. No use worrying over that; it cannot be helped."

With that, she returned to her work.

Damballa heeded his grandmother's hint. He had work of his own to do, and limited time to get it accomplished.

As he set about his tasks, Damballa wondered – not for the first time – whether he was doing the right thing. Once he had discovered what was in Von Dunkel's diabolical fluid, Damballa could have taken measures to stop the fight from occurring. A well-placed call to the law, perhaps to the earnest Detective Bynoe … a sample of the fluid delivered to a government scientist … a tip to a newspaper reporter … the deed would have been easy enough to carry out.

But the consequences of such an exposure would have been dire. The ensuing outrage would have led to severe national and international conflict, perhaps resulting in repercussions unthinkable in the wake of the Great War.

Better by far to give Jackhammer a fighting chance, Damballa decided as he continued his work.

CHAPTER THIRTY

WEIGHING IN

For a heavyweight bout, the weigh-in was nothing more than an opportunity for publicity. In the case of the lower divisions, weigh-ins served to make certain that both participants' poundage was at or under the limit for the class. There was no limit for the heavies, though. Anyone even a few ounces over the 175-pound light-heavyweight limit was a heavyweight – period.

Yet for an event that should have been utterly superfluous, not to mention irrelevant, a heavyweight-championship bout's weigh-in was still a grand spectacle, a ritual that heralded the action that would come hours later, when the combatants would finally enter the ring.

A significant match like Jackson-Krieger was a pretext to turn the weigh-in into a full-blown circus of flacks and hacks. Long before the fighters were scheduled to step onto the scales, reporters from hundreds of newspapers and radio stations from the United States and other countries – especially Germany – began to gather in the lobby of Yankee Stadium, the venue of the fight. Photographers fiddled with their flash cameras. Major and minor dignitaries who had wangled an invitation to the event jostled with the police officers who were there to provide security. Anticipation of the fighters' arrival was almost as intense as it would become before the bout actually began.

The hum of conversation rose as word came that the cars containing the fighters had just arrived. Nobody went outside to catch a glimpse, though. Both fighters' cars were under heavy police escort, and photographers had already been stationed to snap pictures of Jackhammer and Krieger as they emerged from their vehicles.

The fighters did not go directly into the lobby. To avoid the crush of the crowd, they would approach the scale from opposite entrances – a symbolic reminder of the opposite corners they would occupy in the ring.

Officials had already gathered at the scale, a gleaming new model that would not have looked out of place in the examining room of a high-society physician. Among them was the man who would serve as the ringside doctor at the fight. Dr. Vaughn Lyons was a tall, lean personage who seemed even more stiff-faced than usual. That was understandable, given the magnitude of the bout.

Now the doors opened, and the fighters emerged with their entourages. The din rose, and cameras flashed like lightning as the groups approached the scale like military squadrons on the march. In contrast to the nervous smiles that twitched across the lips of the other officials, Dr. Lyons' face remained expressionless.

"Quiet, please," the doctor said, his voice somehow carrying above the noise of the crowd. The murmurs subsided in response to Dr. Lyons' authoritative tone.

The entourages stepped aside, and the fighters stood beside the scale. Each man wore a suit jacket over bare chest and boxing trunks. Calf-high socks and dress shoes were the only other garments the fighters wore. In any other circumstances, an ensemble such as this would have invited ridicule. But it was typical for weigh-ins. And who would have the nerve to make fun of a professional prizefighter within his earshot?

"Mr. Krieger, please step onto the scale," Dr. Lyons said.

❊ ❊ ❊

Chum's eyes scanned the crowd. He was looking for Damballa, even though he knew the crimefighter would be in disguise if he attended the weigh-in at all. Chum guessed that Damballa would, indeed, be there, to forestall any other tricks the Germans might have up their sleeves other than the fluid that fuelled their fighter.

Chum knew Damballa could make himself look and sound like anyone, even a white man. The trainer's eyes were sharper than most, but he didn't spot anything out of the ordinary among the people in the throng. And there were too many in the crowd for him to look at each of them.

Finally, he gave up.

He either here or he ain't, Chum thought pragmatically as he turned his attention to Jackhammer.

The fighter was standing stock-still, his famous deadpan gaze focused on his opponent, who was in the process of removing his shoes and suit jacket. Chum looked at the other Germans. Glares of disdain and outright hatred lanced toward Jackhammer and the other Negroes in his group. The only German whose expression did not convey overt malice was Krieger's trainer, Kohlbrecher.

"Easy, son," Chum whispered to Jackhammer.

Jackhammer made no response.

❀ ❀ ❀

Krieger stepped onto the scale. The lobby became quiet as the doctor adjusted the sliding and counter weights along the scale's beam. When the point of the beam finally hovered without touching the ends, Dr. Lyons made his announcement.

"Two-hundred twenty-seven and three-quarters pounds."

Murmurs of surprise rose from the press corps. This was the most Krieger had yet weighed in his career. Yet there did not appear to be an ounce of fat on his frame. Nor had he become musclebound – at least as far as the gazes of ring-wise sports writers could determine.

Krieger's thews were well-defined, but not bulky. With his smoldering blue eyes and his lips curled in an expression that was half-sneer and half-snarl, Wolfgang Krieger presented the image of a tiger in human form: a warrior who combined the size and endurance of a Jim Jeffries with the speed and dynamism of a Jack Dempsey.

As he stood on the scale, Krieger stared at Jackhammer with all the arrogance of a Teutonic demigod … or an Aryan Adonis.

"You may step down from the scale now, Mr. Krieger," Dr. Lyons said.

If Krieger detected a slightly sardonic undertone to the physician's words, he gave no indication. The German got off the scale, donned his garments, and stood between Kohlbrecher and Von Dunkel.

"Your turn, Mr. Jackson," Dr. Lyons said.

❀ ❀ ❀

Von Dunkel could not understand why the *Neger* champion was not responding to the ferocity that emanated in almost palpable waves from Krieger. Were Jackson's senses so dull that they could not detect that he was in the presence of his master? Standing next to Krieger, *Herr Doktor* could *feel* the sheer physical dominance that radiated from the superman the *Starkenflessig* had produced.

At the dawn of this day, Von Dunkel had suppressed all doubts in regard to what he had done. He had achieved the ideal balance between the *Starkenflessig* and the sedatives. He had created the ultimate ring gladiator: a fighter with the strength, reflexes and ferocity of an animal, combined with the intellect and sagacity of a man.

And Von Dunkel was confident that the balance would last long enough to get Krieger through the fight before a breakdown could occur. ...

Herr Doktor looked again at Jackhammer.

He has no idea, Von Dunkel thought. *The poor brute has no idea what is about to happen to him.*

❀ ❀ ❀

As Jackhammer doffed his jacket and shoes and stepped onto the scale, the lobby erupted in a spontaneous burst of applause. Immediately, Dr. Lyons signaled the crowd to stop. It took several minutes for the clapping to cease.

Through it all, Jackhammer's demeanor did not change. In the ring and in public, he maintained a mask of quiet stoicism. His normally taciturn nature was one reason he kept his thoughts and feelings to himself. The other was the list of "rules" that had been drilled into him since the beginning of his career by Chum and the Salt-and-Pepper Twins.

The gist of the rules was: Do *not* make the same mistakes that undid Jack Johnson. That means no bombast, no triumphant grins over fallen foes (especially Caucasian ones), and – more important than anything else – no dalliances with women of the wrong color.

Those rules were easy enough for Jackhammer to follow – especially the last one. Why would he give a damn about white girls when he had Lola Thorne wearing his engagement ring? But he wasn't sure he would have Lola much longer. ...

The contrast between Jackhammer and Krieger was clear as Dr. Lyons readjusted the weights on the beam. Jackhammer looked like a light-heavyweight compared to the German. The muscles that powered Jackhammer's punches lay deep beneath his dark skin. Jackhammer was no Charles Atlas ... but he hit hard enough to turn larger and stronger foes into quivering, unconscious wrecks.

"Two-hundred pounds even," the doctor announced.

The reporters nodded in approval. It was the weight they had expected. Now that Jackson had entered his prime, he always weighed within a pound or two of 200. If he came in at less than that weight, he would be weakened as he climbed through the ropes. If he were heavier, he'd be slow and sluggish.

As Jackhammer stepped off the scale, one of the officials moved to the forefront. A portly, florid-faced, white-haired man, William O'Gatty was Chairman of the New York State Boxing Commission and had been associated with the sport since the days of the great John L. Sullivan, who was the last of the previous century's bareknuckle champions.

O'Gatty motioned the boxers to come closer to each other. They followed his bidding.

"Shake hands, gentlemen," the commissioner directed.

Jackhammer was the first to extend his hand. Krieger reached out a moment later, and two of the most dangerous hands in the world clasped while cameras flashed like starbursts.

Only once before had the champion and challenger met. It was at the formal signing of the contracts for the fight – another grand opportunity for publicity and photos. The boxers had been cordial to each other on that occasion, though they had exchanged only a few words.

This time, there was no conversation. The hard-eyed glares that passed between them spoke far more eloquently than any words.

When the cameras stopped flashing, the handclasp ended, and Jackhammer put on his jacket and shoes. They no longer looked at each other.

"Good luck to the both of you," Commissioner O'Gatty intoned.

The fighters grunted in response as they returned to their respective retinues. With the weights now known, the event was over, and the fighters and their handlers returned to the doors through which they had come. And the reporters and photographers began to drift out of the lobby.

Some of the sports scribes shook their heads as they made their way outside. Weigh-ins tended to be raucous occasions, with plenty of good-natured ribbing between the fighters' camps. Sometimes, there was feigned hostility. Only rarely was the animosity real.

This time, however, nobody questioned the veracity of the contempt displayed by the Germans, or the resentment that seethed in the eyes of the Americans – especially the colored ones.

As they exited the arena to which they would be returning hours later, more than a few reporters uneasily hoped that any enmity expressed that night would be confined to the ring.

✤ ✤ ✤

Damballa was there. ...

CHAPTER THIRTY-ONE

FIGHT NIGHT

Possessors of precious fight tickets swarmed into Yankee Stadium well before the bout was due to begin. No preliminary matches had been scheduled. A match-up like Jackson-Krieger occurred only once in a generation, if even that often. Whether it lasted one round or the full fifteen, this was an event that would be part of history, and those who attended would own their own small share of its significance.

In bars, in private homes, in tenements, in farmhouses, on ships, in spaces rented for the occasion, across the United States and much of the rest of the world, radios were tuned in to receive the blow-by-blow account of the contest. Staccato-voiced announcers discussed the strategies they expected the fighters to employ. Listeners made predictions of their own, and exchanged wagers. Alcohol flowed freely, even as youngsters were allowed to stay up late to listen to the big fight.

Lights blazed down on the ring set up in the stadium's infield, where the Bronx Bombers usually plied their trade. The ring was a bright island surrounded by the temporary seating that occupied the ballfield, and the stands that rose into the night. Slowly, those stands were filling. This evening, no seat in Yankee Stadium would be empty.

The NYPD was providing security for the fight, thanks to the Mayor's desire to claim due credit for the success of the spectacle. Uniformed officers ushered celebrities and politicians to their seats at ringside. Plainclothes detectives, including Dodson and Bynoe, coordinated the safety measures. If some of the white uniformed cops were unenthusiastic about taking orders from a black man, they kept their resentment to themselves. This was not the night to express such feelings.

At least, not openly.

The Mayor and Police Commissioner Wheelwright sat next to each other in the front row, along with their wives. The rich and famous flanked them on both sides, stretching around the four sides of the ring. One side was reserved for the Negro elite: the Sugar Row crowd and their counterparts who had arrived from cities like Philadelphia, Boston, Baltimore, and Chicago.

Delia Pomphrey was there, resplendent in jewels and a feathered hat. Her escort for the evening was not Adolfo Levere, but Kurt van Vallen, who was the only white person present amid the colored collection of renown. Levere was seated elsewhere, beside a beautiful young blues singer who wore a gardenia in her hair. They were engrossed in conversation as they awaited the beginning of the fight. Others talked about the significance of the two pairs.

Madame Pomp's choice of companion would have been the primary topic of ringside gossip, were it not for the late arrival of Lola Thorne – and the unknown couple that accompanied her. The big man and the round woman appeared to be Africans, and they both looked uncomfortable in the expensive garments they wore. Three empty seats awaited the trio's arrival, and more than a few people wondered how Lola had been to obtain places at ringside for this duo who, by the look of them, were neither socialites nor entertainers.

Kojo and Mary had talked long into the night with Lola. They had told her a great deal about Damballa, short of revealing his true name. Grudgingly, Lola came to understand why she should not attempt to prevent the fight from occurring, despite her fears for Jackhammer.

If she could not stop the fight, she would still witness it. She had to. Kojo and Mary would, however, escort her, as per Damballa's explicit wishes. Lola wondered how in the world the Africans would be able to secure ringside seats next to her on the eve of the bout.

"Do not concern yourself, dear," Mary told her. "The Salt-and-Pepper Twins have taken care of it.

Now, surrounded by tens of thousands of conversations, all Lola could do was wait.

❊ ❊ ❊

Krieger's dressing room was the locker room usually occupied by visiting teams at the stadium. This time, instead of a loud and boisterous baseball team, only three people were in the cavernous space: Krieger, Kohlbrecher and Von Dunkel. The rest of Krieger's faction was waiting in the corridor, along with the police officers who were there on guard duty.

The observer from Jackson's camp who had come to watch the taping and gloving of Krieger's hands was gone. Von Dunkel was glad it had been a white man, not some *Schwartzer.*

Normally, Krieger would have been throwing punches at the air, working up a sweat so that he would enter the ring with his muscles loose and his reflexes primed to respond instantly. This time, however, he sat still as Kohlbrecher massaged his shoulders and Von Dunkel spoke softly into the fighter's ear.

"Remember, Wolf, you must attack as soon as the bell rings," *Herr Doktor* intoned. "Do not waste time trying to anticipate what Jackson will do. It will be over quickly; the *Neger* does not possess enough intelligence to be afraid of you, nor the strength to forestall you. Do you understand?"

Krieger gave a slight nod. He stared straight ahead, his blue eyes narrowed to slits. A muscle jumped spasmodically on his jawline.

Kohlbrecher carefully concealed his disgust. As Wolf's trainer, he – not Von Dunkel – was supposed to be the one to decide the strategy for the fight. Lately, though, Von Dunkel's scorn for him had become more pronounced. Kohlbrecher dreaded what could be awaiting him when he returned to Germany. ...

Since his confrontation with Von Dunkel, Kohlbrecher had thought about escaping ... losing himself among the millions who teemed in this huge and vulgar metropolis. But he could not bring himself to abandon Wolf to *Herr Doktor.*

A sharp rap sounded at the locker room door.

"It's time," a voice declared.

"*Ja,*" Von Dunkel said. He gestured at Kohlbrecher, not deigning to speak. The trainer slipped a stark black robe over Krieger's shoulders. The fighter rose, towering over Kohlbrecher and Von Dunkel. Kohlbrecher opened the door, and the three men stepped into the corridor.

❊ ❊ ❊

Jackhammer was in the Yankees' locker room. Other than towel-boys and janitors, he was the first member of his race to sit in this space. Then again, Jackhammer wasn't a baseball player. If he had been, he'd be playing for peanuts in the Negro leagues, not making a million dollars in the ring.

Chum, Frankie and Joby Washington were with the champion. Arnold Ruland had gone over to Krieger's dressing room, to witness the wrapping and gloving of the challenger's hands. It was customary for a member of the opponent's camp to observe that process, and make certain no illegal objects or substances were placed beneath fighters' gloves.

The German observer – Hans Wimmer – had just departed from the dressing room. He had said almost nothing to Jackhammer's handlers, and that was fine with them. The gloves were now laced firmly on Jackhammer's fists. Like Krieger, the champion eschewed his usual warming-up activities.

"You okay, son?" Chum asked.

"Yeah," Jackhammer replied.

"Damballa tol' me to tell you this: Once you and Krieger commence to fightin', the stuff that's in both of you's liable to take over. Krieger been on the stuff a lot longer than you. So it gon' happen sooner with him. Damballa say that yo' biggest danger ... and yo' best chance. I think I understand what he sayin'. Do you?"

"Yeah," Jackhammer said again.

The champion's demeanor remained impassive. Beneath that façade, however, his thoughts roiled like the undercurrents of a stormy sea.

He thought about Lola, with whom he had not spoken since their confrontation at Compton Lakes. He wondered whether or not she would even be in the audience tonight. She had come to all his fights since they'd first met.

But now. ...

He thought about Wolfgang Krieger. He had always been confident that he could take the German in a fair fight. But what about a fight that was less than fair ... a fight in which Jackhammer came in at a decided disadvantage, which had never happened before?

Most of all, though, he thought about the horrific dreams that had plagued his sleep since Damballa shot him up with the devil's fluid. There was not much in life that Jackhammer feared. However, the creature that he turned into during those dreams unnerved him. He did not understand how the Beast could also be him. Yet if the Beast was necessary for him to win the fight, then he would be the Beast ... but he would not allow the Beast to overcome him.

A sharp knock sounded at the dressing room door.

"It's time," a voice on the other side announced.

❊ ❊ ❊

Like millions of other people, Mamadou had her radio tuned to the broadcast of the fight. None of those other listeners, however, would have had the Silent Ones crawling contentedly across their feet as she did while she rested in a well-padded easy chair.

In her quarters at the Sanctum, Mamadou could finally relax ... at least from the labors that had fully consumed her time since Damballa brought samples of the accursed fluid the Germans had concocted. She knew she would be far from relaxed once the fight began.

Wrapped in a robe bedecked with Bakosi designs, Mamadou seemed somehow diminished, as though her heroic efforts in the laboratory had leached the last of the vitality from her aged body. She would not now have been able to dispatch an attacker as easily as she had the German at the *gri-gri* shop. Even so, she was in no way easy prey for anyone.

Everyone's time comes, she thought grimly. Her time was much closer now. But it had not yet arrived.

The ring announcer was introducing the living former heavyweight champions in attendance, as was customary before a major title bout. Jim Jeffries, Jack Dempsey, Gene Tunney and the ragtag, post-Tunney bunch that preceded Jackhammer all received generous rounds of applause.

The only ex-champion's name Mamadou did not hear was that of Jack Johnson. Mamadou frowned at the slight. But she knew Johnson was there ... just as Damballa was there.

Mamadou's lips moved in silent prayer to the deities she had worshiped long before Walter Horace Shropshire came among the Bakosi with his Bible and his Jesus. She had done everything she could. Now, the rest was up to her grandson.

She continued to pray, even as the Silent Ones slid across her hands.

CHAPTER THIRTY-TWO

FIRST BELL

Anticipation was reaching its crest in the packed stadium as the announcer, a man named Benjamin Franklin Jowett, checked his microphone for the umpteenth time. The boxers and their seconds were in their corners. The national anthems of the United States and Germany had been played by brass bands. The ritual introduction of the former champions was over. Only minutes remained before the bell would clang for the first round of the fight.

Jowett, a walrus-mustached, long time fixture at sports events held in New York City, began his portentous announcement. It was said by some wags that he didn't really need a microphone to be heard even in the cavernous Yankee Stadium. He used one anyway.

"Ladies and gentlemen," he began. "Tonight, we present fifteen rounds of boxing, for the heavyweight championship of the world."

A tide of cheers and applause rolled through the crowd.

"Your judges are: Mr. Frederick Fosse and Mr. Joseph Kane."

The applause came more tepidly this time, for fight judges remained unobtrusive until their scorecards were read. If a bout ended in a knockout, the judges' tallies became irrelevant.

"Your referee is: Mr. Albert Dennehy."

A louder ovation greeted that announcement. Dennehy, a compact, gray-haired man dressed in a white shirt and black bow-tie, was a former middleweight contender who had gone on to become a popular third man in the ring.

"And now ... introducing, in the blue corner, from Hamburg, Germany, weighing in at two-hundred twenty-seven and three-quarters pounds, with a record of thirty-seven victories, all by knockout, and no defeats, the challenger, the heavyweight champion of Europe, the 'Aryan Adonis' ... *Wolfgang Krieger!*"

A hybrid noise that was half-cheer and half-boo erupted as a spotlight shone on Krieger. The German, swathed in his black robe, did not acknowledge the mixed reception the crowd accorded him.

Jowett waited for the hubbub to abate before beginning his next – and final – introduction.

"And, in the red corner, hailing from Chicago, Illinois, weighing in at an even two-hundred pounds, with a record of forty-four victories and no defeats, forty of those wins coming by knockout, the defending heavyweight champion of the world ... *Junius 'Jackhammer' Jackson!*"

The roar the crowd launched into the clear night sky could be heard blocks away from the stadium. It lasted several minutes, and Jowett let it go on. Were it not for the unwritten rules of ring decorum and objectivity, he would have joined the applause for the champion, who raised a gloved hand in appreciation.

Finally, the ovation subsided, and Jowett proceeded to recite a statement that he, the Mayor and the Governor had worked out earlier. He had committed the brief declaration to memory.

"Ladies and gentlemen, tonight's bout is a competition between two men, not two countries. It is a sporting contest, not a political event. Regardless of color, nationality or creed, may the better boxer emerge victorious."

For a moment, silence followed Jowett's words. Then came the sound of more than one hundred thousand people, clapping politely.

"Will the principals please approach the center of the ring, for your instructions from the referee," the announcer said as the applause wound down.

Jackhammer was accompanied by Chum and Frankie as he moved to ring center, where Referee Dennehy was already waiting. Krieger's seconds were Kohlbrecher and an anonymous member of the training-camp staff who was little more than a bucket-carrier. Von Dunkel occupied a seat directly beneath Krieger's corner.

Dennehy looked at the two fighters as they faced each other with about a foot of space between them. The referee had officiated hundreds of ring contests, but never before had he seen such a feral expression on a fighter as the one that twisted Krieger's features. Dennehy half-expected him to begin to snarl.

Jackhammer did not appear to be intimidated by his opponent's display of contempt and bravado. At least, Dennehy *thought* it was a display. ...

"All right, gentlemen, we reviewed the rules earlier," the referee intoned.

"No hitting on the break after a clinch, and you will break promptly at my command. In the event of a knockdown, you are to go immediately to a neutral corner before I begin the count. Is that understood?"

"Yes, sir," Jackhammer muttered.

Krieger managed a slight nod.

"Go back to your corners, gentlemen," Dennehy instructed. "And good luck to both of you."

Moments later, the bell for the first round rang.

❀ ❀ ❀

Mamadou leaned forward in her chair as she listened to ring announcer Stockland Brice's blow-by-blow account of the action. It was as though she could not only hear what Brice was describing, but see it as well.

"Krieger rushes straight at Jackson and is on him before the echo of the bell dies. A left and a right and another left and right from Krieger all land solidly! There's not going to be any feeling-out tonight, folks; Krieger has jumped right on Jackson and caught him flat-footed. Jackson hasn't had a chance to get set. This is something that's never happened to him before. Usually, he's the one that gets the fast start. Now he looks like he's almost out on his feet!

"Another combination to the head and body sends Jackson reeling into the ropes! Krieger is raining punches on Jackson! Jackson hasn't managed to land a single blow in return. The referee is looking closely at the action … he may be on the verge of stopping this fight less than a minute into the first round!"

The din from the crowd threatened to drown out Brice's commentary. Mamadou merely listened, her facial expression unperturbed.

"Jackson is desperately trying to clinch! The referee is moving to break them up. Oh! Jackson has just hurled Krieger away from him like a sack of potatoes! Krieger stumbles halfway across the ring, but manages to stay on his feet.

"Jackson's going after him. There's that famous Jackhammer jab! Rat-a-tat-tat! Krieger's head is snapping back and forth like a paddleball! Look out! A right uppercut by Krieger has just staggered Jackson! Jackson comes back with a left hook. Blood is beginning to show on both men's faces."

Mamadou continued to listen impassively, with the Silent Ones curled motionlessly at her feet.

"Punches are flying with incredible speed, folks! There's no way these fighters can keep up this pace for 15 rounds. They might not even keep it up until the end of *this* round! Oh! Krieger just nailed Jackson with a tremendous right to the jaw, and Jackson is down! It's the first time Jackson's been on the canvas in his career!

"Krieger is not going to a neutral corner. Jackson is on his feet! He pushes past the referee and hammers Krieger with a left hook. Krieger is down! It's a first for him, too. He jumps right back up before Dennehy can order Jackson to a neutral corner or start a count.

"Dennehy looks like he's gotten caught in the middle of a tornado as the fighters are going at each other like a couple of wildcats! There's the bell to end the round. But Krieger and Jackson are still fighting! Their seconds are struggling to drag them back to their corners.

"What a first round, folks! What a first round! I don't know about you, but I've never seen anything like this in my life!"

Mamadou exhaled the breath she had not realized she'd been holding for most of the round's last minute.

"Keep control of yourself, Jackhammer," she whispered.

❊ ❊ ❊

"You still here, Jackhammer?" Chum asked as he removed the water bottle from the champion's mouth.

"Yeah," Jackhammer replied.

"You know what you up against now," Chum said. "Don' let him get to you like he did when the round started. His brain almost gone now. You still got yours. Use it, son."

Jackhammer nodded.

"One thing you got goin' for you, son," Chum continued. "Surprise. Them Germans didn't think you could stand up against the juice in they man. They don' know you got juice of yo' own. They don' know he gon' lose hisself before you lose yo'self. Know what I'm sayin'?"

"Got it," Jackhammer said.

"You can do it, Junie," Frankie encouraged. "You the champ, man."

Blood was dripping from Jackhammer's nose, and a lump had formed under his left eye. Muscles were twitching beneath his skin. His deadpan stare had become more intense, and his lips peeled back from his teeth as Chum re-inserted the fighter's mouthpiece.

Neither Chum nor Frankie could guess what Jackhammer was thinking. ...

❊ ❊ ❊

Von Dunkel sat in stunned disbelief below Krieger's corner.

How? The doctor asked himself repeatedly. *How could the* Neger *have withstood Wolf's attack? How was he able to knock Wolf down? Has the* Starkenflessig *suddenly weakened? Is it not what I thought it would be? Has it –*

A sudden thought struck Von Dunkel like a two-by-four.

What if the Schwartzer has his own Starkenflessig? *No, that cannot be! But how else to explain his performance?*

"Von Dunkel," a voice murmured in his ear … a low voice, but still audible over the crowd's noise.

The doctor knew the identity of the speaker without needing to turn his head to identify him. Only a few people had the status – and temerity – to address him by his surname alone. The speaker operated out of the German embassy in Washington, D.C., but he was really an operative of the *Schutzstaffel* – the SS.

However highly Von Dunkel ranked in the Reich, he was not beyond the reach of the SS. A knot of fear formed in his stomach as he waited for the voice to continue.

"What is going on here?" the voice demanded. "You assured us – and the Führer – that this fight would be over in less than a round. We are now going into the second round. Why?"

"Complications," Von Dunkel said. "It will not last more than another round. You will see."

"We will hold you to your word, Von Dunkel," the voice said.

Then the speaker was gone. And Von Dunkel began to sweat.

❀ ❀ ❀

As they prepared Krieger for the next round, Kohlbrecher and the other seconds were asking themselves questions similar to the ones that troubled Von Dunkel's mind. But he had no time to mull over uncertainties. The break between rounds spanned only one minute. He had to make certain that Krieger understood what he must do.

"Jackson got lucky, Wolf," Kohlbrecher said. "Just stay on top of him, and you will finish him off. Do you understand?"

He heard no response from Krieger. The trainer bent closer to his fighter's ear.

"Do you understand?" Kohlbrecher repeated. Then, ashen-faced, he lifted his head. His hand trembled as he inserted Krieger's mouthpiece.

Wolf was growling. …

CHAPTER THIRTY-THREE

BEASTS IN THE RING

The Beast glared across the snow at the black creature only a short distance away. This one was different. This one was no pitiful prey-creature, though it shared some of the characteristics of that kind. It was black, but its hide bore a sheen that was lacking on the sooty skin of the prey-creatures. As the black one opened its mouth, the Beast beheld a row of fangs as formidable as its own. ...

The Beast realized then that this thing was not prey. It was a rival ...

One bound would launch the beast toward the creature that refused to flee, that glared in defiance, that gathered its limbs in preparation to leap forward, not away. But something was holding the Beast back ... some unknown force that dragged against its limbs. ...

Then a strange sound assailed the Beast's ears ... a sound that was not natural to the snowy domain through which the Beast roamed and hunted. But before its echo diminished, the force that impeded the Beast's movements was gone, and the Beast sprang forward even as its rival's muscles tensed in anticipation of the attack. ...

❁ ❁ ❁

Looking across the ring, Jackhammer saw the difficulty Krieger's seconds were having in keeping their man on his stool before the start of the second round. When the bell clanged, Krieger hurtled across the ring as though he had been shot from a cannon.

In the first round, the speed of Krieger's attack had caught Jackhammer by surprise, even though he knew the German's physical attributes had been greatly augmented. This time, Jackhammer was prepared. And he brought his own enhancements to the fore.

Moving more fluidly than he ever had before, Jackhammer sidestepped Krieger's rush. When the German whirled to face him, Jackhammer rammed a straight left into his opponent's snarling features. A halo of sweat flew from Krieger's head and blood spurted from his nose.

Krieger showed no reaction to Jackhammer's blow. The German began to swing wild, amateurish punches. But they came so quickly that they would have overwhelmed anyone who had not also been injected with the *Starkenflessig*. As it was, Jackhammer was hard-pressed to block and duck the storm of blows, while landing short, sharp counterpunches of his own.

Jackhammer knew he needed to end the fight soon, before the fluid Damballa had shot into him took over, the way it did when he was dreaming. But the German was so *fast* ... Jackhammer could barely keep up with the flood of punches that flowed from the German's fists.

And even with the roar of the crowd drumming in his ears, Jackhammer could hear Krieger's growls. So could the referee.

❊ ❊ ❊

"I've never seen anything like this before, folks!" Stockland Brice shouted into his microphone. "These fighters are whirling around the ring so fast that the referee can hardly keep up with them! Krieger throws a left hook, and then a looping right that Jackson is somehow able to avoid. But Jackson isn't just backpedaling. Every now and then, he stops and fires straight punches into the head and body of Krieger. Any one of those blows would have flattened an ordinary fighter. But neither of these men is ordinary tonight. They're like a pair of supermen. How long can they keep this pace up, though? How long?"

"Not long," said Mamadou as she leaned forward in her chair and turned up the volume of her radio.

❊ ❊ ❊

Jackhammer was beginning to believe he was about to force the opening he needed when one of Krieger's flailing blows crashed into the side of his jaw. Jackhammer's head swiveled and his knees became unhinged. He struggled to stay on his feet, but another blow from Krieger drove him to the floor. His head pounded with pain, and he could feel the canvas grind against his knees.

But he could not hear the referee's count, because the tolling of the doleful decimals had not yet begun.

Again, Dennehy was having trouble steering Krieger to a neutral corner. Finally, the referee got through to the German, who went toward the corner to which his seconds were frantically pointing.

When Dennehy turned to pick up the count on Jackhammer, he saw that the champion as already back on his feet. Dennehy could see that Jackhammer's legs were steady, and there was no sign in his eyes of the telltale glaze that indicated that a fighter's grasp on consciousness was loosening.

Still, there was something different about Jackhammer's face. ...

Gone was the deadpan stare that the champion presented to his opponents and almost everyone else. Jackhammer's features were now twisted into a feral grimace similar to the one Krieger had displayed since the opening bell. Dennehy was beginning to wonder whether either fighter could control himself much longer.

"You okay, Jackhammer?" Dennehy asked as he wiped the ring-resin off the champion's gloves.

A short nod was Jackhammer's only reply. It was as though he could not trust himself to speak.

The referee motioned the fighters to continue. Krieger and Jackhammer resumed action immediately, charging toward each other like a pair of wild bulls on a collision course.

❊ ❊ ❊

The Beast glared at the rival that rushed toward it on the savanna. Unlike the prey-creatures the Beast hunted through the tall grass, this one did not flee in terror. Instead, it stood fast and stared directly at the Beast and roared in defiance and disdain. Thick muscles bulged beneath its pale hide, and a straw-colored mane bristled across its flat skull. ...

The thunderous challenges the Beast and its rival bellowed at each other sent the denizens of the savanna scurrying away in a wave of squealing panic that swept through the grass. As the rival drew closer, the beast glared at the fangs that jutted from the pale creature's jaws and the talons that curved from its paws. Paying no further heed to the menace the rival presented, the Beast sprang to meet the onrushing mass of muscle and bone. ...

❊ ❊ ❊

Paying no further heed to the menace the rival presented, the Beast sprang to meet the onrushing mass of muscle and bone. ...

"It's pandemonium in the ring, folks! Pandemonium!" Stockland Brice shouted, his voice grown noticeably hoarse from a combination of excitement and astonishment. "If I weren't seeing it with my own eyes, I would not believe what is happening in this ring right now.

"Jackson and Krieger are mauling each other like a couple of lions or tigers! There is not even a pretense of pugilism going on here. Referee Dennehy is attempting to break the fighters from a clinch in which they look like they're trying to drag each other to the canvas.

"Look out! The fighters have just hurled the referee away from them like a rag doll! Dennehy hits the canvas hard and rolls under the bottom rope and lands right in the press section! The reporters are helping him back into the ring!

"Meanwhile, both fighters have spat out their mouthpieces and are snarling at each other with bared teeth. They're each raining punches, but neither man is giving ground. Referee Dennehy is still groggy. He's gaping at the fighters, and trying to figure out what to do.

"Can you hear that crowd, folks? One hundred thousand people roaring, screaming, gasping at the incredible spectacle unfolding before their eyes. It's a cinch nobody thought they'd ever be seeing anything like *this!*

"The fighters have closed in on each other again. And they're both down! They're both down! They're pinwheeling around the canvas, tearing at each other with their teeth! The referee is shaking his head in disbelief, and so is everyone else in this stadium!

"Both fighters' seconds are coming into the ring. The round is only about halfway over; the cornermen are not supposed to enter the ring until the bell sounds. The referee is still staring as the seconds try to pull the struggling fighters apart.

"Now Dennehy is waving his arms in a criss-cross motion. He's signaling that the fight is over! But what is the actual result?

"Other people are crowding into the ring now. There's the ringside physician, Dr. Vaughn Lyons. The doctor is approaching the fighters, who are hemmed in now by the crowd of cornermen and others. But Jackhammer and Krieger are still going at it like a pair of junkyard dogs!

"The doctor has something in his hand … must be a hypodermic. Lyons takes two quick jabs, one at the arm of each fighter. It's a wonder the doctor could do anything at all, what with the tangle of arms, legs and bodies around Krieger and Jackson.

"Now Lyons is motioning for the others to step back. As they follow his instructions, the fighters' movements are slowing down considerably.

That must have been one powerful sedative in that doctor's syringe, folks. In the meantime, two medical crews are hurrying down the aisles. Each crew is carrying a stretcher.

"Meanwhile, the referee is leaning through the ropes and having an intense discussion with Commissioner O'Gatty. There's a lot of head-shaking and finger-wagging going on. Finally, heads nod in agreement. Dennehy is now motioning toward announcer Benjamin Jowett. It looks as though we are about to hear some kind of resolution to this bizarre turn of events.

"The crowd is quieting down now as Jowett comes into the ring and confers with the referee. The medical crews are also in the ring. Dr. Lyons is giving them instructions as they ease the fighters – neither of whom is moving now – onto the stretchers. Both these fighters have been knocked out tonight, folks. But not by each other.

"Now Jowett is tapping his microphone, and the stadium is almost silent. Let's hear what he has to say, folks."

Mamadou listened.

※ ※ ※

"Ladies and gentlemen," Jowett intoned, his amplified voice echoing into the night. "Referee Dennehy stopped the bout at one minute, thirty-four seconds of the second round. Because of several infractions of the rules by both the champion and his challenger, as well as their respective seconds, a double-disqualification has occurred."

The crowd remained quiet as the announcer paused.

"Because the disqualifications cancel each other out, New York State Boxing Commission Chairman William O'Gatty has declared the bout to be No Contest. As a result of that ruling, Junius Jackson retains the title of heavyweight champion of the world."

Neither cheers nor catcalls rose from the spectators as they absorbed that information. It was as though witnessing the swift, inexplicable degeneration of a boxing match from a contest of skill to a battle between ravening brutes had left them dazed, as if they themselves had soaked up the blows Jackhammer and Krieger had landed on each other.

Jowett was not yet finished.

"Because of the unusual circumstances in the way this bout was conducted and ended, Chairman O'Gatty and the State Boxing Commission, along with other authorities, will undertake a complete and thorough investigation. Penalties, if appropriate, will be imposed."

Scant attention was paid to that pronouncement as the medical attendants carried the stretcher-bound fighters out of the ring and then out of the stadium to awaiting ambulances. In a slow-moving press, the crowd filed out as well.

In the minds of virtually everyone in the crowd, as well as the millions of people who had listened to the radio broadcast of the bout, a single question repeated itself endlessly: *What the hell happened?*

❊ ❊ ❊

Mamadou reached out and switched off her radio. Letting out a sigh that carried with it all the long years of her life, she leaned back in her chair and closed her eyes. She sat quietly for a time, her only movement a slow stroking of the Silent Ones that lay in her lap.

She knew what the hell had happened.

CHAPTER THIRTY-FOUR

'WHERE IS *HERR DOKTOR?*'

Half a dozen burly, grim-looking men marched into a room at the soon-to-be-abandoned training camp of Wolfgang Krieger. Hans Wimmer and Oskar Schutz looked up from the clothing and boxing gear they were packing in preparation for the imminent departure to Germany. At the sight of the intruders, Schutz and Wimmer stood erect, though they refrained from snapping a stiff-armed salute.

Though they were not wearing uniforms, the six men were obviously several cuts above Von Dunkel's black-clad paramilitary. Then again, they did not need uniforms to proclaim their SS status. The way they carried themselves was more than sufficient to indicate who they were.

"Where is *Herr Doktor?*" their spokesman demanded without ceremony.

Schutz and Wimmer exchanged puzzled glances.

"At the hospital, with Wolf," Wimmer responded.

"*Nein,*" the hard-eyed man countered. "We just came from there. Kohlbrecher was with Krieger. Von Dunkel was not. According to Kohlbrecher, Von Dunkel never appeared at the hospital at all."

A short, uncomfortable silence followed those words. Schutz broke it.

"*Herr Doktor* told us he was going to the hospital to consult on Wolf's treatment there," the underling said. "We had no reason not to believe what he said."

The SS man snorted – a sound that unnerved Schutz and Wimmer.

"You are entirely too credulous," he said.

Schutz and Wimmer did not say anything.

"If you happen to see *Herr Doktor,*" the spokesman said, "be sure to tell him that our ambassador urgently wishes to speak with him before our ship departs for the Fatherland."

"We will do that," said Wimmer.

After a final cold stare, the SS man and his cohorts left the room. Wimmer looked at Schutz.

"Better *Herr Doktor* than us," he said.

Schutz nodded. Both men resumed their packing. Their movements were much more hurried than they had been before the arrival of the SS men.

❈ ❈ ❈

Von Dunkel had no intention of meeting face-to-face with either the ambassador or anyone in the SS. Nor had he ever planned to go to the hospital with Krieger. *Herr Doktor* was well aware of what the inevitable blood tests on Krieger would reveal … and he had no desire to be anywhere near the reach of the American authorities when those test results became available.

The reach of the SS was another matter. …

It had been simple enough for Von Dunkel to slip away from the crowd that pressed close to the ambulance into which Krieger was loaded. When the ambulance's doors slammed shut and its siren began to wail, it was too late for anyone to react to his absence.

And what would they do about it? he thought derisively. *Stop the ambulance and go looking for me?*

No, the top priority was to get Krieger to the hospital. Then they – and that meant more than a few people – would be seeking him. But he intended to make certain they would never find him. America was, after all, a vast country, and Germans had lived here since colonial times.

He was on his way to a train station – not Grand Central, but an obscure stop that would not be frequented by many riders. The train ride out of New York would be only the beginning of his journey into anonymity. He was on foot, for he did not trust inferior American automobiles or stupid taxi drivers. His hat was pulled down low enough that the shadow of its brim obscured his features. He encountered few people, and they paid him scant heed despite the black doctor's bag he carried.

In that bag was the last of the *Starkenflessig* – his soaring triumph, and his abysmal curse.

How could it have gone so wrong? he asked himself yet again. *I thought I had not made any mistakes at all. … How in the name of the Führer did the Neger's people get their hands on the* Starkenflessig? *How were they able to keep that a secret from the finest mind in Germany?*

How? How?

Those questions were monopolizing Von Dunkel's mind when a hand suddenly reached from behind him and clamped over his mouth. Another arm seized him around the waist and lifted him from the ground. He'd had no awareness at all that anyone had been trailing him.

Something was in the hand that covered Von Dunkel's mouth ... something dry, powdery, sweet-smelling. He tried to hold his breath, but it was too late. Vaguely, he heard outcries, but they soon faded to echoes as his senses slipped away and a curtain of blackness descended over his eyes.

How did they find me? Von Dunkel screamed silently.

Then he lost consciousness.

❊ ❊ ❊

"*Aufwachen*," a voice said. "Wake up."

Von Dunkel tried to ignore the command, even as awareness returned whether he wanted it to or not.

No pain assailed him. But he quickly realized that his arms were bound behind him, and he was leaning upright against some sort of pillar or pole, to which his legs were tied as well. An icy knot of fear formed in his stomach as his mind registered that the voice had spoken to him in his native tongue – which was the last language he wanted to hear at this time.

He could feel air on the skin of his arms and legs, and thus realized that he had been stripped to his underwear.

Von Dunkel knew there was no further use in feigning oblivion. Reluctantly, he opened his eyes.

In the dim light that met his vision, Von Dunkel expected to see a squadron of SS men, led by the one who had threatened him during the fight. But only one person stood in front of him ... a person cloaked in blackness ... a person whose face was hidden by the shadow cast by the cloak's hood. ...

"Damballa," *Herr Doktor* whispered.

Von Dunkel had never before been in the presence of his nemesis. He had, however, been given sketchy descriptions of the cloaked crimefighter by the people the German had paid to seek such information. Those descriptions matched this apparition, whose outline appeared to shimmer in what Von Dunkel assumed to be either candle- or torch-light.

Why does he speak to me in German? Von Dunkel wondered as he struggled to dam the tide of terror that threatened to overwhelm him. He struggled to keep his voice calm as he spoke.

"It seems I am at a disadvantage in more ways than one," *Herr Doktor* said in German. "Your hands are free; mine are not. You can see my face; I am unable to see yours."

The cloaked man appeared to consider Von Dunkel's words for a moment. Then his hands – which held no weapons – went up to the hood and slowly drew it back. When he saw the face that was thus exposed, Von Dunkel gasped in shock.

For the visage upon which the German stared wide-eyed was that of Dr. Vaughn Lyon, the ringside physician at the Jackson-Krieger fight.

CHAPTER THIRTY-FIVE

THE RECKONING

"**Y**ou," Von Dunkel hissed. "*You* are Damballa?"

The cloaked man did not reply.

"Was that a sedative you injected into the fighters?" Von Dunkel asked. "If that is the case, there will be complications when it wears off."

"It was not a sedative," the cloaked man said. "It was an antidote."

"An antidote?" Von Dunkel repeated. "How could you produce an antidote without a sample of the *Starkenflessig*?"

"I had a sample. More than one, actually."

The cloaked man was continuing to speak in German. Von Dunkel shook his head slowly as he attempted to comprehend what had occurred; how this man could have obtained the *Starkenflessig*; then injected it into Jackson, as had obviously been the case.

Suddenly, *Herr Doktor* began to laugh in a tone that indicated hysteria rather than mirth.

"I knew it!" Von Dunkel crowed. "I knew you were really a white man! I knew that no *Neger* could possess the intellect necessary to function as brilliantly as you do; or to elude the clutches of my operatives. ..."

A laugh from the cloaked man interrupted Von Dunkel's raving. Something in the timbre of that laugh silenced the German.

Then one of the cloaked man's hands reached to the back of his head and began to pull forward. As Von Dunkel's eyes widened in amazement, the cloaked man's hair and face gradually peeled away, like the scaly hide shed by a snake. When the likeness of Dr. Lyons was gone, Von Dunkel was confronted by the true face of Damballa.

Anthracite eyes burned in a face as dark as midnight. Full lips remained curved in a smile of disdain. Damballa opened his hand, and the white mask floated to the floor.

For a moment, Von Dunkel could neither speak nor move. Then he found his voice.

"This cannot be," he said shakily. "You are playing a game with me. This black face is but another mask – or burnt cork."

Damballa yanked the skin on one of his cheekbones to demonstrate that the black face Von Dunkel beheld was not a mask. Then the crimefighter rubbed one hand over the other. No granules of burnt cork were dislodged.

"Do you not recognize me, Professor von Dunkel?" Damballa asked.

"*Nein!*" Von Dunkel snarled, his arrogance temporarily superseding his fear. "Why should I? It is difficult to tell one *Neger* from another."

"I was the '*Neger*' you would not allow into your chemistry class at the university years ago," Damballa said quietly.

Von Dunkel still did not recognize Damballa's face. But he did recall the university incident. It was the only time a black man had ever attempted to enroll in one of his classes.

Before the German could say anything in response to this revelation, Damballa went on.

"As it turns out, Von Dunkel, I did not need the tutelage you refused to grant me. I learned from others. Indeed, I learned more than you could ever have taught me. Even so, I followed your career from afar, and became aware of your … ambitions.

"When I learned that you were connected with Krieger, I suspected the worst. And when I encountered the enhanced capabilities of the one you called '*Der Tod*,' my suspicions were confirmed. You had created a concoction that would ensure that Krieger would win the fight.

"Despite your scheme, the fight needed to go on – but only if I could secure a sample of your fluid. I did so, and I also discovered how it was made. And I gave it to Jackson."

"Impossible!" cried Von Dunkel. "No vials were missing from their storage cabinet."

"If you had the chance to examine all the vials, you would have found that some of them contain water, not what you call the *Starkenflessig*," Damballa said calmly.

❖ ❖ ❖

Von Dunkel shook his head as he absorbed information that was patently incredible … but could only be correct, considering what had happened in the ring earlier this night.

"What happened to the real Dr. Lyons?" the German asked.

"He is safe and unharmed."

"You mentioned an antidote."

"The *Starkenflessig* has a side effect you did not anticipate. When it interacts with a heightened flow of adrenaline, the augmentation of the bestial qualities stolen from the predators you drained becomes magnified beyond the body's capacity to sustain. Sparring sessions were not sufficient to generate this effect. The fervor of actual combat in the ring was more than sufficient. Were it not for the antidote I injected, both fighters' bodies would have broken down like engines that lacked sufficient lubrication."

"How did you create the antidote so quickly?" Von Dunkel demanded, curious despite his current predicament.

Damballa let out another unnerving laugh.

"It was not I, *Herr Doktor*," the cloaked man said. "At least, not I alone."

Von Dunkel blinked in confusion. Since regaining consciousness, he had focused solely on Damballa. Now, in the wavering candlelight, he became aware that his place of imprisonment was a large room with a low ceiling. Vaguely, he could make out low-relief carvings on the walls. Primitive-looking sculptures cast grotesque shadows on the floor.

Then his gaze was drawn to a figure standing near Damballa. Von Dunkel wondered how he could have failed to see the elderly, oddly clad black woman before now. Disgust showed plainly in the woman's stare. It was as though he, not she, was the one who belonged to a lower rank of humanity. ...

"Mamadou possesses knowledge far beyond yours," Damballa said. "I have learned some of it ... but not enough to have developed the antidote on my own."

Von Dunkel drew himself up as straight as he could. He continued his efforts to contain the unseemly dread that churned within him.

"This does not matter," the German said, his voice rising. "The two of you do not matter. You have thwarted the Reich this time. But the Reich will prevail in the end. The iron heel of the Aryan will crush all who oppose the Führer, and the world will belong to us!"

"If that day comes, you will not be there to see it," said Mamadou.

The calm certitude of her tone cut like a stiletto through Von Dunkel's bravado. She reached down and picked up an object Von Dunkel had not noticed before. It was his doctor's bag. She opened the top, then upended the bag. A cascade of small vials fell out and shattered on the stone floor.

Von Dunkel gaped in consternation. Then he realized there was no liquid amid the bits of broken glass. The vials had been empty.

"We have disposed of the *Starkenflessig*," Damballa said. "Hopefully, none of your colleagues in Germany will attempt to duplicate your work. Because of the adrenaline effect, your potion is of no more use to your military than it ultimately was to Krieger."

"I have no – "

Von Dunkel cut himself off. It was not for these two *Schwartzers* to know that he had not shared his findings with other scientists, lest they attempt to steal the renown that was rightfully his – especially that loathsome Mengele.

"What now?" *Herr Doktor* asked sullenly.

"It is time for your reckoning," said Damballa.

"Who are you to speak of 'reckoning'?" the German spat. "*You*, whose savage race stands only a small step above the great apes!"

"Even the most 'civilized' men and women can be savages, in their own way," said Mamadou.

She did not see fit to remind Von Dunkel of the depredations of the Belgians in the Congo. The import would be lost on the likes of him, as his next words amply demonstrated.

"Bah!" he snorted. "You speak out of ignorance, as do all your kind."

Abruptly, Damballa reached into his cloak and extracted a thin, quill-like tube. He lifted the tube to his mouth, aimed it downward and puffed a strong breath into its narrow confines.

A small cloud of green powder emanated from the front end of the tube and settled on the skin of Von Dunkel's bare legs. Only a moment later, his legs began to tingle, as though their blood supply was dwindling.

"What have you done to me?" Von Dunkel cried, his hauteur banished.

Neither Damballa nor Mamadou replied. Mamadou bent and untied the ropes that bound Von Dunkel's legs. The German's first impulse was to aim a kick at the elderly woman's face. But he found that he was no longer able to move his legs. And the tingling was intensifying.

In the meantime, Damballa had moved behind Von Dunkel, and was cutting the ropes that restricted the German's arms. Then Damballa gave Von Dunkel a slight shove. Unable to brace himself with his legs, Von Dunkel fell forward. His arms were barely able to break his fall as Mamadou stepped nimbly out of his way.

Von Dunkel rolled onto his back. He glared at the two *Negers* looking down on him. As the German sputtered a string of sulphurous curses, Damballa and Mamadou silently departed from the chamber. Von Dunkel heard the click of a lock after the door closed behind them.

❊ ❊ ❊

Still swearing, Von Dunkel used his elbows to hitch his way forward.

His legs prickled as though he were suffering an electric shock – yet he experienced no pain. Still, he could not move his legs at all. It was as though he were dragging a pair of logs behind him.

Suddenly, sharp points jabbed into the skin of his arms. He cried out, believing for a moment that rats were attacking him. He lifted his arms – and saw bits of bloody glass clinging to their undersides. Von Dunkel realized then that he was crawling over the shards of the vials that had once held the *Starkenflessig.*

He struggled to suppress a burst of laughter at the irony of being wounded by the remnants of those shattered, empty vials. The moment of levity passed as quickly as it had come.

"Do they intend to keep me here until I starve to death?" he muttered to himself.

As if in answer to that question, the sound of drumming suddenly assailed Von Dunkel's ears. Again he cried out, and he swiveled his head in search of the sound's source. He saw nothing but shadows, slow-burning candles, and the shapes of the sculptures.

He realized now that one part of the room was totally unlit … a huge patch of blackness in which he imagined he could discern deeper, darker shadows – but no drummers.

"Must be hidden loudspeakers," he said aloud.

Perhaps they intend to drive me mad before I starve, he said in his mind as the drumming continued.

Desperately, Von Dunkel strove to think of a way to escape. Had he not developed the *Starkenflessig?* Had he not risen to a position of power in a ruthless regime? Was he not the most accomplished scientist in the Reich?

Had he not been bested and humiliated by a pair of *Negers?*

Von Dunkel cried out again. This time, it was a wordless scream that embodied frustration and despair. When he regained control of himself, he heard another sound that was somehow audible beneath the infernal booming of the drums. It was a sound that was not familiar to him. Even so, it caused cold fingers of terror to brush across his spine.

Slowly, reluctantly, *Herr Doktor* turned his head toward the scraping sound. And his tongue clove to the roof of his mouth at the thing he saw. All he could utter was a weak, strangled outcry that could not be heard over the drumbeats.

From the unlit part of the chamber, a serpent was sliding toward him … a serpent larger than any he had ever seen, or even imagined. It was as though the gigantic creature were drawing its substance from the stone from which the chamber was made. That impression was heightened by the gray color of the reptile's patterned scales.

Using his elbows for leverage, Von Dunkel scuttled backward. His eyes formed white circles of trepidation, and his mouth opened and closed like that of a hooked fish. The giant serpent moved faster, easily catching up with its helpless quarry.

"*Gott in Himmel*," Von Dunkel whispered as the serpent raised enough of its vast length from the floor to stare down at him. The flick of the serpent's tongue mesmerized *Herr Doktor*. Ophidian eyes stared into his own with a gleam that suggested intelligence rather than simple instinct.

Then M'satha looped his coils around the body of his prey and crushed the life and evil out of Claus von Dunkel.

❊ ❊ ❊

Detective Bynoe stood in front of the door to a maintenance room at Yankee Stadium. The room's number – 1725 – had been emblazoned on his mind earlier in the night.

He looked over at Detective Dodson. The two of them were the only ones in the area. Everyone else was at the front gates, trying to exit the huge arena as quickly as they could, while trying to make sense of the bizarre events that had occurred in the boxing ring and were continuing to occur even now.

Bynoe and Dodson would have been among that throng, had it not been for a piece of paper surreptitiously slipped into Bynoe's hand. Bynoe had searched for the person who had done the deed. But the crowd was too dense, and he could hardly question each of the people surging around him and his partner.

Opening the folded sheet, Bynoe saw only a number and a name. The number was "1725." The name was "Damballa."

Bynoe showed the message to Dodson. Then, as the detectives watched wide-eyed, the paper suddenly crumbled to dust that sifted through Bynoe's fingers.

"Now we know for certain this came from Damballa," Bynoe said. "No one else would feel the need for this kind of trickery."

"I think you're right," Dodson had agreed.

Now they stood in front of the door to Room 1725. Bynoe had the master key he had obtained from the maintenance supervisor. He inserted it into the lock, turned it, and swung the door open.

And, along with Dodson, he stared incredulously at the bound and gagged form of Dr. Vaughn Lyons, whose eyes glared indignantly even as they blinked in the sudden illumination.

CHAPTER THIRTY-SIX

'I'M WITH YOU'

Celebrations usually followed Jackhammer's victories, especially in the colored sections of America's towns and cities. When Jackhammer won, it was as though Negroes as a whole had won, even if the champion's triumphs represented little more than a brief respite from the ongoing burden of race.

There were no celebrations this time, though. Jackhammer didn't lose his fight with Krieger, but he didn't win it, either. The reason the fighters had gone wild in the ring was still a mystery to the general public, and tight-lipped authorities had as yet provided no answers to the questions that reverberated through streets, bars and living rooms.

Both fighters remained in guarded rooms at the hospital. Neither man was under arrest; the police guards were there to fend off the press and curiosity seekers while the fighters ostensibly recovered from the grievous injuries they had inflicted upon each other.

What they were really recovering from was the effects of the *Starkenflessig* that lingered even after the antidote had been administered. Only a few people knew that fact, and those few were sworn to secrecy … at least until a plausible "official" explanation could be devised to account for what had occurred on fight night. When that explanation would be forthcoming, no one knew.

In the meantime, the search for Von Dunkel continued.

❖ ❖ ❖

"You should be able to leave within a few more days," Dr. Lyons said to Wolfgang Krieger.

"That is good news," Krieger said in heavily accented English.

The boxer was lying in his hospital bed. Even though his body bulked large beneath the thin hospital sheet that covered him, the German appeared ... diminished. His cheeks were hollow, and dark circles curved beneath his eyes.

At least he's human again, Lyons thought. *Not the raging beast that awakened after he was first brought here. ...*

"I must thank you again, *Doktor*, for saving my life," Krieger said. "When I think of what could have happened. ..."

His voice trailed off.

"*Ja*," said Kohlbrecher, who was the only other person in the private room. "Were it not for you. ..."

Lyons waved off the gratitude. On the advice of Police Commissioner Wheelwright, Damballa's impersonation of Lyons had not been revealed to the public. Even though the doctor understood the reasons for that deception, he was still uncomfortable with the necessity to take credit for what Damballa had done to save both Krieger and Jackson.

Lyons remembered the slip of paper he had found in his pocket shortly after the police had rescued him from the closet. It did not take him long to understand that the writing on the paper constituted a set of instructions for the treatment of both fighters. Unlike the one given to Bynoe, this sheet did not dissolve once it came into contact with air.

Ordinarily, Lyons would have dismissed advice from someone whose medical credentials he did not know. But there was nothing ordinary about Damballa, whose name appeared at the bottom of the instructions.

The treatment worked, Lyons thought. *That's all that matters.*

He added some notations to Krieger's chart. Then he nodded to the two Germans.

"I'll be back later," the doctor said.

Then he departed, leaving Krieger and Kohlbrecher alone in the antiseptic-smelling room. They were silent for a time. Then Kohlbrecher spoke, measuring his words carefully.

"I will not be going back to Germany, Wolf," he said.

Krieger showed no sign of surprise ... which surprised Kohlbrecher. Then the trainer continued.

"There is something I must tell you ... something I've kept hidden from everyone, even you."

"I know your secret, Franz," Krieger said softly. "I have always known."

Kohlbrecher stared open-mouthed.

"But how – " he stammered.

“How do the Americans say? ‘It takes one to know one.’ ”

The two men stared at each other.

“ ‘Aryan Adonis,’ indeed,” said Kohlbrecher.

Then they burst out laughing, in relief as much as humor. Then a serious expression crossed Kohlbrecher’s face like a cloud.

“You must seek a way to stay here, too, Wolf,” he said. “Given what happened in the fight, your risk of exposure is high.”

“*Nein*,” said Krieger. “I must go back … for Ilse.”

Kohlbrecher nodded in understanding and respect.

“Can you get me a pen and paper, Franz?” Krieger asked. “There is something I must write.”

Puzzled, Kohlbrecher complied.

***

Two people were with Jackhammer in his hospital room: Chum and Lola. The trainer and Lola had not gotten along particularly well before. Although Chum had nothing against women, he was an old-school trainer who was convinced that boxing and romance did not mix well.

Lola resented that attitude, but she kept her feeling to herself. She didn’t want to disrupt the bond between the two men.

Now, even though they sat on opposite sides of Jackhammer’s bed, they were united in their concern for him. But there wasn’t much need to worry about him anymore. Dr. Lyons had just given Jackhammer a clean bill of health, and the champion was due to be discharged from the hospital the next day. The doctor had recommended another night of bed rest.

Lyons remained unaware that Damballa’s part in the events surrounding the fight was known to Jackhammer and his associates. And they preferred matters to remain that way.

“I be glad to get out of this place,” Jackhammer said. “It’s like some kind of prison.”

“No it ain’t,” Chum said gruffly.

Jackhammer nodded. He knew Chum had seen the inside of a prison more than once.

“Well, I still be glad to get out,” Jackhammer said.

“Me, too,” said Lola.

Chum looked at her, then at Jackhammer.

“Y’all know it ain’t gon’ be no ‘happily ever after’ out there,” the trainer said. “They still lots of questions people gon’ ask.”

"And I got the answer for all of 'em," Jackhammer retorted. "One of that German's punches knocked me outta my head. And I got no idea what made *him* go crazy."

"People will believe you, Jackhammer," said Lola. "The Germans are in enough trouble already. They have to be careful about what they say. Besides, Damballa told us the treatment Dr. Lyons gave you has already purged that fluid out of your system."

"The thing is, son, do you wan' keep fightin'?" said Chum. "You still the champ. That investigation ain't gon' find nothin' that will take your title away from you. And Damballa say you gon' be good as new, cause you didn't have that stuff inside you as long as the German did."

"We already know what the Salt-and-Pepper Twins want," Lola said with a touch of asperity.

Chum gave her a sharp glance. He knew that Ruland and Washington were already mapping out their plans to take full advantage of the controversy the double-disqualification had triggered. They were lining up future fights, and were even talking about a motion picture starring Jackhammer as a costumed hero, like Damballa.

But he hadn't known that Lola knew it, too.

They's more to this here chick than her looks, Chum thought with grudging admiration.

"Don' know what I gon' do yet," Jackhammer finally said. "Got to think about it for a while."

Lola slipped her hand into his.

"Whatever you decide, Champ, I'm with you," she said.

"Thanks, Baby," said Jackhammer.

Then a knock sounded at the door. Chum got up.

"Must be one of them nurses," he grumbled as he went over to open the door.

After a brief murmur of conversation, Chum closed the door and returned to Jackhammer's bedside. The trainer held a folded piece of paper between his thumb and forefinger, as though it were noisome.

"This supposed to be from Krieger," Chum said. "You wan' read it?"

"Yeah, I'll read it," Jackhammer said.

He opened the note and read it silently. Then he held it up so that Lola and Chum could see Krieger's words.

Dear Champion:

We met as beasts in the ring. If we ever meet again, may it be as men.
–Wolfgang Krieger

"As men," Jackhammer echoed.

❀ ❀ ❀

Mamadou was sitting in her easy chair, the lights low and the radio off. Damballa sat at her side in a chair he'd carried in from the kitchen. The Silent Ones slid between and around them. Mamadou's face was gaunt and drawn, but her eyes shone with their usual intensity as she looked at Damballa.

Damballa broke the silence.

"It is time, Mamadou."

"Yes, my grandson," she said. "It is time."

EPILOG

A black car pulled up in front of a small house in the Ohio countryside. A tall black man got out of the vehicle and quietly closed its door. Dusk was falling, rendering the ebony-skinned man's features indistinct. He was dressed in a black suit. His shirt and tie were black as well.

He strode up the sidewalk to the front door of the house. Light shone through the curtains covering the downstairs windows. Someone was home. The man hesitated a moment before knocking on the door.

A moment later, the door opened. A black woman of medium height stood at the threshold. Modestly attired and umber-skinned, the woman looked up at her unexpected visitor.

"Yes?" she inquired. "Can I help you?"

"Is your name Amelia Shropshire?" the man asked.

The woman nodded.

"My name is Shropshire, too," the man said. "Walter Horace Shropshire Jr."

A sharp intake of breath greeted those words. The woman gazed intently at the man's features. Then she opened her door wider and stepped aside.

"Come in, Walter," she said. "We have a lot to talk about."

Damballa entered his sister's home, and she closed the door behind them.

The End

AUTHOR'S NOTE: ENTER DAMBALLA

Ron Fortier and I have been friends since the mid-1970s, when we each began to get short stories published in small-press fantasy and science fiction magazines such as Gordon Linzner's legendary *Space & Time*. Indeed, Ron and I both served terms as president of a group called SPWAO (Small Press Writers and Artists Organization).

So, it became just about inevitable that when Ron began Airship 27 Productions, I would become involved. Over the past several years, I've proofread many of Airship's books before their publication. But Ron and I both knew that sooner or later, I would come up with a book idea that could prove Airship-worthy.

Almost everything I've written since those early small-press days has been in the fantasy genre – primarily sword-and-sorcery, in African-inspired settings. Seldom had my imagination ventured into the world we know. Of course, it can be argued that the pulp world isn't all that close to the world we know, either. But it's closer than I usually care to approach.

I had long-since created a black sword-and-sorcery hero named Imaro. The challenge now was to develop an African-American contemporary of 1930s-era crimefighters such as The Shadow, Doc Savage, The Spider, Captain Hazzard, etc. A counterpart, not a copycat.

The *Damballa* story sprang from my subconscious well before the eponymous character took shape. As a life-long boxing fan, I knew that the biggest bout of the 1930s was the June 22, 1938, encounter between Joe Louis and Max Schmeling. Louis, an African-American, was the heavyweight champion of the world. Schmeling, a German who had held the title for a brief time earlier in the decade, had defeated Louis before the "Brown Bomber" won the title from Jim Braddock.

Thus, Louis-Schmeling II was a highly anticipated grudge match that carried racial and political overtones as well. For the first time, white and black Americans were united in rooting for a black man as their country's fistic standard-bearer against Schmeling, who symbolized Nazi Germany whether he liked it or not. And there are indications he didn't like it, though he remained a loyal German citizen.

In the world we know, Louis annihilated Schmeling in one round in 1938. That outcome provided Louis and his fans sweet vengeance for Schmeling's 12-round stoppage of Louis in 1936.

The core of my story became a fictionalized version of Louis-Schmeling II, with Jackhammer Jackson standing in for Louis and Wolfgang Krieger as the equivalent for Schmeling. In this different scenario, their bout would be their first meeting in the ring, not their second. Both fighters would be undefeated going into the contest. And a fanatical Nazi scientist in Krieger's camp would be in the process of providing an unfair advantage to the challenger. ...

A crimefighter who operates on the fringes of the law would be needed to stop this sabotage. An image of the man who would become that hero was forming in my mind, but he didn't snap into full focus until I read a book called *William Sheppard: Congo's African-American Livingstone*, by William E. Phipps.

Sheppard was a black American missionary who served in the Congo region during the late 19th and early 20th centuries, working with the Bakuba people. His dedication, generosity and empathy led to comparisons with his better-known Scottish counterpart, Dr. David Livingstone. Sheppard became famous in his own right because of his crusade against the atrocities committed by minions of Belgian King Leopold II, who ravaged the people of the region in the name of the profit resting in the region's rubber trees.

A whiff of scandal cut Sheppard's mission short. Married and the father of a young daughter, the churchman had an affair with a Bakuba woman, who gave birth to a child by him.

The components of my story were now in place. William Henry Sheppard morphed into Walter Horace Shropshire. The Bakuba became the Bakosi, a people with an ancient and secret history. And the out-of-wedlock child left behind by the missionary became ... Damballa.

With both African and American heritage, and a burning ambition to make his own mark in the world, Damballa became the champion of people of African descent on both sides of the Atlantic Ocean. And the remarkable interaction between a crime-fighting champion and a prize-fighting champion became one of the focal points of the story.

From that juncture, *Damballa* flowed onward – sometimes smoothly, sometimes slowly, at all times inexorably. Writing outside my customary genre was tricky on occasion. It was hard work – and a lot of fun, even considering the story's serious undertones.

Racism was one of those undertones. These days, most rational people reject the belief that one race is inherently superior to another (or all others). In the 1920s-1940s heyday of the pulps, however, racism was a form of political correctness, not to mention conventional wisdom. It was part and parcel of popular culture, not just the pulps. The barrage of slurs and stereotypes was constant, and applied not only to blacks, but people of many ethnic derivations, including whites such as the Irish, Italians and Russians – and also to women of all backgrounds.

I could not have avoided the race issue in *Damballa* even if I'd wanted to – and I didn't want to. Racism was more a fact of everyday life then than it is now, and is thus a necessary part of the story's context. As the action progresses, Damballa, Jackhammer, Detective Bynoe and other characters find it necessary to pick their way through the racial minefields of their time.

Concerning nomenclature, the "n-word" was certainly common coin during the 1930s, and I had no intention of shying away from it. In *Damballa*, I use the term sparingly, not gratuitously. Of course, the Germans had their own equivalent to that particular epithet, and characters like the reprehensible Claus von Dunkel use it accordingly.

The terms "colored," "Negro" and "black" for Americans of African descent were employed on an interchangeable basis until the mid-1960s. I follow that convention in *Damballa*.

I'd like to commend Ron, and Rob Davis as well, for their sensitivity to the race issue in both the reprint and new pulp stories Airship has published. And I'm thankful to them for extending me the opportunity to bring *Damballa* to print.

What's next for the mysterious cloaked crimefighter? He and Mamadou will assuredly let me know. ...

ABOUT THE AUTHOR

Charles R. Saunders has been writing fiction and non-fiction since the early 1970s. He is best known for Imaro, his black sword-and-sorcery stalwart who plies his blade in Nyumbani, the Africa of a parallel Earth in which magic works and myths are real. The four current novels in the series – *Imaro, Imaro 2: The Quest for Cush, Imaro: The Trail of Bohu*, and *Imaro: The Naama War* – are all available at www.lulu.com.

Also available at www.lulu.com is *Dossouye*, which recounts the adventures of a black woman-warrior in another alternate Africa.

Forthcoming books include the fifth Imaro novel and the second Dossouye novel, along with *Griots*, a "sword-and-soul" anthology co-edited with Milton J. Davis.

Damballa is Charles's first venture into pulpdom. He lives in Dartmouth, Nova Scotia, Canada.

To learn more about his work and views, stop by his website: www.charlessaunderswriter.com.

SET SAIL FOR ADVENTURE

The greatest seafaring adventurer of all time returns to the high seas, *Sinbad the Sailor!*

Born of countless legends and myths, this fearless rogue sets sail across the seven seas aboard his ship, the Blue Nymph, accompanied by an international crew of colorful, larger-than-life characters. Chief among these are the irascible Omar, a veteran seamen and trusted first mate, the blond Viking giant, Ralf Gunarson, the sophisticated archer from Gaul, Henri Delacrois and the mysterious, lovely and deadly female samurai, Tishimi Osara. All of them banded together to follow their famous captain on perilous new voyages across the world's oceans.

So pack up your you traveling bags, bid ado to your loved ones and get ready to sail with the tide as Sinbad El Ari takes the tiller and the Blue Nymph sets sails once more; its destination worlds of wonder, mystery and high adventure.